The Fish Committee

IRIS POLISKI

IRIS POLISKI

Copyright © 2009 IRIS POLISKI

Prosperity Luthier Productions Press, Mid-Western Division

All rights reserved.

ISBN: 9781521869550

ACKNOWLEDGMENTS

I salute the inspired language skills and ear for the kind of action that grabs the reader's attention while making sure the event was not actionable.

THE FISH COMMITTEE

CONTENTS

	Acknowledgments	ii
1	Connections	1
2	The Fish Committee	10
3	Wheels Within Wheels	18
4	Sal Falls in Love	23
5	Invasion	37
6	South and North	48
7	Various Plans	55
8	Heat and Light	64
9	Delivery Mechanisms	75
10	Omnium Gatherum	81
11	Dry Run	89
12	Some Properties	97
13	Love's Labors	109
14	Public Relations	116
15	After the Mouse	125
16	Into the Woods	132
17	Passing for Normal	145
18	Picnic	151
19	Gains and Losses	160
20	The Money Trail	165

CONTENTS

21 Victoria Ascendant   169

22 Conditional Clauses   177

23 More Gains and Losses   183

24 Elsewhere   189

25 Unconditional Clauses   192

26 The Storm Front   196

27 Aftermath   214

28 The Dinner   224

29 Home Again   239

30 Fiin   243

1 CONNECTIONS

The people scattered along the edges of Yellow Perch Lake had developed a network. Inspired by curiosity and necessity in equal parts, it was a relatively efficient tangle of socializing, exchanged favors, and random boat-to-boat conversations about fish, weather, and the horrors of summer visitors. And every one spied, discreetly.

For instance, it was interesting to see that Lucia Constantini was setting up additional deck chairs; a party was probably in the works. Across the lake from Lucia, Evangeline Juska flagged Miranda Thrip, a next door neighbor, to compare grocery lists before a dash to the Co-op in town. Why make separate trips?

Judge Press, around the point, kept an eye out for Al Gustave's fishing boat. If there was no sighting in 24 hours, someone—usually Webb Tintinger—would wander over to the Gustave property to make sure Al was still breathing. Gustave was a tough old geezer, but not immortal, despite his own opinion. And since Webb and Sophie Tintinger lived practically within yards of Sydnor Feffer (who was their niece), they kept an eye on Sydnor's cottage when she wasn't around.

Dieter and Mrs. Vilnus, who looked as if they'd escaped from a painting by Breughel the Younger, operated as an independent nation-state. However, because Dieter headed the Lake Association's Fish Committee, he was afloat a great deal and thus in constant communication with the permanently fishing Milt Hendrickson, who barely touched dry land from Memorial Day through Labor Day weekend. The general opinion was that Maureen, his wife, was the most patient woman in the world.

Lucia Constantini's son, Sal, came and went on an irregular schedule with or without his young sons, and Sydnor's foreign correspondent friend turned up even more irregularly, which drove her mad. The remaining lake residents, spouses, and resort owners were engaged by their various diversions. Maureen busied herself with long, complicated afternoons of bridge. The fishing guide who lived on the lake was generally ignored. Everyone who cared had long ago figured out where the muskie holes were; the guide was redundant. If it rained for more than two days, resort owner Eloise Walsh, neighbor Adeline Press, and maybe, but only maybe, Louse Garfield, the woman who ran the antiques shop, would join Maureen for bridge. But that was a desperate measure. Louise Garfield, who was gullible in ways that staggered her neighbors' collective imagination, believed that spirits lived under the earth and that she could depend on them to influence a winning bridge hand.

Because the Yellow Perch Lake Association gathered at the general convenience of its membership, the annual meeting was always scheduled on or around the pinnacle of high season, the Fourth of July.

People might arrive early or late in the short northern summer, but by the fourth, the sun blazed over the north woods and everyone was in residence, swimming, fishing, dabbing enamel on window trim, hacking away at underbrush, or simply slumped in lawn chairs, staring tranquilly at the water.

On some years, the Association met after the town's annual July Fourth parade, an event generating feverish excitement among the townsfolk. The summer residents anticipated it with equal enthusiasm; the parade was a classic, if peculiar, bit of Americana.

The locals developed their image of a parade from the movies, their current ego needs, and long winter months spent contemplating materials that could be stuffed into a chicken wire frame and towed. The results were often amazing.

One summer the town fire department created giant pinecones to adorn the corners of the two fire trucks. Judge Press, Cook County, Ill., Circuit Court, (retired) had been classically educated, and was heard to exclaim, "The thyrsus bearers are many, but the Bacchae are few!" Maureen Hendrickson declared that the getup looked like something you'd find in kitty litter and that they should have carried a Smokey the Bear Says Help Prevent Forest Fires sign or something.

For the town's parade during its centennial year, nearly the entire population turned out in crinoline and mutton chop sideburns (per appropriate sex), and then dropped like flies in the 90-degree plus temperatures. Glimpses of up-ended crinoline were available behind cars and shops, as lady marchers stripped heat and history from sweating waists and thighs.

After the parade, Larry Running Bear, the mostly Chippewa manager of the local grocery—he'd come in a loincloth discreetly tucked into a Speedo bathing suit and a feather headdress—remarked to the pinkly perspiring mayor that the Independence Day festivity looked mostly like the rape of the Sabine women. The mayor, unfamiliar with this bit of Native American history glanced enviously at Bear's undress, and said he didn't know about anybody else, but he was going straight over to the Wintergreen Bar and douse himself in a keg of beer.

The township's be-flagged snow removal vehicles rumbled past, including a smattering of Jeeps and trucks with appended snowplows, all heading barward. Sweaty high school twirlers, knees sunburned, fingers purpled by pom-pom dye, staggered home to showers and tiny bathing suits.

And in the county fairground buildings, just to the west of town, an occasional wasp looped low and sluggishly over home made jams and jellies and berry pies stickily protected by plastic wrappings. Buyers and admirers rambled about, fanning themselves. The pleased (if overheated) exhibitors told each other it hadn't been this hot since the summer main street was resurfaced. Sticky from popsicles, children waited impatiently for it to be dark for the fireworks.

In one aisle, Minnie Rosenheim, the local businesswoman who ran a popular pastry shop, had transported an enormous block of ice to cool several prize-winning cheesecakes and her toes. In another, Sophie Tintinger and Sydnor Feffer considered the largess on display and for sale.

"You know, I love this," Sydnor murmured, sweating into an old blue kerchief, knotted Cochise-like around her head. She was holding a jar of Estelle Malmaison's elderberry-rhubarb preserves with an air of one who had discovered a great treasure.

"Syddy, you never use jam. You had the raspberry-blackberry stuff in your refrigerator for a year and a half," Sophie said in a reasonable tone, examining a frighteningly large snap bean.

"I meant the county fair part. And I did too. It crystallized into a wonderful raspberry sugar candy and I ate the whole jar with a spoon. God, it was good."

"Did you ever hear the story about the time old Mrs. LeClerc was making jam and the bear walked in to her kitchen?" Sophie asked.

Estelle Malmaison, handing Sydnor change for the jam purchase, automatically leaned into the conversation.

"It was in '30 or '32," she said. "Took out the entire kitchen screen door, I heard."

"The bear?"

"No, old Mrs. LeClerc when she ran out. Stepped right through it, crosspiece and all. Yelled to beat the band. Near gave the bear heart failure. It chomped onto a full quart jelly jar and lit out through the front door dripping jam the whole way. They had ants for weeks," she added with satisfaction.

"A wonderful story," said Sydnor, "and probably true, too."

"Oh yes, your grandmother used to tell it," Sophie put in.

"Was that the lady who used to come to early service at St. Pete's?" asked Mrs. Malmaison, "with the hats? Navy blue straw, mostly, and flowers?"

Her customers beamed.

"Navy with lavender lilacs," Sophie said.

"Navy with a crown of forget-me-nots," Sydnor added.

"Navy with scrunched up netting?" Sophie remembered.

"I sat behind the one with the lilacs. I swear, I forget the gospel but I remember that hat."

And they each considered the navy straw with lilacs. Estelle, remembering a fragrant Sunday morning, thought she might as well try that rose hip jam recipe. Sophie speculated on nylon netting and wondered if some nice cotton floral lace wouldn't be just the thing to back the French doors at home. Sydnor had rather misted over because she quite suddenly remembered that the navy straw with the forget-me-nots was, in fact, packed in tissue on the top shelf of an old cedar-lined wardrobe that was stored in a dark corner of the upstairs sleeping loft.

And so the July Fourth holiday, warm and sticky and damp from combinations of tanning lotion, watermelon juice, and sweat, ground to a close.

If the town basked in its accomplishment, the Yellow Perch Lake Association did not. Everyone who could went to the yearly meeting; it was serious business: a time to elect new officers, debate weed-kill methods, see if Judge Press's 37-inch northern was a bald-faced lie. The meeting would determine the owner of the abandoned row boat that had banged into Eloise Walsh's pier, argue about the menu for the annual lake dinner, and comment lengthily on the summer report from the Fish Committee.

Not only, said Webb, was all this better than television, but residents missed the meeting at their peril. One year, for instance, the Hendricksons returned from a Canadian fishing trip to discover than their select and secretly cultivated mushroom lowland had been filled with a sand a yard deep because the Association had decided that the adjacent slough was a virulent mosquito breeding ground (it was), and filled it.

Two years later, the group decided, as a test, to spread sheets of tarpaper on the frozen lake edge of Dennis Melton's property, so the spring melt would send the covering to the bottom and smother the persistent weeds that sprang up in front of his property each year, fouling motorboat propellers.

Melton had somehow missed this proposal and when an early April storm picked up tarpaper frozen to assorted small icebergs and stones and hurled the entire mess against the new conservatory he'd built onto the boathouse, he became apoplectic. Melton was fortunate to have the local veterinarian in his snowmobile party ("Let's just zip down the hill to the cottage and see what the ice break-up looks like," Melton had said), because not many people respond well when their host's eyes roll back into the head, leaving only the whites showing like the bottoms of fried eggs.

The Association, chastened by this small medical emergency ("and it didn't do a damn thing for the weeds," Al Gustave pointed out), repaired the conservatory damage and bought several incredibly ugly orchids for Melton, who calmed down, especially after being named Chairman of Lake Improvements.

In fact, the weed-fish relationship at the south end of the lake generated considerable animosity among the Association membership. One group said that the waterweeds were superb shelter for small fish and a good breeding area.

The opposition retorted that the weeds were too dense for the kind of schooling that represented healthy fish behavior, and what's more, the weeds literally screwed up boat propellers. It was a kind of reprise to the death-by-tarpaper attempt in the winter.

Lake Association members discovered, during a New Business session, just how strong the anti-weed feeling ran.

"If we spent some of the money clearing out those weeds," said Eloise Walsh, whose property was next to Melton's, "that we've devoted to pumping walleye fingerlings into the lake, there'd be better fishing all the way into our bay."

"The stuff grows back," said Kurt Wraddle, the local guide, reasonably. "We can't use poison . . ."

"Little Squash Lake did," someone interjected,

" . . . because it's illegal and anyway it didn't work very well and it stank up the lake to high heaven." He'd been pressed to serve as acting chairman for the session and was regretting it.

"There are weed-cutting services," Eloise continued, more determined. She was short and fierce, rather like a bulldog.

"Eloise, they run into thousands," said Judge Press. "We checked."

"Well, what are we going to do? Wait till half the lake is clogged?"

"Too bad there's no such thing as an underwater harvester," Al Gustave volunteered. "We could just whack 'em off at the bottom—keep the stuff from reseeding." All the summer residents who had ever mastered Roto-Tilling examined this vision.

"Look," said Wraddle, "the best you could do and I don't know how workable this is, would be to tow something heavy—a steel pipe, something—along the bottom and pull the stuff up. Or break it off. You'd need a couple of powerful towing boats, though."

The genius of this suggestion was that responsibility fell to the weedy-shore people. A week later on a Saturday morning, the Eloise Walsh crew and the Dennis Melton crew, in watercraft powerful enough to hoist multiple water-skiers into position, each hooked tough ropes to the harvesting object. This was a steel box spring, chosen for its innumerable coils, a water weed puller with a vengeance.

Interested parties boated over to watch from a safe distance. At a prearranged starting point, Eloise and Dennis nodded to each other and gunned it. Both boats roared, and both hulls lifted from the water at alarming angles, hovering there in mid-leap, then splashed back down, after sun glasses, life jackets, and water skis slid out and into the lake.

The delighted audience bobbed on the ensuing wash, and some kindly teenagers leaned over to gather the escaped floatables. Dennis Melton swore, richly. Eloise, who'd been thinking along the same lines, eased over within the parameters of the box spring tether, and both conferred. Then, maintaining a boat-to-boat distance of some fifteen feet or so, they carefully eased both boats forward and lo! On the lake bottom, the harvester-box-spring followed. There was applause and some cheering, and since the remainder of the project looked to be lengthy and uninteresting, the audience drifted away.

Overnight, an easterly breeze sprang up, strengthening toward early morning, and the first risers along the western shore of Yellow Perch Lake beheld what the weed harvest had wrought. Mounded along the water's edge were hundreds, nay, thousands of pounds of lank, greenish, dying, slimy water weed roots and tendrils. It had begun—this early—to smell.

Astonished and outraged, cottage owners attempted phone calls to Melton and Walsh. The overflow callers found Wraddle, just in from discovering the stuff was too heavy and slippery to be shoveled or pitchforked. He was reduced to explaining over and over, "It's mostly all water. It'll dry out in a couple of days and just crumble away."

This was a little optimistic, because shortly great swarms of flies descended to feast on minuscule dying things clinging to the weedy mess, and the affected householders retreated indoors, exasperated and swatting. That the other half of the lake had escaped the debacle just made it worse.

Within the week, Eloise Walsh was called to the bedside of a surprised cousin in the Upper Peninsula. Melton, who had renters, was not visible during daylight hours and took to leaving notes on doors before finally dashing off to Green Bay on some sort of business. Kurt Wraddle finally fled 500 miles north into Canada with two visiting fishermen he had ambushed at The Bait

Box out on Rt. 70. He'd offered them a really good guide price if they could be ready to leave in a day.

Eventually, the green stuff decayed away, the flies left, and the principals returned, all vowing never to say another word about the water weeds, one way or another. Much later, a small truck pulled into the Highway G landfill, deposited a battered steel box spring, paid its dumping fee, and left quietly. The subsequent weed growth actually diminished; it seemed to be something that everyone could live with.

So, on balance, it was better to attend the annual meeting.

2 THE FISH COMMITTEE

During relatively normal years, the Association turned its attention to fish. With the weed problem on hold, fish took center stage. True, there were other life forms to be gloated over: a pair of eagles set up shop in Lucia Constantini's tallest pine, loons nested in the next lake over but came to Yellow Perch to show off, and a blue heron had taken to shitting all over Webb and Sophie's pier, an intimacy that rather pleased them. Still, fish in all forms, manifestations, life cycle, and representative weirdness won group interest hands down. The major concern involved managing the actual fish population.

The Association had started cautiously, first studying and cultivating the current fish mix. Dieter Vilnus emerged as a natural project leader. He was a resident four properties and some forest down the lake from Sydnor and the Tintingers, was a central European, a refugee of war or associated upheaval and had been so cosseted within a Chicago community of (one supposed) fellow countrymen that he had never completely mastered English. But he was voluble, and after a lengthy conversation with Dieter, one was apt to come away speaking a kind of Euro-pidgin with odd attendant accents and glottals. But, by God, Judge Press said, the man knew his fish.

For instance, structure makes fish very happy; fishermen know this. Fish love, if not solid walls of weeds, then watery tendrils and irregular shapes on lake bottoms; they hover over them blowing little bubbles with their fish lips, happy and comfortable feeling invisible against this background. The Association leadership thought about structure at length, studied the benefits of fish cribs, and prepared to construct some.

Too late. Dieter Vilnus, operating on instinct, had sunk two old wooden rowboats in strategic fish areas mid-lake.

"Fish cribs," he announced to the meeting. "Yah. I work like two Belgian horses. Good fish cribs, you catch good pike there, if you like pike." Vilnus was a crappie man; he caught dozens of enormous crappies and, with his pleasant round wife, pickled them. They could both be found, late summer afternoons, scaling and scraping, swathed in long butcher aprons, hovering over fish cleaning tables, a touch of 19th century Europe.

The bullhead problem was brought up during the fish crib meeting; Sydnor was not paying much attention, but Al Gustave was, and she found him afterwards, swearing quietly to Webb, Sophie and Maureen.

"Damn bullheads," he snarled, "They get in through the outlet. Some fool tourist prob'ly bought little ones for bait."

"We'll have to try to clean them out," Webb said. "They'll wreck the fishing."

"The little ones are adorable," Sydnor protested. Gustave shot her a venomous look.

"Bottom feeders, junk fish, they'll breed like cockroaches and ruin the lake for sport fish." But the babies were perfect miniature catfish, complete to their tiny spiky whiskers. They wiggled together in minnow schools: yard-wide black clouds of darling little bullheads, looking a little like tadpoles until you got up close. They hovered in the warm shallows, perfectly visible over the pale sand.

Three days later on a Tuesday morning, Dieter Vilnus appeared on the lake path, strode up and handed Sydnor one end of a seine net saying, "Here. We walk together through your water, catch the bullheads."

Sydnor, too surprised to protest, found herself a partner in this sweep. Vilnus was skillful. He scattered the valuable game fish minnows that the cove's shallows sheltered in great numbers, then scooped up a small cloud of the baby bullheads and dumped them in buckets of water.

Webb took over the end of the seine net and worked the next scallop of shoreline with Vilnus. Sydnor found the operation depressing and sat in Sophie's kitchen drinking reheated coffee.

"At least they didn't just dump them in the woods," she said morosely. It took the better part of several weeks, but Dietrick Vilnus chivvied residents, armed them with his net, and even surprised summer renters found themselves part of the great bullhead minnow roundup. At the end of the hunt, the lake was as empty of bullheads as was reasonable, and Dieter Vilnus, who had removed gallons of the creatures, was unanimously named permanent Chairman of the Fish Committee.

Then the Association edged into the restocking project. After much discussion with the Natural Resources people and general calling around, the ad hoc Fish Committee put 1,000 five-inch walleyed pikes from a local resource into the lake. In the following weeks, the fish committee squinted into the shallows and around half-submerged trees hoping for glimpses of the pikelets.

Early one morning when the fog was just beginning to lift and the loons had retreated through the woods to recover from their dawn reveille, Milt Hendrickson, the perpetually fishing husband of Maureen, came bow-to-bow with Dietrick Vilnus. They floated many feet above one of Vilnus' structures.

"You know, I think maybe I start to bring coffee and crullers. I see every fisherman on lake before breakfast right here."

Milt sighed. "We can't figure out where you sunk the other rowboat. If we could find it, you'd only run into us half the time."

"Oh. You should say something before. It's other side of little point, where Gustave always loses French spinner. No good fishing though. I just see northern big as a baseball bat over there;

it eat everything. The northern getting big; we feed them baby walleye, I think."

"You serious?"

"Last week I see 30-inch northern under Constantini pier. Monday I see two. The crappies they hide. I think Lake Association buy 1,000 swimming pieces breakfast food. You ask: I bet nobody catching anything."

"Jeez," said Milt, and rowed over to the Tintinger pier, startling Webb who was rinsing heron traces off the pier with lake water. He'd not seen Milt Hendrickson this close to dry ground since Memorial Day weekend.

"What's wrong?" Sophie demanded, sprinting out of the cottage clutching her coffee cup.

"Dieter says the northern pike are eating the walleye fingerlings. Don't you think, Soph, that a northern as big as a baseball bat is more likely a muskie?"

At 9 a.m., Webb trolled over to Al Gustave, anchored in the general area of the fish structure. He was attaching a lure to his line with a reef knot and a look of determination. Gustave received the walleyecide information calmly. Both men stared at the trees and fished aimlessly for a while, then Webb dropped anchor and stepped carefully into Gustave's boat, which they turned toward the judge's dock, "Bench Press" carefully stenciled on the side.

The emergency meeting of the Fish Committee at the Vilnus lakefront was a surprise to the permanent chairman who had to be hailed off the lake to attend. Dieter had caught six crappies and a 36-inch northern pike. "I catch for experiment," he explained. Al Gustave raised his eyebrows, never having considered landing a large northern, or a small one for that matter, subject to whim.

Dieter slung the fish on his cleaning table, knocked it on the head and slit its bottom. "Ah ha!" he said, and everybody looked as a partially digested smallish walleyed pike emerged with the entrails.

"I begin to understand the workings of the haruspex," Judge Press remarked.

"Somebody take northern," called Mrs. Vilnus from the porch. "Nasty big fish. No taste, too many bones. Is fresh coffee here." Milt Hendrickson was bobbing against the pier, wanting to know what was the deal. Webb went to tell him, Gustave finished cleaning the fish, Judge Press and Dieter retired to the porch and were randomly sprinkled with powdered sugar from Mrs. Vilnus' crullers by the time the committee reconvened.

"Those walleyes are expensive," Gustave said.

"And fading fast," Webb added.

"Well, apparently all the major northerns in the lake have been yearning to sink their teeth onto a five-inch walleyed pike," said the Judge. "Now what are we going to do about it?"

"I think northern pike lazy fish," said Dieter. "Panfish good enough food before, but easier to chomp up dumb new walleye. We put in lots, though. Next year they chomp back."

"So when they're bigger it won't matter?"

"It matters now," said Gustave, irritatedly, "because nobody can catch anything, and we're losing the walleyes. How many can a good-size northern eat in a week?"

"We've screwed up the balance of nature," said Judge Press, "whatever that was."

"How 'bout we feed everybody," said Dieter. "We buy balance of nature. We get cheap panfish, everything eat them. We throw in some little bass, they grow like crazy. Maybe pike, new walleyes eat some, but everybody eat panfish, and game fish, they grow up big. By spring we got lake full of hungry grown-up fish; they leap out of water chasing each other."

"Is there any budget left?" asked Webb. They all considered.

"Oh, what the hell," said Judge Press. "Why not?"

"Fisherman. All crazy," said Mrs. Vilnus, taking the empty cruller plate.

Around sunset, Webb walked through the woods to Bench Press where the judge, on his pier, had stymied the mosquito population with a good deal of pungent cigar smoke.

"I found out what Dieter did with the little bullheads."

Judge Press blew a perfect smoke ring. "Does it involve an old European custom that will raise warts on our hands?"

Webb laughed. "He's got this big screen livebox under the pier where they keep the crappies till they can clean them. Dieter put all the bullhead minnows into his old rain barrels and fed them a bucket at a time to the crappies. Took a while. Vera told me. The crappies were fat as pigs. Waste not, want not."

"So much for the old 'they don't eat in captivity' theory."

"Either fish are real, real, stupid or Dieter is very, very smart."

"I vote for the second. Fish that tricky to catch can't be that dumb."

"Yup. There's a mosquito as big as a 747 on your arm."

* * *

Directly across the lake, a half-glass trilevel confection faced into the morning sun and threw shards of reflected sunlight at Mason Thrip, owner, who contemplated it from a safe distance on his pier.

He squinted at the cathedral ceiling, the cook-your-own-ox limestone fireplace and the terrace, begging for tubs of expensive yews and blue spruce. What had he been thinking of? This was a fishing lake. This was a lake where whole families had lived for years and years. Hell, people didn't even put up signs, there were just mailboxes with washed-out names on the side away from traffic.

The enormity of his miscalculation had been slowly creeping up on him and had finally sunk into his functioning consciousness early this morning.

"Randi," he yelled.

"In the garage," his wife called back. He fumed, quietly. He didn't want to go into the garage again. He had spent the entire morning in the garage. It was full of his boat, a construction so ornate that it resembled a floating ballistic missile system. It was bewhiskered with gauges, antennae, dials, sounders, and various gear that, with impressive beeping noises and read-outs, described lake conditions, weed conditions, fish conditions and the overall condition of its conditions. With an estimated top speed of 135 m.p.h., it could hurtle across the lake in two minutes flat and churn right through sand, moss, and pine needles up to the front door of the cottage across the lake and quite possibly right into its living room.

"What is this thing?" Miranda asked from the drive. She was holding a long object at arm's length as if it were a dead snake.

"Did that come off?" he cried.

"Unless it's meant to lie uselessly under the boat, I guess you could say it came off. What is it?"

"Part of the temperature gauge. You know. Calculates the difference between the surface and bottom." He took the snaky fragment reverently.

"How much difference could there be? The DNR map says the lake's only 23 feet deep."

Mason Thrip made one of those snap decisions that reverberates through a season if one is fortunate and through a lifetime if one is not.

"Randi, we're going to put the boat on the Chain. This lake is far too small. I'll just hook 'er up and we'll slide it in at the Dockworks."

"Oh, Mason, do you really need me? I kind of wanted to transplant some of that wild columbine."

"Oh, come on honey; we'll drop her in and take a little run down the Chain to the brewery at the portage. It'll be fun."

Sighing, his wife went to get a sweater. Mason Thrip backed his van into the general vicinity of the boat hitch so that his unwieldy craft, gleaming with chrome and christened in stencil "The Rolling Boil," might float in more appropriate waters.

3 WHEELS WITHIN WHEELS

It was a relatively familiar name; the steep chrome letters on the building's façade were designed to impress. The name represented power, fuel, speed, pollution, enormous return on investment, and the American Way. Inside, on the eleventh floor, three men were seated around a map at a board room table. It was a detailed document, heavily annotated to indicate larger or smaller mineral deposits in the northern half of a state famous for lakes, streams and dense forests. These were small details, however; the company had long and extensive experience sweeping those kinds of impediments out of the way.

"Promising," said the man in the navy blazer. "Very promising. Has engineering seen the prelims?"

"They're all over it," said a tweedy type, whose name was Drochek and who represented Research and Development. "Champing at the bit. We'll go after on-site cores and samples as fast as we can. First leasing letters are out; we should be seeing replies soon."

"You don't anticipate difficulty?" inquired the third man, a lawyer. He was carefully nondescript. Indeed, his protective blandness was such that, had he immediately left the room, neither the man in the navy blazer (whose name was Shutter and who was in charge of Exploratory Planning) or Drochek could have—with any certainty—described what he looked like. The lawyer had deliberately constructed his personal camouflage. He saw himself as an éminence gris, a conceit born of his fascinated reading of Cardinal Richelieu's biography. He found the 17th century schemer and statesman's deviousness extremely impressive. The lawyer's name was Ross; he felt that he'd been a little shortchanged in that respect.

"Difficulty?" said Drochek. "Naw, we have some friends in the governor's office and our lobbyist has touched base with his lobbyist."

Ross smiled. "The governor's lobbyist?"

"One of the Natural Resources people is—I guess sympathetic—is the right word. He used to be with the state Commerce and Industry Association. Plus these locals are pussycats; they haven't got a clue. And the profit thing is a great motivator. The lease is impressive; I think it looks to them like they might make a lot of money—relatively speaking, of course," Drochek added.

"Leases, initial exploration, long term mineral rights, excavation," said Shutter, ticking off the high points.

"What's the time line?" Ross asked.

"The aerial surveys took a year plus," Shutter said, "you know the rest, so I'd expect to start excavating in a few months."

The trio leaned over the map again.

"Copper, zinc, a little gold?" Ross inquired.

"Mostly copper and zinc," said Drochek.

"Extraction?"

"Well, the usual methods. You know. It make take a little more work by engineering, but it's early days yet," said Drochek cheerfully. Engineering had actually said, "Water! It's all water. You're gonna have to pump the entire county dry." No point bringing that up now—early days. He reverently folded the map, crosshatched carefully to indicate greater or lesser presumed mineral deposits around, over, and under myriad lakes, waterways, streams, and forests, and tucked it into his briefcase.

It was a very good map, and thorough. It had been compiled over a long period by low-flying aircraft equipped with relatively sensitive cameras and magnetic equipment. In fact, the small planes with the odd gear fastened beneath the wings had generated considerable comment. After all, people sitting on tractors or in fishing boats had ample time to look up and ponder the sudden new interest in their terrain.

The planners had anticipated curiosity, and throughout the region, small articles appeared in local papers announcing an inclusive (though otherwise vague) geophysical survey in progress. The articles rather cleverly implied that the rest of the state had been surveyed or studied or something, and that the "geophysical survey" had just gotten around to mopping up these leftover counties in the north.

An alert reader might have caught a tone, made famous by "The Wizard of Oz," suggesting that the viewer pay no attention to the little man behind the curtain.

"One other thing," said the lawyer. "If the locals demand public meetings and if we have to have a few, let's remember to insist on scheduling them in afternoons or mornings. No benefit in having an entire town turn out to confront our people. Let's try and keep it low key."

* * *

Mason and Miranda Thrip were on the verge of a different adventure.

"Am I close? Am I close?"

"Four feet. Three feet. Now just go real slow . . . " Miranda was making little measuring motions with her hands.

"There! There!" she called. "It's just touching."

Mason Thrip, leaning out the van window, was easing—gingerly, gingerly easing—trailer hitch to boat. The boat, settled in its winch-rigged cradle, looked like a Thanksgiving turkey nesting on three marbles. It dwarfed Mason, the van and the garage. He peered again and climbed out.

"We'll just pop 'er on," he muttered, gripping the trailer shaft. Thrip had done this before with the salesman's assistance. Getting it off had been a lot easier, though pretty alarming. There were procedural bits with the trailer cable that he hadn't quite grasped, and would have to study later.

"Ngghh."

"Mason, You'll hurt yourself!" said Miranda.

"Ngghh! Ngghh!" said Mason, and van and trailer joined with a nasty little clack.

"Isn't that a pretty thing," he said, quite red from the effort, and stepping back to admire the attachment.

They climbed into the van. The sun shone, birds sang, the lake sparkled. Mason settled his fishing cap at a rakish angle and accelerated. The boat swung like a vast compass needle and pointed north, into a space already occupied by the garage. The door frame splintered from the impact and the winch cable, twanging off various metal objects, whiplashed around the remnant of door, the trailer hitch and, since Mason's van was still rolling forward, its right rear axle.

"Oh god," said Miranda. Metal bits were still humming from the impact. The woods seemed suddenly very quiet.

Mason tottered out of the van, white-faced, inspected the damage, and cursed. In the classic bad timing that came to mark the day, Mr. Bleu's mail jeep puttered up the driveway. Mason cursed again, but more quietly and from a different perspective.

"Mm. Look's like you got a situation here," said Mr. Bleu, staring appreciatively at the garage door, now at half-mast and resectioned. Mason moved his mouth, but since he'd not yet settled on outraged, frightened, or furious, nothing of substance came out.

"Do you know of any . . ." Miranda began.

"Sure thing," said Mr. Bleu. "Call the City Service people at the 70 intersection. Jimmy—his dad's the owner but Jimmy runs the towing—tell 'em . . ." he gazed appraisingly at the garage and the door slid gently onto the ground, its springs protesting—"tell 'em to bring the big truck. Look's like you might be going to need a carpenter too. Want'cher mail?"

4 SAL FALLS IN LOVE

Sal Constantini had checked all his vital signs, established that he wasn't catching cold, he wasn't having some kind of allergic reaction, but was simply mentally disheveled. The only logical conclusion (an awful one) was that he had fallen in love. The realization plunged him into deep gloom—another sensation that he vaguely remembered from some time ago. It was a disaster. Well, wonderful, but a disaster after all. And it wasn't as if he wasn't seasoned. Boy, was he seasoned.

He'd been married, he was happily divorced, two children, boys, amicably shared; he'd been pursued, he had pursued in turn, he was pursued still; after all, he was a catch. No need to pretend. His company, net worth, and eligibility were public knowledge. (Constantini mattresses was a hugely successful concern. "Constantini Cares About a Good Night's Sleep" blared from the sides of all the company vans.) The annoying element this time was that he seemed to have fallen in love with someone who, first, was not pursuing him, second, probably knew who he was, and third, didn't give a damn.

She was, moreover, absolutely unlike anyone that he had found attractive in the past. She wasn't a blonde. He liked a certain amount of—well, not dependence, more a certain melting appreciation for his possibilities. She wasn't a melter. She regarded him—the time that she had regarded him—levelly, appraisingly, as if sizing up a small animal for rabidity. He suspected she'd filed him in a stack of rejects somewhere.

He'd come upon her in the Co-op parking lot. Her jeep—battered—was parked next to his van. She had just finished changing a tire and was stowing her jack in the rear. She was a little dusty.

"I borrowed your tarp," she said. "Thank you."

"My tarp?"

"The back of your van was open. I used it to kneel on. I think it's clean. If it's not, I'll hose it down and drop it off."

"Drop it off?"

"To the address on the side of the van," she said, "unless it's a front." She seemed quite serious. The "Constantini Cares" address was in smaller but legible type.

"No, glad to . . . I'm sure it's fine . . ." he trailed off, beginning to realize his blunder.

"Thanks then," she said, climbed into the jeep, started it, and drove away. Now there was no reason for him to see her again, which is what he suddenly wanted to do.

Sal was struck dumb. An entire herd of buffalo had walked over him, and all he could say was, "I'm sure it's fine?" What kind of a bozo remark was that?

This was nuts. Where were his brains? He was going to have to find her, and in a town of some 1,300 people, it could be slow going. But, he considered, not impossible. Unless, unless, she lived out of town, in the woods or on a lake somewhere. Hell.

Sal stood next to his van transfixed, holding a 10-pound bag of potatoes. Snapping back to reality, he frowned at a surprised shopper, and angry with himself, shoved the potatoes into the van and drove home.

Home, this week, was the family summer place on Yellow Perch Lake. He would collect his boys from camp next Saturday. His mother, Lucia Constantini, had asked why he needed to send them off to a camp, for heaven's sake, as they fronted on a lovely lake and were surrounded by miles of deep woods. "To teach them how to fight," said Sal. Lucia, who'd grown up with numerous brothers, saw the logic. "And their mother thinks it's a great idea." So. Bargaining chip.

He could hear his mother from the driveway turn-in. She was organizing the asphalt people quite loudly. There would be a newly surfaced turnaround behind the guest cottage. She was in competition with some heavy equipment and she was winning. Lucia Constantini won frequently; it was her combination of organization and energy. In a perfect world, she would have headed up the Joint Chiefs of Staff.

Sal was staring into the refrigerator when Lucia trotted into the kitchen, holding a bouquet of invoices, the regular mail, a box of invitations, and two ball point pens.

"Where are the potatoes?"

"Oh. The potatoes. They're still in the van."

"Can't have a cookout without potato salad."

"I'll get them," he said, not moving.

"I hope you find what you're looking for in the refrigerator. It's defrosting nicely with you holding the door open. What *are* you looking for?"

"I don't know," Sal said helplessly. "I thought I did but now I don't." Lucia observed her son narrowly. This was not typical behavior. But then, what was typical behavior these days? And she was not about to engage in amateur psychoanalysis. Grown-ups, Lucia believed, fell into crazy spells, and since such things were part of life, they had to figure out how to deal with them. Especially if they were at or past voting age.

"Potatoes," she said. "Potatoes, potatoes." Sal went.

※ ※ ※

The cookout—a picnic, actually—was the following day. They were blessed with a sun-saturated afternoon. In Lucia's gazebo fizzy drinks sat in tubs of ice; friends and neighbors milled about, exclaiming about the weather and the terrific food. Sal drifted over to a conversation between two of his neighbors,

Sydnor Feffer and Al Gustave, who were arguing about septic systems. Gustave was forwarding considerable advice, remarkable in that he had only the most primitive toilet facilities at (or near) his cabin.

"Now the Canadian dry toilet," he was explaining, leaning slightly to the left to level his drink, "just needs this little electric fan that vents out the residues . . . "

"Yech," Sydnor said.

". . . . and come spring when you open up, you just take out this tray of perfect loam and throw it into the woods. And toss in another handful of starter."

"Starter?" she queried.

"Some sort of bacteria and moss mix; just munches everything right up."

"I'd have to dig a basement, Al. It needs to drop down into something and fester."

"Um," Gustave said. He was a gnarled old woodsman, and this new consideration made him resemble an extremely thoughtful tree trunk.

"Or you could close down your bathroom and dig an outhouse," Sal offered. "Do you need another drink?"

"Much help you are," Sydnor said, "but thanks, I'm fine. Rummaging around for a septic system upgrade will take forever, but there are always margaritas to help the experience along. How are you? You're looking a little peaked, if you don't mind my saying so."

"I have a woman problem," he said, "and don't tell my mother."

"Pah!" Gustave snorted, and went off to find a conversation about fish.

"You know, I've never thought of you having woman problems," Sydnor said, studying him more carefully. To her, Sal looked like a cross between a mafia prince and an extremely intelligent pirate. "I'd have thought they'd fall out of trees into your lap. Or is that the problem?"

"No, not exactly. I met somebody in the Co-op parking lot that absolutely knocked me out. I've never seen her before, I don't know her name, there's no way to find her, and I may have to kill myself."

"You're in love!" Sydnor declared, and immediately lowered her voice.

"How can I find this person? What would you do?" Sal asked, moving to a quieter corner.

"Oh, there are all kinds of options. First, I'd see Walter Hansen in town and find out what he knows. I think his real estate expertise covers every living creature who walks the streets."

"She has a jeep," said Sal, morosely.

A jeep: practically a philosophy, thought Sydnor. "Tell him that, and you could also casually ask around the gas stations if anybody's seen a nice used jeep that they'd been willing to part with."

"Tan or khaki; sort of beat up."

"You're beginning to drift. Look at it this way. Worse comes to worst, you could hang out in the Co-op parking lot and when hunger drives her back, well, there you are. *Now* I need another drink. Come on, let's see if my uncle can shed some light on this hunt. What about license plates?"

* * *

For the next several days, Sal saw jeeps—real and imaginary. He'd catch a glimpse of one turning into a side street, and the jeep would have vanished when he turned in after it. He looked searchingly at one in a gas station—it was tan, but new. Once, in a fit of excitement, he followed a beat-up looking jeep down a private drive and then had to make excuses to the teenage driver who climbed out of it and asked him if he was lost. It was too much. He went to see Walter Hansen holed up in his real estate office in an explosion of paper.

Walt had a wonderful week once, selling Lucia Constantini a lot adjoining her lake property so that a septic field for a year-around home could be created. He considered it remarkable that he remembered it at all, as the Constantinis believed that quantities of red wine were essential to all business transactions, and Hansen had spent the entire time slightly looped.

"Well, there's vehicle registration," Hansen offered, flattered by Sal's plea for assistance. "But they're reluctant unless it's a police matter."

Sal mentally riffled through the business Christmas Card list for various legal types in good standing, debating whether or not to make it a police matter. Tacky, very tacky, so no.

"But if you have time for research," Hansen was saying, gazing thoughtfully out the window, "figure out what kind of work would be easier if someone had a jeep. Or maybe not easier, but where a jeep might be necessary."

"Walter, I get what you mean, but we're not exactly in the badlands."

"Well, you've obviously never been to the Porcupine Mountains," said Hansen testily. "Call the Forest Service people. Call the local surveying companies. Call the Yuper Rally Club."

"A jeep isn't actually a racing car," Sal began.

"It might as well be," said Hansen, who was out of his league. "Sal, I don't want to be discouraging, but maybe this is a woman who just likes jeeps."

It was nearly two weeks before Sal was able to break away from work for an extended weekend at Yellow Perch Lake. "Just so you know," Lucia had said on the phone, "The St. Pete Woman's Guild is on retreat this weekend near Crystal Falls and I'm going, so you're on your own. There's a grocery list stuck to the refrigerator. If it gets too quiet, go talk to Webb and Sophie. I hear he's worked out a new pattern for Adirondack chairs. It's always nice to have you around, dear."

Sal took himself off to the Co-op, carefully checked the parking lot, and went in to edit the grocery list. It would be ok, he thought, if he never ate bratwurst again. With all the good soppressata and prosciutto in the world, why would anyone need bratwurst? He went to haggle over a slab of fresh salmon with the amiable counterman.

He was missing a single item, one not to be found at the Co-op. No useful knife sharpener is ever found in a grocery store. He nipped over to the local hardware store, found a sharpener immediately, and spent a fulfilling 30 minutes among the table saws. Then someone in the next aisle said, "Tarp." Or she had said it in the middle of a sentence. Sal stopped breathing and leaned into a wall of clamps to listen.

"Are they only blue? Don't you have tan or something? Tarp blue is a nasty color." Good god, it was the jeep woman. A hardware salesperson said regretfully that there had been a sort of murky green, but it sold out; there was only blue. Sal leaned further toward the conversation and unhooked a large clamp with his elbow. With a wild gyration, he caught it before it hit the floor.

He had to intercept her somehow—how? Where? Here? No, it would look dumb: a three-way conversation including a sales guy? Sal put the knife sharpener in a wheelbarrow full of small socket wrenches, moved quickly to the far end of the next aisle, and peered along a perfectly uniform row of toilet seats at the tarp conversation that seemed to be ending. The woman (Yes! The same woman!) was shaking her head and turning toward the main aisle.

In a sprint that would have credited an Olympic trainee, Sal dashed past the plastic laundry baskets sale, ducked his head to avoid a rack of hanging cookout aprons, leaving a row of festive potholders swaying in unison, and zoomed out into the parking lot. There, third row down, was the tan battered jeep. He took a deep breath, stood next to it, and waited.

She emerged carrying a rag rug, spotted him, and kept coming. Sal felt a little faint. She was in sandals, faded red capri pants, and a T-shirt printed with the NASA photo of Earth. The breeze ruffled her hair but not her composure. "Yes?" she inquired pleasantly. It could have been worse; she could have said, "Who are you?"

"I can find a tan tarp for you, but it might take a little time, because the nearest one is probably 150 miles away," said Sal, trying to breathe normally. He would find a tan tarp if he had to make it himself.

She considered his offering calmly. Was she was being enticed with a tan tarp? He looked considerably better than at their first meeting. Good nose, she thought. In fact, good everything. His hair curled; she wondered what it might feel like. "I'll bet you're going to give me your card."

"No," said Sal, "but I'm going to ask your name, otherwise I'll have to leave it with the hardware store, addressed to Woman with Tan Jeep."

"And you know I want a tan tarp because. . ."

"I heard you from the next aisle," he admitted. "I was in table saws. It would be nice if I knew your name."

"Ah. You're thinking about asking me out, aren't you."

"How do you know?"

"Because there's a little vein in your left temple that's throbbing noticeably."

"Jesus," said Sal, clapping his hand to his head.

"Victoria," she replied. "I think dinner would be a good idea, if you're free tomorrow evening, and then we can get this tarpaulin adventure straightened out. Six would be good; I'm at Tamarack Lake Lodge; one of my relatives runs it. I'll be in the bar. Is that all right with you?

"Yes," said Sal, who was operating in a twilight state. "I'm . . ."

"I know. It was on the side of your van. See you tomorrow." She smiled, and Sal wanted to grab her, the rug, and all of her worldly possessions and roll down a long, long, green hill into a meadow full of flowers. He understood—intellectually—this vision was absolutely insane. How was he going to get through the next 24 hours?

Driving back to the lake, he kept hearing a strange buzzing sound, and after two miles or so, Sal realized that he'd left the parking brake on. He'd been trying to see the vein in his temple by readjusting the rear view mirror; the vein seemed to have settled down. He considered all the idiotic stories he'd ever read about people dying or throwing themselves off bridges in fits of passion. They seemed crazy then; they didn't seem so crazy now.

At home, he dashed into the bathroom and took two aspirin on the off chance they might be useful, then marched down to the dock, climbed into his over-powered inboard, leaned back and stared at the sky and took a deep breath. It was all still there. Sky, trees, clouds. He started the engine, eased out into the lake, and at a furious speed, made four long, long figure eights, chopping back over his own wake. He drifted back home. Twenty four hours. Oh, boy.

* * *

In the end, the event was more tranquil, but laced with what the French call *frission*, a thrill, an anticipation of the unexpected. It was Sal's own fault; he wasn't sure what he was facing here, and he was fueled by rapture and nerves.

Fortunately, Lucia Constantini, back from her determined meditations, was dealing with business and had been engaged in a series of phone calls to landscapers, evergreen farms, and the two or three nurseries in a 20-mile radius that were able to whip up banks of established-looking plantings in a single afternoon. Had she been paying attention, she would have seen her son, in uncharacteristic wardrobe indecision, wander past the kitchen in a black shirt, no collar; then in a dark maroon shirt, open collar; and finally in a black knit shirt, no collar, casual jacket.

Lucia's comments on this parade of fashion would have been seven or eight degrees beyond sarcastic. However, the mailman banged on the screen door to get a signature for a box of expensive fabric samples, and Sal changed back into Levi's and a T-shirt. He walked aimlessly down to the lake and back, then split some wood he'd ignored for a year or so.

***

She was in the Tamarack Lodge bar sipping Campari. (Campari! he thought. In this state?) Her name was Victoria Caruso and she was camped out in one of the Tamarack cabins for the summer in exchange for some sort of work that Sal wasn't very clear about. She was wearing a tiered Navajo skirt and a cotton sweater, and looked wonderful.

They stepped into the bright late afternoon sun, paused, and looked at each other. "You're taller than I thought," Victoria said. She came up to the bridge of his nose.

"You're exactly the right size," Sal replied, smiling.

In for a penny, in for a pound, Victoria thought. This was the first time the old saying seemed crystal clear to her. Heigh-ho, she thought, delightedly.

"We have reservations," said Sal, opening the passenger door.

"Please do not ever call me Vicki," she said, climbing into Sal's small fast car, dusted off in honor of the occasion. "And our Caruso is from the Spanish, so I'm no good at Italian irregular verbs, or anything like that."

"I don't think I know any," said Sal, wondering what his mother would make of this forthright and possibly crazy person. "Do you?"

"Just establishing some guidelines here," she said seriously. That was hopeful, he thought. It meant there could be more Victoria available in the future. Calm, calm.

The tarp was necessary because of the dissertation she was researching on blue heron habits, those involving breeding and nesting. Heron research tended to be dampish, she explained. They were water birds, after all.

"They stop feeding the chicks at a certain point, to make them hungry enough to leave the nest. How do they know when to do that? Do the nests get too small? Does the intensity of daylight change? It's very interesting; I think I have an new angle." Angle was an appropriate term, since the nests were in the tops of very tall trees. "There's a large rookery in the Nicolet National Forest," she added.

"It's across the road," said Sal modestly. "I mean, the forest is the boundary of the east side of Yellow Perch Lake."

"Ah," she said, considering. "Do you know any of the roads in?" He did not, but had a very fine Forest Service map, and promised to memorize it and/or hand it over.

They had gone to the next town known for its Cajun restaurant. The menu included whole schools of blackened fish varieties which they declined in favor of pasta. Victoria had thick dark hair, cut short; it grew away from her face on the left side, then reversed direction to reappear on the right in a curved, elegant arc. Sal had a sudden desire to brush it back from her ear, but reached for an olive instead, and was forced to wash it down with red wine.

And then they relaxed. It was the wine or the sunset or on Victoria's part, the realization that he was interesting and probably wasn't going to lunge at her. Across the table, Sal continued charmed, while realizing there was a lot he needed to find out (Herons?) and even if he wanted to lunge at her, and he did, he had no idea how such a gesture would be received.

So they ate and told each other stories. Victoria described the peculiar life of a graduate student. It sometimes made her feel, she said, like a visitor trapped in a middle school. Her parents, in Ohio, were supportive but a little puzzled. "There are teachers in the family," she said, "but what I'm doing seems pretty exotic to everybody."

Sal sympathized. "You've got a bunch of Herons on your side at least," he said wryly. "They're probably a lot more sympathetic than our competitors."

"They're undercutting you with imported hammocks?" Victoria inquired, and Sal laughed. They drove back in moonlight.

Tamarack Lake Lodge had a long dock and they'd walked to its end when Victoria said, "I have to be back on campus for a seminar for about a week. So if you're serious about the tarp, consider it a relaxed deadline."

Sal felt a stab of panic. "And you're coming back?'

"Of course. I have to count eggshells. The fledglings are just starting to thrash around. And I'll cook something for you as a thank you gesture for this evening."

"Where?'

"Here." She waved randomly toward the cottages. "Don't I look like I can cook?"

"Where's your seminar?"

"No sneaking in permitted. I have to concentrate. This thesis has to be defendable."

"Victoria, I want to see you again, very soon, immediately. Why can't I deliver the tarp to you at wherever, and just quietly leave?'

"You don't strike me as a person who would just leave, quietly or otherwise. That's why we're standing on this pier making small talk. Listen Sal, I think you are probably the most gorgeous man I have ever seen in my life, so it's important to . . ." At which point he grabbed her and kissed her variously and thoroughly, putting an end to sensible precautions, and thus unbalanced, they pitched forward into the lake, fortunately missing a tethered canoe.

"God, how romantic," said Victoria, laughing and splashing upright in four feet of water.

"It's warm," said Sal. "Peel off your clothes and let's swim. We can't get any wetter."

"No no; there are leeches here; big black leeches. Come on, we'll towel off in my cabin. I'll work you over with a hair dryer; no lust. Your gorgeous quotient has decreased."

"It's all your fault. You took advantage of my weakened state. It burns the wine off, though." He looked very wet and pleased.

"I'll know better next time." Victoria looked like something pulled through a swamp; Sal's hair had sprung into a mass of tight curls. They exchanged wet for fresh towels, gestures they found hilarious all out of proportion to simply getting dry. Victoria kissed Sal damply and soundly and sent him home wrapped, toga-like, in a large beach towel with a big bright orange smiling sun face, his wet clothes draped over the passenger's seat.

Victoria re-washed her hair and immediately fell asleep, flattening it on one side, so she washed it again in the morning. Both counted the evening an enormous success.

Sal returned the next evening with the towel, laundered, and bearing a bottle of very good wine. Victoria had zipped around town, gathering ingredients for an impromptu bouillabaisse, and found some fine French bread. They fell upon the meal like hungry wolves, and then, rather more gently, upon each other, so completing the promising start made the previous day.

Because neither were amateurs, no bones were broken. (Victoria later discovered that the small crackling sound she'd vaguely heard was a saucer full of safety pins, spilling off a chair.) Bits of clothing led, like a breadcrumb trail, around the table, past the fireplace, and into the small bedroom where it ended.

When it was late enough for the moon to light a path across the fine glaze of sweat on Sal's right shoulder, Victoria, slightly muffled, said, "You're staying?"

"I left for the city at six o'clock. I'm possibly there by now. Maybe I stopped for dinner someplace. I hope you're not planning on throwing me out."

"Good god, no!" Then, thoughtfully, "You have a toothbrush."

"In the overnight bag. Not on me, notice. Plus one at the lake house, one in the city, and one in the trunk to clean maple seeds out of the hood slots. You think I would shake you down for a toothbrush?' He slipped his arm behind her head to get a better view. "I'll bet you're loaded with toothbrushes."

"Not anymore," she said, and stroked a handy spot in the small of his back. Which put the matter aside for the evening.

Early in the morning, Sal, tranquil, left with a piece of buttered toast in his mouth, two paper napkins in a pocket, and plans for the near future. Victoria washed, dressed, and packed. She put down her bag, looked around, considered for a moment, and then pulled off the bedding and stuffed it into a laundry sack that she tossed into the jeep with her suitcase and notebooks. Privacy was important; Victoria was strong on privacy. Yea, even unto the last new toothbrush—which Sal had found and taken away with him. It was a portent, probably.

5 INVASION

From the bathroom window—especially the bathroom window—morning flowed into Sydnor's cottage. The sun shown on leaves tender as lettuce, and tossed their images across sink, counterpanes and comforters, across linoleum and the deep speckled colors of the much-enameled kitchen chairs.

These mornings made you want to hug yourself, Sydnor thought, warming her fingers on her coffee cup. The surge of well being made all projects logical, benign, possible. She would string a hammock between two trees. She would find the cottage property survey. She would move the entire woodpile to the new tool shed. She would get a two-story addition underway. She would do it all at once. Today. This morning.

Heady stuff. All her neighbors reported similar bouts of euphoria. It was the air or the altitude or a stiff belt of ozone. It was the woods smell as night evaporated from ferns and hollows. It was the blue heron delicately picking its way around the piers, and the sounds of frogs in the reeds at the point. It was because they were all crazy about the woods. Not only personal woods in front and in back, but next door, along the roads, across the lake, trees and forest singly and collectively, straight up to the timberline, a passion for deep green *in toto*.

Sydnor suspected that ancient forest worshippers would have been perfectly happy cohabiting with, for instance, Al

Gustave, who was so much part of the woods he could easily disappear by just standing still. Gustave, a retired postmaster, had devised a cunning all-terrain forest vehicle from his extensive collection of parts from Model A Fords. It rode high on antique wheel rims and he maneuvered the contraption through the woods, visiting his trees, avoiding fire-blackened stumps with vast colonies of lichen, remnants of a 50-year-old burn.

"Old fire lane's almost grown over," he'd observe, peering up a vanishing path. Sydnor, riding with him on several of these excursions, marveled at how specific his landmarks were. "See the blue spruce? Watched it from six inches. All the hard woods are coming back; all logged out in the 20s. See all them baby maples where that old pine top got tore off?"

Gustave would make an odd deep sound, like a wood dove with catarrh, shift and steer sideways up a gully to examine some rough bark festooned with animal hairs. Indian paintbrushes, wild yellow violets, toadstools as big as turkey platters drifted past in slow motion. The forest was all.

So it was ironic that on a bright, Monday morning, Al Gustave was one of the first to get the letter from the Random Mining Company with a mining lease form attached. He stormed over to the Tintingers and burst into Webb and Sophie's little pick-me-up lunch with Sydnor. He shook the documents, nearly incoherent with rage.

"I'll bet every one who owns property in the county will get the same mailing," Webb said.

"Listen to this part," Gustave demanded, "about wanting to poke around in *my* land for 'all ores, minerals, mineral rights, surface and subsurface upon and under those lands, considered as a whole,' and then this part about exploring for—wait, here it is —'explore for and develop any and all ore or minerals in, upon and under the premises,' and they go on about mining and . . ." (his face was getting dangerously red) "and 'concentrate, smelt, refine or process'—and get this!—'store, stockpile, and exercise all other rights and privileges which may be useful or convenient!' *Convenient*!"

Sydnor was afraid he might have a heart attack. "Steady," she said.

"Al," Webb interrupted, "calm down. You're not going to sign that thing, obviously."

"Well sweet Jesus, no," Gustave shouted. "But if this is going to all the property owners in the township or whatever, some fools are going to sign it—and then where are we?"

"Time to call in legal aid," said Webb, and went to phone Judge Press. Sydnor handed Gustave a cold beer, thinking that an ice pack would have made more sense.

Not too far away, another person held the same document, had read every word of the 6-point type, and circled "Section Three. Annual Payments" with a yellow marker. The Reverend Z. X. Weathersill, pastor, Reformed Brethren Church, was sitting on some 80 acres of absolutely (in his estimation) useless forest and river frontage. It boasted five old and permanently abandoned cottages, a decaying pier, and a raft sunk in 24 inches of water. Occasionally, a hearty family from the church hiked in to camp, but not often.

He reread the bit about "the total annual payment . . . determined by multiplying the respective per acre payment," and made a few rough (and completely unfounded) estimates, and dazzled, added some imaginary "production royalty" numbers. Mercy. They'd pay a royalty on "all the ore mined or extracted." It could be a lot. Let's see, it was a percentage—not a terribly large percentage—of what the mining company got for the ore or minerals or whatever.

This could be really profitable. Weathersill debated about running the whole thing past his board, but after considering pros and cons, dismissed the idea. No point getting them all worked up. First things first. Here was opportunity. He gave a little wiggle of pleasure and uncapped a fountain pen.

And so, though presently invisible but soon to appear in strong bright colors, the battle lines were drawn.

In town, Hansen's Real Estate considered every scrap of land vis-à-vis location, assessment, history, and current taxes owed. Walter Hansen, owner, operator, actual agent and broker, had maps by surveyors and civil engineers that were at least three and four generations old and were coveted by the state historical society. Hansen's Real Estate had a proprietary feel for the acreage underfoot, so the letters from the mining company same as a shock, as it did to friends and colleagues.

"What the hell is this, Walter?" demanded his friend Charlie Haney, who was the county assessor. Both men were in front of Mint's bar, where a nice greasy lunch was served from 11:30 till 2 p.m.

"Charlie, I was figuring to ask you the same," countered Walter. "Doesn't the county assessor get a sneak preview of this kind of underground approach? No pun intended, but some heavy hitters have been researching around, and pretty thoroughly, it looks like. Did you *read* this thing?" And Walter flapped the stapled documents at Charlie.

"I read 'em," Charlie said, "and assessor is an elected position, it doesn't come with second sight. I don't like this much"—he flapped his copies back at Water—"in fact, I don't like it at all. It could be some kind of land grab, or maybe it's harmless, but I don't think so. And I also don't think if I was a tourist I would plan my vacation in a mining town."

"A mining town. Like Riverbend?"

"Don't even say the name," Charlie replied.

Riverbend was an example of the worst kind of takeover. It had been an innocuous little town along the state's major river: a haven for canoes, fishermen, pleasure craft, and, it turned out, for a very large mining corporation. Riverbend had a deposit of gold. The local residents, business people, township, environmentalists, all put up a good fight. It seemed Riverbend might be safe. But then the state governor, well tended to by the mining corporation, jiggered a few critical votes and the local governing council, gutted, caved in.

Riverbend's ore was so rich it was shipped directly across the U.S. border to smelters in Canada. The remainder was not so rich, and the tailings were sealed into a giant septic tank-like silo of questionable quality. (Previously the company had asked if they could just dump the stuff into the river.) Not too long after the profits had been taken and the company removed its equipment, odd chemicals turned up in the ground water, and fishing declined. Then business declined, and Riverbend slid into a kind of Grade B tourist stop.

The governor, on the other hand, moved on to a national post in Washington D.C. where an entrenched bureaucracy refocused his contacts into an area populated by organizations eager for government influence. Subsequently, had he ever set foot in Riverbend, he would have been stoned.

"Well," said Walter, "there's our township council that they're going to have to get past before digging up the place. We're self-governing, last I looked. They'd have to vote permission."

Charlie considered. "Doesn't Minnie Rosenheim's boy have to do with some of this mining stuff? At the University? And he could fill us in on . . . this," he finished lamely.

Minnie's boy, Arthur Rosenheim, possessed a degree in geology, was a full professor, but did not hold a named chair because there wasn't one in that particular branch of the sciences.

"Good." Walter said. "Maybe we can coax him up here for a bit. Minnie'd like that. To fill us in; do sort of a tutoring session."

At about the same time as this conversation was taking place, a hearty business type wandered into the Chamber of Commerce office and wondered to a bored-looking secretary if there was a list of apartment rentals, and by the way, of available office space. She regarded him for a moment, then turned around and yelled, "Harold!"

A round, officious gentleman bustled out of a back room where he'd been eating lunch. Brushing muffin crumbs with one hand, he seized the visitor's with his other and pumped it up and down as if he were jacking up a car. "Harold Whitenaw, what can we do for you this lovely day?"

"Gerald Mactate," the visitor beamed. The abundance of bonhomie generated by the two threatened to suck up the available oxygen in the room. The secretary rolled her eyes and slipped out back for a cigarette. After some chat and appreciative mutual chuckling, the Chamber of Commerce established that first, Mr. Mactate was new to the area, second, he wanted to rent in town, and third, he was planning to transfer his business to the area.

""What do you do, Mr. Mactate?" Whitenaw enquired.

"Oh, I invest," said Mactate modestly, "in a small way. Start-up businesses, sometimes land, it keeps me out of trouble," he smiled. "Call me Gerald." The secretary, who had returned silently, handed Whitenaw a modest list of rental properties, residential and business. Whitenaw passed it to Mactate as if it were printed on beaten gold and offered further aid whenever and wherever he could. Mactate took the list, thanked Whitenaw profusely, and made a mental note that the Chamber could be wrapped around anybody's little finger. He gave a little wave from his car.

As expected, the Tintingers, Sydnor, and the people of the lake community, town and township all received Random Mining Company offers with attached lease forms. They were delivered to people who cared about the woods, waters, and animals. These were people who grieved over dead deer, fed the chipmunks, tested their well water, tidied up in campgrounds, and threw back undersized fish. And, perhaps more to the point, people who hated change. Especially bad change. Mining was bad, bad change; it was a leveler of landscapes, drainer of wetlands, polluter of water, destroyer of forests. What did a mining company care about the blue heron? The leases were not welcomed.

In town and lakeside, various local phalanxes formed and moved to investigate further. Maureen Hendrickson drifted into the county collector's office ostensibly to pay the last installment of the tax bill. She chatted with the office manager, an orange-haired, sharp-eyed woman whose newsgathering capacity was legendary, and who was known far and wide simply as Gertrude. Maureen shared her astonishment at the mining company offers. Wasn't that something? And out of the blue. Had anybody noticed strangers wandering around? Mining company people, very likely?

Gertrude made sympathetic noises. "I hear there's some activity down at the old church camp on the Chain," she allowed. "Somebody's trucking in equipment." Her tone was disapproving.

Back at Yellow Perch Lake, Al Gustave turned his woods vehicle right onto the lake road instead of his usual left into the firelane, and nearly ran down Mr. Bleu, the postman. Gabby by occupation and nature, he engaged Gustave in lengthy philosophic speculations on the mail delivery system and its shortcomings seeing (he said) that Gustave had been in the Service in the Old Days and there'd been so many improvements. Gustave, mustering great self-control, suppressed sharp replies and instead made pointed inquiries. By evening Maureen, Sydnor, the Tintingers, and Gustave had deciphered some of the local signals. They met around Webb and Sophie's picnic table.

There was definitely something going on at the old church camp that backed up to the Rolling Log Flowage. There were surveyors: orange markers had sprung up along the road. There was talk that major forest clearing was planned and had already begun.

"That's all Reformed Brethren Church property," Gustave said. "All along the Upper Chain of Lakes and up to the flowage."

"That's practically around the corner," Sydnor said.

"It's not as if they were underhanded," Maureen said. "Gertrude says that the Reformed Brethren Church Trust has been trying to develop that frontage for years."

"But surely not with a mining company!" Sophie protested.

Al Gustave had been silent. "Do you save newspapers?"

Sophie Tintinger looked at him as if he were mad. "Not if I can help it," she snapped. "The woodshed's the worst fire hazard in the county, and the *porch* . . ."

"Why, Al?" Webb asked.

"Remember, in May, that funny article about the airplane survey?"

"Yes," said Sydnor, "that thing about the geological survey planes with packages of instruments and how it was all normal operating procedure."

"You know," murmured Maureen Hendrickson, "Milton said that whole thing sounded phony." It was impossible to know what Milton had really said, as his waking hours were spent casting into submerged logs, but the point was taken. The item *had* been strange. Webb said he'd look and disappeared into the garage.

"I thought it sounded like some secret army project," said Sophie. "Remember the movies where somebody discovers a giant pea pod and the military gets called in?"

"And people who found it get younger . . ." Sydnor said.

"Or older . . ." Maureen added, getting into the spirit.

"Or get mental telepathy?" Sophie finished.

"Jesus," said Gustave in disgust.

"Here it is." Webb held a badly stained Washington County Woods-Gazette. "It was under the tackle box."

He read, skipping bits, "Survey Planes Scan Northern . . . series of low-flying planes bearing instrument packets . . . says these northernmost counties are in a 'zone of magnetic and gravity anomalies . . .'"

"Whatever the hell that means," said Gustave who was systematically breaking small branches into twigs.

"Says it's a 'late Precambrian continental rift zone in the North American plate,'" added Webb.

"It was a cover for some kind of metals survey," Gustave said.

"There's uranium," said Maureen.

"There's gold," countered Sophie.

"Or copper or nickel or something," Sydnor guessed.

"We've been took!" Gustave exclaimed.

"Or had," Webb said.

"That's what I said."

"Can we deflect this thing?" Webb pondered.

There was a banging and a muffled curse at the Tintinger pier. "Does no one install tie-up brackets anymore?" Judge Press demanded, marching over to the group. "I had to throw the damn anchor over the live box."

Every one looked at him bleakly. "Yes, I got one too, and we're all here to develop a campaign of some kind to fight back, right?"

Everybody spoke at once.

"Lawyers," Sydnor said. "The company's huge; they'll be hip deep in lawyers!"

"Who put their pants on one leg at a time," said Judge Press. "And there wouldn't be truckloads of them; that looks bad. At least there wouldn't be truckloads of them right away. But I've been thinking about this. How do we all feel about a little preliminary rabble rousing? You know, outraged letters to the editor, big business versus the little guy." He paused. "Which, of course, is perfectly true. And we could include other papers too."

"Hell, I'll do outrage," Gustave said. "I'm plenty outraged now."

"What a good idea," said Maureen, "so then what do we write?"

"Well," Sydnor said, considering, "first there's outrage at the mining company's sneak attack. That's good for a bunch of letters right there. Then there's protest against the threat of environmental ruin, forest wreckage, water pollution. God knows, we're all drinking from the same water table. Do you suppose people don't know that?"

"Ah," said Webb. "The Riverbend debacle. Lots of people know about that. I'll bet there are some deadly before and after photos of that mine. Can we get a hold of those?"

"I'll bet I can," Sydnor said. "If there's any question, the request will be from my Institute's upcoming publication on geological strata or something." She was pulling over a paper napkin and beginning to make notes. "Buster will print anything, bless his heart. Too bad the paper's only weekly."

"How about a special issue of the Yellow Perch Lake newsletter," Sophie suggested. "Webb usually knocks one out in an afternoon. We could circulate it around the lake—and the Upper Chain of Lakes, for that matter."

Webb raised his eyebrows. "There's faith," he said. "But something else—let's put together a rabble-rousing 'Don't Destroy the Woods' ad."

"Buster'll love that," said Sydnor. "Or will he?"

"Could we get into trouble?" Sophie asked suddenly.

"Well . . . " said Webb.

"We're just responding to the original story which has turned out to be a cover or obfuscation or something for an underhanded land grab attempt," Sydnor offered.

"We are concerned citizens rising up against an environmental threat," Maureen said.

"A proven environmental threat illustrated by the accompanying previously published newspaper photos," Webb added.

"A paid ad is a paid ad," said the Judge.

"There are, you know, people who will think digging up the north forty is a wonderful opportunity and an on-site cash cow," Webb cautioned.

"Cash cows often have limited lifetimes," Judge Press said, "and we'll cross that bridge when we have to. Maybe somebody should go see what the action at the church camp looks like. And if Random Mining has gotten this far, the Natural Resources people must have an Environmental Impact Statement ready to launch at the public."

"A what?" asked Sydnor.

"What it sounds like. If somebody plans to dig a mine, you have to say what it will do to the environment: fish, water, wetlands, food chain, all that."

"Let's get a copy," said Webb. "It has to be a public document."

"Right," said Judge Press. "I'll find one and I think it behooves us to locate some expert witnesses in mining operations, toxic runoff, and the leftover tailings stuff. I'll bet the Houghton campus has experts thick on the ground. So to speak. Meanwhile," he looked around, "the resistance movement is now open for business."

Maureen looked worried. She was having trouble imagining Milton enthusiastic about resistance activities.

"I'm all for it," said Gustave quietly. "I feel real strong about this. I grew up against smoke and factories and never saw nothing but cement till I was fifteen, and the best things and the best times I ever knew was these woods. Now, I know the bit about how nature is our leasehold for the future. But since I'm the only future I got, I would sure like to enjoy it as pretty as it is now, and when I come to be buried up here, I sure as hell would hope it wouldn't be under some big ugly pile of mining tailings." He still looked like a tree trunk, but a very determined one.

"Al, I believe that's the most I've ever heard you say at one time," said Sophie, dabbing at her eye. Gustave looked profoundly embarrassed. It seemed to call for a stiff drink. Sophie splashed vodka into glasses; Maureen got terrible hiccups, Sydnor knocked over the bug lantern, Judge Press untangled his boat, rammed the pier, and the evening was called on account of darkness.

6 SOUTH AND NORTH

Sydnor worked for a research institute with scientific interests so arcane that it was referred to in solemn tones. Visiting academics arrived weekly to compare new theories on the shape of the universe or time reversal or shrinking black holes. There were always more than enough theories to go around; the most speculative ideas frequently often filtered, months later, into the popular press, to the astonishment of the reading public and the embarrassment of the researchers who had just been arguing among themselves, sort of, to see how it sounded.

Her role in this organization was to prepare cautious summaries of research for interested contributors and for the scientific press, and also to ship the more lucid (or photogenic) work to the "Advancement" office to help fundraising efforts. From time to time, staffers would hear hopeless moans issuing from the money arena, as fund-raisers came to realize just how unsexy (from a donor-interest point of view) the trilobite extinction really was.

Amidst the daily hubbub of conference schedules, staff reports, and churn, Quinn turned up at the conference on potential life forms in carbonaceous chondrites. He had great height, a fine skeptical inquiring mind (it turned out), a notebook, a press badge, and a tolerant editor.

"Are you actually taking notes?" he had asked from the row behind her. She was.

"Well then, I don't need to. What's a Fischer-Tropsch reaction?"

Sydnor started to explain, but stopped as a beleaguered research assistant dimmed the lights for the main event. An aesthetic looking chemist with astrophysical tendencies started his slide presentation. The carbonaceous chondrites looked very much like truffles studded with little spots of mold.

The speaker was passionate about these spots, and his assistant kept flashing different views of chondrites on the screen, saving a whole turd-like family of them for a grand finale. Quinn was suppressing, with difficulty, great snorts of laughter; Sydnor could feel him doing it; it was contagious.

When the lights came up, they were grinning like gargoyles and Sydnor was quite breathless from keeping a straight face.

"What pray," he asked, "*are* carbonaceous chondrites?"

"Peculiar and possibly seeds-of-life-bearing meteor fragments," she said.

"My stars and garters," he said with genuine surprise. "Where from? Come have lunch and tell me everything."

So began a beautiful friendship, though punctuated by Quinn's frequently far-flung assignments. She sent him odd items from the activities that surrounded her: arguments and discoveries and wild surmise. Quinn was especially pleased to learn that the Relativity Group had decided the universe was probably saddle-shaped, but that the group leader would only discuss the subject while lying on his office floor, staring up at the ceiling. In exchange, Quinn shipped bits of hilarity from copy that poured off the newswires. One of Sydnor's favorite items was the story about an Ohio flagpole sitter who built a small addition to his platform so that his dog could flagpole sit with him.

"I think we've learned enough," Sydnor said one Saturday. Quinn was in town but not for much longer. They were tilted back in chairs in the comfortable blackness of the local planetarium. The narrator was chatting confidentially about the position of major stars during the vernal equinox. "Let's drive up to the summer cottage and see some real sky."

Quinn thought.

"I'll make a deal with you. Can you steal some vacation and fly to Mexico with me while I do a story? It's due Thursday but they'll hold it for the next weekend section. Then I can take off and we could go up—how long a drive is it, anyway—for a long weekend."

So it was that Sydnor, under a large hat, and holding a large bottled drink, found herself south of the border watching Quinn, one presumed, working. It was surrealistically hot. Sydnor stayed in the shade and read murder mysteries. Quinn adapted and flourished; in the hotel bar, his height was an advantage.

"Nothing happening here," he'd say, eyeing the perspiring heads of a dozen people nursing sweating glasses of various beverages. And he'd wander out and chat casually with the parrot dealer across the square. The parrot dealer's brother-in-law knew of some interesting smuggling. Would the señor wish to observe? Perhaps a guide? Quinn, in workable Spanish, leaned confidentially into the conversation, establishing friendship, trust, and an improved cash flow. And a story, Sydnor knew, informed, exclusive, and likely syndicated, would appear. Quinn would be elsewhere.

Later, meandering across the city, they drank margaritas. The heat metabolized the alcohol directly into sweat and a kind of loopy energy and gave the sidewalks a blinding moiré shimmer. At midnight, back in the marginally cooler hotel room, Quinn shut his eyes and began contentedly to dance to the seductive murmur of a guitar somewhere outside. Supple and confident, he swung into impromptu patterns; it was as if a Yeti had suddenly learned to tango. Arms outstretched and hands adrift, he stepped into a pasa doblé, embraced a lamp and reversed into a fast allemande with a parlor palm. Sydnor, pressing a can of cool beer against her right temple, watched, transfixed. It was an exhibition of unconscious grace as elegant as any she'd seen: a kind of grown-up teddy bear's cakewalk.

He drifted across the carpet, smiling with satisfaction at the rhythm he'd found, spun once in the middle of the room and ricocheted off the edge of an end table, as light as a leaf. She watched, enchanted. Here was adventure, a sensibility capable of —who knew? —practically anything. It was going to be a hell of a lot of fun.

So on the weekend when Quinn dug a pit in the Sydnor's cottage driveway to roast corn Indian style, it was all of a piece. He had commandeered a cushy monster of a car and they'd sped north, through kettle moraine, farms and dairyland, Quinn reciting the names of the various breeds of dairy cows from some odd repository in his brain, along with useless animal husbandry tidbits.

While the corn steamed, he filleted the morning's bass catch and tossed it, nicely wrapped, onto a small grill. Given the fishing gear—antique fishing poles that had to be untangled from a corner of the living room—dinner was remarkable. It had been a terrific weekend, with perfect weather. Throughout the weekend, Quinn uncorked some of his adventures and they came spilling out in fascinating installments.

"So there we were," he said, continuing a saga of a trek in strange and ominous country, "negotiating with some local tribal chieftain, with all his serious artillery tucked into the hills . . ."

"Why were you there? I mean, particularly *there*?"

"Because of a very specific, very interesting little engagement on the other side of the mountain. You couldn't drop in from a helicopter; they'd shoot you down. But the partisan front and fellow travelers always liked to know who was covering the action. Curiosity is a civilizing factor. And," a trifle grimly, "it was part of an assignment. It may have gone a little over the edge."

"So he took his knife out of his mouth long enough to offer you tea?"

"He had this palatial hideout chopped into the side of a hill. The choice was Earl Gray or the local stuff. He spoke French, probably perfectly. I don't, so we settled on pidgin, but his English was better than he was admitting. After the brandy . . ."

"After the brandy?"

"Smuggling as a second language. It's a universal fallback position, I think. He was eager for news. After the brandy, my photographer and his translator passed out and we discovered we had 34 words of Russian in common and had each read *Dr. Zhivago*. Brotherhood. We wept. He eventually gave us a guide with many rounds of ammunition and Joe got some of the best pictures of his career. Or mine, for that matter. Happy ending sort of because we got the hell out, and so survived. This is depressing. Let's finish the corn and then drive out to that bar on the river where you can toss strudel to the turtles."

"Bread crumbs to the panfish?"

"That place. It's a nice view. Tourists, sunset, all that."

So they sat on a deck over a deep dark river, sipped cold dark beer, toasted a far-away Asian night, and drove back, slowly, to avoid hitting a deer. Sydnor felt aglow. And then looked at her arm. She *was* aglow. Could happiness create phosphorescence? Something was going on.

"Quinn, look at the sky. See the light?"

"It's still twilight, we're pretty far north."

"No, see those ribbony things, there to the right."

He looked. "Northern lights, I swear, out of season. Is there any beer left? Let's get onto your lake. If it's a real aurora that'll be the best view."

It was more than a real aurora. It was the great grandfather of auroras. They passed cars slowed to a crawl, whose occupants, wide-eyed, stared up at the sky. Not only were there ribbons of light, but empyreal pyrotechnics overtook them as they drove. It was an all-out, no-holds-barred, gala aurora, one of the planet's little surprises, a lavish gift from the natural conspiracy between the sunspot cycle and the magnetosphere. Back at the cottage, vast iridescent streamers were filling the night horizon around the lake; they were an amazing shade of pink.

By the time Quinn and Sydnor snatched the beer and rowed out to the middle, they were encircled by great shimmering sheets of pink and turquoise-tinted light, blazing up, unbroken. It was as if the boat, lake, and everything surrounding had been dropped onto the poop deck of a huge decelerating spacecraft, so they could watch as cosmic scenery disappeared into space over their heads.

"It's the end of the world," Quinn yelled, exhilarated.

Sydnor stood up; the phenomena seemed to call for it. She wobbled, and dumbstruck, sank back down into the boat. They stared, goose-like, into the pulsing sky. The aurora streamed up on all sides, silhouetting the great pines surrounding the lake, and rushed into a swirl of knotted tendrils high above. Great pastel pennants dissolved above their heads. It looked as if some extraterrestrial hand had unplugged a moon-sized basin stopper to drain the dazzle into somewhere else. It went on and on.

"Listen," said Sydnor. There was enormous silence like thousands of caught breaths. No mosquitoes hummed. No dogs barked. All creatures were mute, and the colossal illumination rumbaed overhead.

"It is a damn good thing that half the state's seeing this. Otherwise nobody'd believe it," said Quinn. The turquoise was paler now, and the tendrils tightened and began gently to tilt eastward.

"Hallelujah," Sydnor said.

The boat had drifted back toward the dock. Daunted by the competition, the lightening bugs had switched off. A kind of ozone sizzle hovered in the air. The aurora billowed further east like ladies' skirts in a vast, animated cartoon. Quinn sang the first verse of Bahia softly in Spanish and rowed in.

"It's ending," Sydnor sighed.

"It'll be light in an hour."

A small frog made tentative noises under the pier. The beer was gone and neither could remember drinking any. Final fading streamers lifted off the horizon and slipped into invisibility at treetop level. Still watching, they leaned against each other in the cottage clearing, rubbing serious stiff necks.

"I don't want to tell anyone about this," he said.

"Granted. I think I'm going to fall down."

"My dear. Permit me." He dropped to one knee, hoisted Sydnor over his shoulder like a sack of flour, and marched toward the cabin.

"The porch ceiling! Quinn! The porch ceiling!"

"Dwarves, dwarves, the place was designed for dwarves," he muttered, dodging nimbly and unloading a shrieking and laughing Sydnor onto the top of a particularly ugly chest of drawers.

"How can you say that? This place is magic."

"Maybe this is one of those once-in-a lifetime things," he said. "Do you ever expect to see anything like that again? I don't."

"There are always," said Sydnor, carefully tracing the top of his ear with her index finger, "there are always things we shouldn't expect to see again. You're testing divine providence or dumb luck. And like that."

"Promise me," said Quinn, "that you will never write for a newspaper."

"It has got to beat working," she yawned.

He snorted. "Come to bed oh mistress mine," he said, and, wonderfully tangled in mismatched quilts and blankets, they slept until noon.

Some days later, a small item from the Associated Press reported that an astonishingly clear display of the aurora borealis, out of normal phase, and so forth, had been seen as far south as Amarillo, Texas. Sydnor clipped the article and put it her top desk drawer. Quinn was on assignment somewhere near the Cambodian border, using up another of his nine lives. By the end of summer, a slight depression appeared in the cottage driveway, marking the remains of the corn pit.

7 VARIOUS PLANS

Gerald Mactate was checking in with the Mother House.
"Do you have an office yet?" Ross asked.
"Got a couple of possibles," said Mactate, "but I can operate out of the apartment for a week or two."
"Don't put it off; you really need to look established—smoothes a lot of rough edges to have a name on the door. Use 'Investments' by the way."
"Um," Mactate said. He refrained from suggesting that a name on the door would be more critical for a dentist.
"Try to warm up the township council members or board or whatever they have there," Ross added.
"There's a Chamber of Commerce guy who's going to be a good friend," Mactate said. "He'll get me into Rotary for starters."
"I don't think there's time for starters. It should be the Council; you're pro-mining, pro-profit. Opportunity. You know the drill. Get in there."
"You know, maybe all this is overkill."
"The internal work is very, very valuable. You'll be an old timer there before you know it."
"God, I hope not. Do you know how small this town really is?"
"Gerald, that's the point. Small doesn't take very long."

"Good," Mactate said. "Because I'm getting claustrophobic already."

* * *

The first letters to the editor appeared in the following Wednesday's edition of the Washington County Woods-Gazette. They were angry, horrified, and sorrowful that such underhandedness was necessary by a major U.S. etc. etc. "For believability," Sydnor explained. She had a real knack for virtuous hand-ringing. Everybody signed their real names—some friends from other parts of the township had been recruited into the letter-writing blitz. Sydnor bought twelve copies. The Riverbend photos would follow in a week; the anti-mining ad would be held until heavier ammunition was required. This was just a start.

"I always thought it was loony to publish a paper in the middle of the week," she said to Maureen, who'd been returning an enormous Phillips screwdriver, "but it gives us time to sneak around the church camp."

At 4:30 back in town, Gertrude rinsed out her coffee cup, folded the newspaper to the letters page, and scrawled, "Digging—Brethren Church Camp" on it. She closed the county collector's office, dropped the paper on Charlie Haney's desk next door in the assessor's office, and went home, anticipating a satisfactory evening speculating on local gossip with her Bridge regulars.

Charlie nipped into the office at 5:10 to pick up his jacket because his checkbook was in the inside pocket. (He lived in fear of some stranger discovering the county assessor had a personal balance of only $163.78.) He found Gertrude's message, and took the paper with him.

At Hansen's Real Estate, five blocks away, the postman Mr. Bleu had delivered, along with the mail, considerable opinion about big city mining interests and the Yellow Perch Lake Association's admirable stand on home rule. Walter Hansen remembered home rule from freshman history, and didn't think this was it; he skimmed his newspaper, folded it to the letters page and set out for Mint's Bar at a thoughtful trot.

Charlie Haney's check was good at Mint's Bar (almost anybody's check was good at Mint's Bar), and he was reading Sydnor's letter to the editor and frowning when Walter sat down next to him.

"I don't get it," Charlie said to Walter. "If somebody's taking cores or samples at the old church camp, the first thing they're going to run into is water. It's right on the river. Walt, how far down does that church property run anyway?"

"Not quite a mile along the Upper Chain waterway," said Hansen, frowning. "It stops up against the flowage and just before the national forest; I don't understand why they held on to it so long; the camp hasn't been used in 20 years."

"No taxes to speak of," said Charlie, who believed that anything with an address should kick in a little something to the tax base.

"Minnie says she's called Arthur," Walter said. "He got really interested; he's coming in for the weekend."

Walter Hansen and the long-widowed Minnie Rosenheim had maintained a comfortable relationship for so many years that townspeople no longer speculated whether or not they would ever marry. Walt, publicly a bachelor, would have been astonished to learn of this agreeable status quo; he believed that the arrangement was slightly risqué and never referred to it directly.

*** * * ***

Several mornings after the formation of the Yellow Perch Lake resistance cell, Sophie Tintinger poured a second cup of coffee, stepped out the kitchen door and, attempting short gliding steps, managed to carry it unspilled, onto Sydnor's back porch. She tapped on the screen and let herself in. Sydnor, at the big round country table paying bills, pulled out a chair with her foot for Sophie.

"I think we should get Sal Constantini *deeply* involved in this," Sophie said.

"I'm sure he will be. He and his mother both have a huge real estate investment here on the lake and probably a bunch of other places around town," Sydnor replied.

"I don't think it's lost on anybody that there are deep pockets in that household and we may need some kind of hefty financial aid before this is all over."

"Well, you can ask him," Sydnor said. "I'm not going to. We used to sneak out in his boat and listen to Cubs games in the middle of the lake and smoke. Our hearts were young and dumb, and fortunately we didn't see each other as lifetime companions."

Sal's divorce was about two years ago, she calculated. "But I don't think he'd consider a happy misspent youth as an excuse for an underwriting opportunity. Sal knows perfectly well when to wave a checkbook around and when not to. His mother's still planning an addition to the boathouse, by the way."

"Really? For dining and dancing?"

"Lucia thinks big. At least the waterfall project's on permanent hold." They chatted about the relative looniness of various friends and neighbors. Briskly, Sophie said that if they were going to reconnoiter the action at the Church Camp property, they should do it now.

"Before the place is overrun. And while there are still trees to hide behind. And before my courage evaporates."

"The old evaporating courage problem," Sydnor said, and went to put on grubby clothes and sneakers. "We should cut through the woods to the old landing. If we're going to trespass, we should do it as invisibly as possible."

At first they ambled, tourist-like, along the edge of the lake road. And then stopped. They could not possibly have overshot the path to the landing, because heavy equipment had chewed through underbrush and trees on each side. It looked as if tractors—two abreast—had attempted a new road but not gotten around to finishing it.

Great swags of broken pines leaned away from the cleared area. Uprooted maples and oaks, bark torn and leaves dying, were thrust crazily out of the way. A stand of tamarack had been bulldozed into a pocket wetland, and ferns, cattails, and wild forget-me-not reduced to mush. It smelled of raw earth. It smelled wounded.

It had been done in a hurry, and whatever had done it was still in there, grinding away. A hydraulic snarl started abruptly. "My god," Sydnor said. "What's that?" There was a crash as a tree —a large tree, from the sound—fell nearby. A metallic shrilling sound over to the left blotted out anything else, but when another tree came down close by, their cover thinned considerably.

"The old lodge," Sydnor said, as both dropped to their knees in the bracken fern. A backhoe and several skid steer loaders were visible through the woods. The women crept around the corner of the rickety building and slid into an enclosed splintery sun porch. "I once found a stack of ancient St. Nicholas magazines on one of these porches," she whispered, batting spider webs aside. All the old church camp cabins were overgrown and abandoned; the underbrush was reclaiming the steps and the floors sagged.

"Keep down and don't stab yourself on the floor boards," Sydnor whispered.

Sophie was peering out a ruined porch window. "They're digging or something," she said. "They're digging up dirt—and rocks and gravel—that kind of stuff, at least as far as I can see, anyway."

"Why are they taking down trees?" There was another crash closer toward the water.

"Maybe to get the drilling stuff in?" Sophie offered.

"This is carnage," Sydnor said, forgetting about keeping down. "Look over toward the water. They've cleared a couple of acres; you can even see to the other side of the channel. Oh my god. We've got to get pictures."

A large station wagon maneuvered down the newly-sliced road and stopped near a beached and rotting raft at the water's edge. As one, both women crept to the other side of the porch for a better view. Three men emerged from the station wagon and squinted into the glitter of sun on water. One was Reverend Z. X. Weathersill of the Reformed Brethren Church who was not exhibiting the joy that might be expected from a new member of a successful mining consortium.

He was trying to say something to the two other men and had been reduced to waving his arms. They looked at him blankly, then one went over and banged on the window of a wheel loader. The driver rolled down the window and turned off the engine. Even with a skidder growling further off, it was suddenly quiet.

Weathersill was explaining or protesting or both. ". . . had no idea . . . extensive . . . really much too high handed . . . "

The other men—strangers—were carefully camouflaged as local woodsmen in crisp new plaid Pendleton shirts, corduroys, and new waterproof boots. Flashing neon lights on their fishing hats could scarcely have rendered them more conspicuous. The Reverend Weathersill wore disreputable-looking wash pants and a 15-year-old flannel shirt over a garment doubling as something clerical. The man in the red plaid shirt responded to Weathersill at length. His second, in a brown plaid shirt, looked bored and went over to the station wagon, rummaging something out of the rear. Weathersill's voice rose. He had after all, Sophie considered, preacher training.

"Totally unnecessary clearing!" The Reverend's voice carried well, and the first man adopted a reasonable and conciliatory tone, obviously explaining that clearing was the only way. Weathersill, who had apparently expected to have more control of this process, was not appeased and said so, gesturing at tree stumps and at a once gentle rise that had been leveled when its top was scraped off.

This futile dialog might have continued, except that the brown plaid shirt extracted a 12-gauge shotgun from the rear of the station. Weathersill looked stunned.

"What kind of game do you get up here?" asked the would-be shooter, sighting along the shotgun barrel. They were moving closer and the conversation was quite clear. The women dropped to the porch floor.

"Um," said the Reverend. "I don't hunt, myself, but deer, of course, and . . . " he contemplated the woods, "Uh, birds? I think wild turkey and pheasant. I can't imagine you'd want to shoot any thing else." he trailed off...

The potential shooter sighted along the barrel again and swung it abruptly toward the lodge. Sophie and Sydnor flattened. There was a loud shot.

"Dammit!" said Weathersill. A fine birch leaf confetti drifted gently down through one of the wrecked windows. Bits filtered into Sophie's hair. She clutched Sydnor's arm.

"Shhh," Sydnor hissed.

"For god's sake, Tom!" said the red plaid shirt.

"It was a bird! A really big bird!" said the shooter, excited.

"Nothing's in *season*," said Weathersill, speaking as if to an imbecile. "And big birds up here are eagles—the symbol of our country, a protected species, and shooting one is subject to ENORMOUS FINES," he said, infuriated, his voice rising.

There was some muffled muttering and sharp words. "Put it back in the car," said Weathersill, in the same voice that brought his congregation smartly to its feet during Sunday service. The trio moved closer to the lodge. Sydnor and Sophie froze.

"*Now* can we continue?" asked the red plaid shirt.

Weathersill said, "Please remove some of the equipment and keep the digging away from the bank. If you get a bunch of curious observers in here there is likely going to be trouble. This isn't," he gestured in a random circle, "the most beautiful example of exploration."

"Can't make an omelet," said the red plaid, and the three men set off on a pilgrimage along the shoreline, stepping over tree trunks.

"Not the issue," Weathersill replied, his voice growing fainter. "National forest," he then said, adding, "Indians" and then, perhaps, "night fishing." A gabble of indistinguishable conversation followed, with a question that ended in "town meeting."

"I wouldn't," said Weathersill quite clearly, and added—possibly in answer to a question from the other man—"poison ivy."

The wheel loader started again and another excavator shrieked through a stone. They sounded further away. Sydnor and Sophie rose carefully, eased open the porch door, and did a crouch-shuffle down three stairs, keeping close to the building. They had inhaled numerous seasons of acorn fluff, pine needles, mouse dust and aspen fuzz. The men had disappeared into the woods.

Sydnor murmured, "Do you see anything? Can we do a quick getaway?"

"Hush," said Sophie.

After some rustling, Weathersill emerged from the woods, proceeded slowly down the driveway and back to the station wagon. He was alone. Escape seemed, at the moment, impolitic. Sophie had deflected a sneeze, but her eyes had begun to water. A door slammed and the station wagon started. There was a crunch. "The raft," Sydnor whispered. Reversing and accelerating muddily, the vehicle rattled up the mangled drive to the road. The sound faded.

"The damp has soaked right into my bones," Sydnor muttered, straightening up and peering out. "This is absolutely god-awful."

"We're all going to be arthritic," replied Sophie grimly, wiping her eyes on her shirt. She fingered bits of leaves out of her hair.

"This is going to be very difficult. Somebody's going to have to talk to Weathersill. And his bishop or president or whoever he reports to. Let's volunteer Judge Press."

"You don't like the idea of a simple poison pen letter?"

"Only if it's published in the local paper with the rest. I'll bet we could get Louise Garfield to write it. She's nearly always fever-pitch ready for environmental disaster. And boy, do we have disaster."

"I don't know what we were thinking of," said Sophie. "These people are serious. Or dangerous. Or both. Let's get out of here."

A small spider dropped down to eye level with Sydnor. It saw it had made a terrible mistake. "Flee!" Sydnor hissed at it. It fled.

8 HEAT AND LIGHT

On Wednesday and Thursday, Minnie Rosenheim made cheesecakes. They sold rapidly at "Remember When Pastries," a purveyor of incredibly rich confections at high prices.

She and the other two women who helped at the shop felt guilty about this at first, but when summer residents flung fifty- and one-hundred-dollar bills at their antique cash register and bought out the entire stock three weekends running, they realized that guilt had nothing to do with it.

The shop had closed at six as usual, and Walt Hansen and Charlie Haney nibbled crunchy crust scraps from the latest batch of cheesecakes while Minnie swabbed off the counter tops and wiped her hands. Walt had been describing a meeting with an enthusiastic newcomer named Masticate or Mactate or something. "One of those types who wants to be your real good friend. Talks a little too close."

"Bad habit," said Min. "Like my aunt Lotty, but she was a bit deaf. I've seen him. I believe he's been in the shop."

"What did Arthur say, Min," Charlie asked abruptly, scattering crumbs down his shirtfront.

"You could wait two hours and ask him yourself, but it was something about an waterway law that he says needs to be looked at."

"What kind of waterway law?" Walt asked.

"I don't know, but Arthur says they're going to run into problems with water. Seems obvious."

"Is that good?"

"Maybe for us," Charlie said thoughtfully. "Maybe not for them. Anybody who so much as tries to plant a septic tank runs into problems with water."

"You think we could get some of the council people together on Saturday to talk to Arthur, as long as he's got all this technical expertise?" said Walt.

"On a weekend? In summer?" Charlie asked, stunned.

"Call an emergency beer and brats lunch," said Minnie. "That'll get them."

"You going to volunteer some dessert?"

"No indeed. Brats and cheesecake? Now, really. 'Remember When' wants people to enjoy the finer things, maybe even in moderation, not keel over dead from a double shot of artery lard. Get some coleslaw from the Co-op, round out your menu. Want some leftover coffee?"

In all of these arrangements, neither Charlie or Walt had considered for a moment about conferring with the Yellow Perch Lake people or any other lake association, though they'd read their letters amid the editorials in the newspaper, and knew that everybody in the area had gotten the Random Mining offer. The summer people were not permanent residents, so could not be expected to understand the intricacies of town politics and territory, and were thus out of the loop.

* * *

At the most eastern edge of Yellow Perch Lake, in a green wooden rowboat, Al Gustave trolled back and forth above submerged tree trunks, pretending to fish for walleyed pike, usually a nocturnal species. He had exchanged a few words with Milt Hendrickson who was plowing tiny furrows in the lake bottom, "fishing deep." Murmuring encouragement, Gustave trolled slowly away and eventually came to rest against the Bench

Press dock. Judge Press was crouched in a small aluminum craft carefully bailing several smelly inches of water with a bent tin can. He stopped, pleased to be interrupted.

"We get, I'll swear, more precipitation than anywhere else on this lake. How are you, Al?"

"Harry, that there is just heavy dew. You know it never rains up here during tourist season. How 'bout an afternoon troll; as lake association counsel, it behooves you to report on where you been and what you got up your sleeve." Gustave steadied the boat and the judge climbed in.

Judge Press often missed the vicious and absorbing legal life as lived in the Cook County Courthouse; this mining company adventure made a nice change. "Been chatting with some environmental types at the Department of the Interior and some other people. People in Houghton, in Madison, some experts."

"Al, do you suppose that anybody up here ever considered that some sort of case could be made for Native American ownership of certain state mineral rights and deposits?"

Gustave rowed slowly toward the middle of the lake. "That's real interesting. You want to reach into the bottom of that tackle box? There's a fifth of some medicinal Chivas I keep around for cuts and scratches."

* * *

Webb Tintinger had not been idle. He was delivering—early—the Yellow Perch Lake Association newsletter, which practically seethed with information on mining toxins, first-hand reports from fishermen who'd watched entire trout brooks poisoned, and official-looking bullet points enclosed in black boxes listing symptoms of mercury and arsenic sickness. He'd also included an article describing the use of arsenic and sodium cyanide in various types of mining operations.

It was an enormous departure from the usual collection of blather and gossip that the community looked forward to receiving. (In a recent classified ad swap corner, two antique railroad lanterns, one 12-foot aluminum rowboat, a pair of World War II German helmets, and a 21-inch-wide kitchen range changed hands.)

Evangeline Juska across the lake had offered to help run off the 500-odd copies on her genuine antique duplicating machine. "Keep the master," Webb had said. "You never know."

He had included a "For More Information" paragraph that invited those interested to call, and suggested that persons might want to present their fears, comments, and general apprehensions to those serving on the Township Council. He felt only mildly guilty about this; he knew perfectly well that the council members, staring at mining company questions, were going to be caught flat-footed by alarmed and concerned citizens. Better get them energized.

For good measure, he'd addressed copies of the newsletter to the editor of the local paper, the Township Council Chairman Maxwell Skyler, and for the heck of it, to the chairman of the local Rotary. Intercepting Mr. Bleu, who could easily be deflected by rain, snow, or conversation, Webb thrust the letters at him, said "Today!" and dashed back to the lake.

He returned to find Sophie fielding the sixth of what would be 23 phone calls from agitated readers. Minutes later, Al Gustave appeared in his all-terrain forest vehicle, leveling the Sophie's last patch of still-surviving impatiens.

At the lake edge, a sound similar to that made by a modest personal jet aircraft announced the multi-horsepower arrival of Sal Constantini, the lake's one genuine heavy-hitter, especially if one included his mother. Sydnor handed him a cold beer as he stormed onto the Tintinger porch.

"You need any heat?" he demanded, breaking off the top and rendering the beverage inoperable.

"At the moment, just light," Sydnor replied, beaming at him, "and I think we're generating our own. How's the family?"

The impromptu assembly of the Yellow Perch Lake resistance group began at 6:30 p.m. in blazing sunshine and ended (more or less) at the 9:30 twilight that reminds summer visitors just how far north they really are.

Judge Press arrived bearing, he said, papers on chemical contamination and both bad and good news. Dieter Vilnus, Maureen Hendrickson, and Evangeline Juska with her silent husband Ernie followed him in.

"I threw the company mining papers away," said Vilnius. "Is crazy to dig holes: you get wet holes and piles of dirt. What you want with piles of dirt?"

"You've put your finger on one of the problems," Press said. "The piles of dirt would be tailings from processing and they're full of remarkably long-lived toxins. The poisons leach into the soil. And into the water, of course. This brings up the bad news and good news.

"Turns out," he continued, "that the natural resources people, at some significant level, have been subverted by Random Mining."

"What? How?" demanded Gustave, his color rising.

"Random Mining did a bunch of surveys that dealt with endangered species and contaminated wastewater. Naturally, they didn't find any—what they called 'significant'—impacts on either. And Natural Resources bought it. It went into their draft Environmental Impact Statement."

"Oh, that is bad news," said Webb.

"How incredibly stupid," Sydnor said. "Can we or anybody expose this? Natural Resources is supposed to protect the environment. They were always on our side. What happened?"

"I think a lot of mining lobby money applied to major political pockets is what happened," said Webb.

"Does anybody know?" Sophie asked.

"Oh no doubt," said Judge Press. "I'm sure a crew of pro-mining folks in the state capitol knows, as does the opposition, which we are part of. There are things to be done, but we have to enlist agencies who are friends, move fast, and get very noisy."

"And the good news?" Gustave asked.

"That last bit was the good news," said Judge Press.

Webb was taking notes like crazy. "This is copper, right? What else?"

"And a little nickel and whatever else they can discover."

"Is there anything we can do?" Sophie asked. "I mean, right now? A petition or something?"

"It's like bailing a boat with a soup spoon," Sydnor said.

"Actually, we should get up a petition stating disapproval, reasons for, etc. etc., and get it to members of the Council," said Webb turning to Judge Press. "Professional opinion, please?"

"Only if you can get an enormous number of signatures. Remember, the population of the town is only thirteen hundred. If that."

"Oh but," Sydnor protested, "there are herds more summer people on the lakes. There must be at least that number all over again."

"Well then, if you can get more than a thousand signatures," said Press, "you'll have a fairly compelling document to present to the Township Council."

"We're going to have to do it then," Sydnor said, decidedly. "But I hate canvassing." She chewed her bottom lip.

"We'll all do it," Maureen said. "We'll get forms printed, and canvass in town and the lakes—although that'll take some doing. We'll each take a location and a lake, how about, and take along copies of the newsletter. What happened to the Riverbend photographs?"

"Coming up, but maybe only in time for the Woods-Gazette," Webb said.

"Now, isn't it handy I have the newsletter master," Evangeline smiled. "And if somebody would whip up a petition form—you know, all those signature lines—I'll run off a bunch by tomorrow noon."

"That's me," Sophie said. "And by the way, don't you think we should pool a little cash to cover paper and ink supplies? It's not fair for the Juskas to pay for all this."

"The Yellow Perch Lake Association slush fund is pretty well padded," said Webb, "but a little something extra wouldn't hurt. Goodness knows where this is going to lead and what it's going to cost."

"Excuse me," said Sal. "Let me contribute to this. I'm in and out a lot, and it will make up some for not being around to get signatures. But my mother could. She's terrific at that. And she knows everybody. She's hired every construction guy for miles around; there're whole unions that'll sign on the dotted line for her."

"Yay," said Sydnor. "We're underwritten."

Sophie had propped a ruled tablet up on the patio table, littered by cans, bottles, and some crumpled newsletters. Judge Press was dictating a legal-sounding paragraph to her for the petition. Vilnus, across the table, was untangling a lure, hopelessly knotted in a hank of fishing line.

"I row over to people fishing?" he inquired, "tell them they should sign petition against mining?"

"You should try," said Webb. "Not everybody is going to love you for it."

"Speaking of which," said Press, "let's one of us check with Gertrude to see if we need a permit. First thing tomorrow."

"Me," said Sydnor. "I hear she's not terribly sympathetic to the mining interests."

"Done!" said Sophie, handing the petition draft to Evangeline, who handed it to her husband.

"Ernie types like the wind," she said, proudly. Ernie looked embarrassed.

"Let me know what happens," said Judge Press. "Now excuse me; there are some people in town who I have to get to know a little bit better. Like Arthur Rosenheim. Who *is* Arthur Rosenheim?"

* * *

Larry Running Bear was in his small Co-op office overlooking the grocery aisles. With him were Stan Wolf and Errol Seize A Dog, friends and fellow tribe members. Their visit was a surprise, since the only reason to show up at the Co-op was to buy food and to poke around in the beer section. They were hearty types, filled up the office pretty thoroughly, and were obviously there on a mission.

"Our council meeting is tomorrow at six," said Stan, "and everybody's coming to get a grip on this Ramrod . . ."

"Random," Errol put in.

"Random Mining Company thing. You're coming, right?"

"Sure," Larry said, "What kind of grip? Are we protesting or demonstrating, or suing, or what?"

"The Elders Council," Stan said carefully, "believes it's our land that the church camp and the mining company are excavating. That's for starters. Plus we're against the mining. It'll wreck the wild rice. And the water," he added.

"Oh boy," Larry said.

"Thing is," said Errol, "there's some kind of a land agreement or deed that one of the local lawyers came across. Looks like we need to sue the Natural Resources people. We've got to look at it and talk about it and decide what to do next." He thrust his hand into his jacket pocket.

"Here's your copy."

"I need a copy?" Larry asked, surprised.

"That's the other thing," Stan said, shuffling a little. "We want you to be a spokesperson—along with one of the older people, of course."

"Me?" Bear's exclamation was emphasized by a crash from near the apple sauce display. "I don't see why you need anybody besides the elders."

"You got a college degree," said Stan, bluntly. "Everybody in town knows you. You got heft. We're going to be asking around for help from environmental people and some of the other tribe leaders. We figure you can talk better with them, you guys all got the same background. And you get along with Nelson . . ."

"Nelson? Nelson's the spokesman for the Elders Council?'

"He does real well in these kinds of disputes," Errol said rather defensively.

"Especially if there's a TV camera somewhere," Larry said. "He always gets dressed up in his museum Native American costume. He looks like an exploded feather sofa."

"Traditional," Errol said.

"And what lawyer found this document thing? I never knew we had a lawyer."

"Well, we don't, or we didn't," Stan began. "He's from out of town, I mean on one of the lakes."

"He's summer people?" Larry's voice rose. "How did we hook up with summer people?"

"He found us. He called the Township Council and asked who was spokesman for the local Native Americans. He said Indians, though. Maxwell Skyler put him onto Nelson Two Snakes," Stan explained patiently.

"I'll bet he loved that," Larry said.

"Who? Nelson?"

"No; the lawyer. What's his name, anyway."

"Guy's named Press. He was a judge too; maybe still is a judge," Stan Wolf frowned. "He says he found these old records and stuff in the state archives. He's all hot to trot. Says he'll stay around as long as we need. Nelson likes him."

"That's something, anyway." Larry said. "Try not to let Nelson make him an honorary member or break out a peace pipe. Last time he lit up, he was sick for two days."

"Well, it's ok then. We'll see you tomorrow."

"Ok," Larry sighed. He foresaw great tribulation ahead.

There was a curse from the last aisle, as a customer slipped in some applesauce.

* * *

Arthur Rosenheim and Larry Running Bear went way back. It was the kind of odd friendship that springs up in small communities especially if the principals are different enough to be interesting to each other. They'd swum the lakes, hiked the forest trails, been on the football team, and in winter they'd skied cross-country and fished through the ice. Fishing was better in summer though, and they were —at the crack of dawn— on a small body of water that was listed on surveyors' maps only as "Wetland." It teemed with bass.

"So," Larry was saying, "it seems I got voted to be spokesman with Nelson."

"Nelson? Nelson Two Snakes?" Arthur swiveled around. "Do you have to wear your headdress?"

"Cut it out. Hey! Strike!" And conversation stopped while Arthur's line sang out toward deeper water and Larry reached for the net. It was hard to talk when the fish kept biting like this.

"Stringer," Arthur said, and threaded an angry bass onto a makeshift lariat. "And you guys got some lawyer involved?"

"He volunteered, but he's legit, and Nelson likes him."

"Then it'll be ok," Arthur said, fixing his bait.

"Maybe he'll agree to wear war paint or something. Help him fit in. But you found something too?"

"Don't say anything," Arthur cautioned. "This is shaping to be the kind of fight where if the mining company gets wind of something, they'll go all out to neutralize any law that gets in their way. You folks are going to need that lawyer."

"What you mean, 'you folks,' Kemo Sabe?" Larry asked. "This is your bass; this is your territory. You should meet this lawyer guy and tell what you dug up (sorry about that) since you're the expert."

"I have to see Max Skyler and some of township people; maybe he'll be there too. It's some kind of working meeting with food."

"After that one, why don't you stop by ours," Larry said. "It's not till six. No food though."

"Am I allowed?"

"Oh hell yes. Nelson likes you too. Anyway, outstanding water rights plus tribal land infringement could be really educational. You wouldn't want to miss it."

"You know," Arthur said, "this whole mess probably is a fast education in environmental law. There goes your line!"

"Net!" said Larry.

9 DELIVERY MECHANISMS

After a few days, Sal managed some tissue paper thin scheduling that got him face to face with Victoria in an obscure corner of the university's natural science research wing.

"Your tarp," he said, producing a large bundle with a flourish. "What are all these stuffed birds?"

"It's part of the museum collection. Thank you. You're just using the tarp as an excuse, aren't you?" She had a smudge of dust or something across the bridge of her nose. Sal found it endearing and resisted the impulse to brush it away.

"Of course," he said. "I really wanted to see you. The tarp is a little more gold than tan, but at least it's not blue." He'd had it shipped from a safari outfitters in London, at a cost approaching a round trip to Trafalgar Square. "Can you get away for an evening?"

"Where? Here?"

"Victoria, I live here. I mean, not *here*," waving at a particularly lugubrious looking stuffed pelican. "I have a nice apartment. I spend most of my time in this city; this is the business headquarters. I'd like to live up north the whole year, but the boys are here and I'd have to shuttle about a dozen managers back and forth every week to keep the company running. So let's have dinner. Do they let you have dinner?"

"Your reasoning process is really remarkable," Victoria said, shifting the bundled tarp to her other arm. "Doesn't it bother you that I'm not asking you to my hangout for an evening?"

"I've been to your hangout, and it was beyond my wildest expectations. I'll bet you're bivouacked in some kind of graduate student housing and I can offer you better. Dinner? Friday? Can I pick you up in front? Why is that person waving his arms at us?"

"Oh good grief, it's the curator. This room is sort of off limits. Ok, go. I'll see you Friday—I'll deal with this.'

"Tell him I'm a potential donor. Ask for a prospectus."

"Sal, this is a research institution, not an initial public offering."

"You'd be surprised," he said, kissed her on the cheek, and loped off toward an exit sign.

* * *

Victoria found a day and a half of anticipation distracting but controllable. She might have been surprised had she been aware of Sal's schedule: a night baseball game with the children plus a brother-in-law and *his* children, an early five-hour meeting with the accountants and then a plant tour 10 miles across town, certain negotiations with a union shop supplier, ordinarily accommodating but not this time, and two hours working out at the racquet club. He appeared there irregularly, depending on how his favorite Levi's fit. He found time to make a fast trip to confer with a crazed mechanic named Einar, the only person Sal trusted to touch the Porsche. Plus all the regular stuff.

Still, he was twanging with energy at the appointed rendezvous. Victoria was in something slippery and black guaranteed not to wrinkle. He sprang out and opened the car door for her, kissed her properly, then paused and kissed her improperly as well.

"Holy cats," she said, wheezing a little.

"I couldn't do that with all the stuffed birds watching. Your lipstick is gone; is it all over my face?"

Sal had phoned instructions to the cook and owner of a small northern Italian restaurant tucked away in a tiny strip mall. Victoria looked inquiringly at him. "We're eating Tuscan," he said, making vague motions with his hands. "Very simple, very good, you'll like it, I think." They submerged in beef carpaccio, after figs and prosciutto. "Just an appetizer," said Sal. "Careful with the ribollita, it's filling." The waiter brought a chianti along with freshly baked bread dabbed with gorgonzola and inserted among a variety of greenery and fresh melon slices.

"It's sort of a gangbusters tasting menu," Victoria said, as small platters of seafood and pastas came and went. And toward the end of the meal, or what she hoped was the end, she leaned back, wiped olive oil off her mouth, and asked, "Who are these people? This food is wonderful."

"Secret," he said. Diners in the other five tables were savoring their meals with the ecstatic expressions of persons just discovering Mozart.

"We need to digest a little. There's a sort of private park close by that's perfect for walking. Then come and see the apartment. There's dessert if you can stand it." He looked at her a little apprehensively.

"Ah . . ." Victoria wavered.

"Tomorrow is Saturday."

She smiled, and let herself be swept into Sal's orbit with curiosity and misgivings, mixed.

The private park was a wooded area in a highly exclusive golf course, completely open because no one would have dreamed of invading its sacred precincts. "What if we're discovered by security or guard dogs or something," she asked, glancing over a shoulder.

"I give them the company membership number. It's for customers; it's a real kick for a lot of them; I don't use it myself."

"Mark Twain or somebody said that golf was a good walk spoiled," Victoria said severely.

"He spent too much time in river boats."

Sal lived in a fairly new building. That was logical, because the really old elegant buildings in that city were either Romanesque reproductions housing government offices or elaborate log cabins cantilevered over kettle moraine. Sal already had an elaborate log cabin, so all the modern glass shouldn't have been a surprise, but it was. Victoria stepped into the apartment and saw a most remarkable object: a large sculpture that hung on the opposite wall. It was alien and familiar all at the same time.

"What is that?" She approached it curiously, appraisingly.

"It's a catamaran," he said, "hung sideways. It was the only way it fit." He was watching her for indications of approval, disapproval, or a desire to leave immediately. The living room seemed to be a sort of a test.

"A catamaran. Do you use it? I mean, sail it?"

"I used to take it up to Superior a lot. But there hasn't been time for a couple of years." He watched her touch it. "It needs a big lake."

"It's beautiful," she said. "It's like—finding a pterodactyl on a roof."

"Ready for dessert?" Sal asked, while mentally flipping through images of dinosaurs.

"Can I tour?" Victoria inquired, peering into a compact kitchen. The place was very clean. It made her nervous. And it was trim, comfortable, but, well, trim. Boys' room with posters stuck onto the walls, games, and half-finished models of cars and spaceships. Master bedroom and living room practically interchangeable: you could sleep on anything anywhere. There had to be a cleaning woman, Victoria thought. White, ecru, umber and the color of fall maple leaves. Decorator too, she amended. There was a stack of management books in the living room, uninspired except, next to them, an oversize volume of sailing photographs.

"I'm not here that much," said Sal apologetically, hauling a couple of hassocks over to a small fireplace. "It's mostly a large, convenient closet."

"You have to live somewhere," she protested.

"The office, up at the lake, the family house. When the boys are here, it gets lively. I think it would be more fun living like you do." There was a small silence.

"That flapping sound," Victoria said, "are warning flags going up. You know the Beaufort Scale? Wind velocity for sailors? You've generated warning number five: 'small trees in leaf begin to sway.'"

"The only thing more annoying than a smart woman," said Sal, settling two dishes of lemon sorbet onto a hassock, "is a very smart woman who name drops. Try that. It's homemade."

She ate, licked the spoon, and said, "It's glorious. Do I pass?"

"Pass?"

"You've been watching me drift around looking at things. Are some rooms worth more points? What are you checking out? If I hate it, are you going to redecorate? Or toss me off the balcony?"

Sal put his spoon down and laughed. "Almost nobody but family ever gets past the front door," he said. "So it's strange to see some one in here besides the boys and the cleaning people. I'm trying to figure out how it feels."

"And how does it feel?"

"It makes me want to redecorate," he said thoughtfully. "It never seemed finished, even when it was finished. You don't look comfortable enough to want to stay here tonight."

"You are terminally romantic or addled or both," Victoria said, tapping her spoon on her sorbet dish. "First, you didn't ask me. Second, you are mixing up a seduction with an open house. Third," and she touched his temple, where a small vein had begun to throb, "might I make a suggestion?" Sal took her hand.

"Make a suggestion."

"There is a florist shop next to the hospital that's open till midnight. Never mind; I just know. Please call and ask them to send over two big bouquets of the splashiest flowers they've got. Then invite me to spend the night. And later you can give the flowers to the cleaning person who will be delighted and adore you for it."

"Victoria, will you stay here with me tonight?"

"Yes, thank you, I will. And in the morning I will sneak back in through a dorm window just like at summer school. Would you like to drink your sorbet?" It and Sal had melted simultaneously. He kicked off his shoes, gathered her into his lap, and smelled her hair. It smelled of—what? Lemon and strawberries and something else. The other bouquets arrived, adding the fragrance of carnations, roses, and stephanotis. The perfumes filled the room, softening corners, mellowing the dying fire and, through some phereomonic alchemy, touched the night with mild euphoria.

Victoria carried a bouquet into the bedroom, put it in a corner, and stepped out of her shoes. Sal scooped her up; she hovered above a quilt.

"We have to talk about this," said Victoria into Sal's chest, floating on perfume and carbohydrates. "We're veering off into complicated. I can't do complicated."

"Shhh," said Sal. "In the morning."

"Do you hear splashing? Is this a water bed?"

"It's pouring rain out," said Sal, and, still holding Victoria, closed the balcony door.

"Oh, how wonderful," said Victoria, and meant it.

10 OMNIUM GATHERUM

Little piles of sawdust dotted Mason and Miranda Thrip's driveway. Ted Sinkiewicz from Northwoods Construction ripped through two by fours and plywood, finishing the new garage door as quickly and expensively as was feasible. He was whistling something tuneless and repetitive and making professional-looking black pencil marks on bits of scrap lumber.

Mason had circled the van, boat, and trailer, now freed of garage door wiring, peering carefully at all sides, and couldn't detect any damage other than the scrape on the bow. The hitch seemed to be fine. He'd gone grim around the mouth, decided it could have been a lot worse, and called Dockworks. He'd drive the thing in for an estimate.

"Lunch first," said Miranda firmly. We're both getting shaky," She dished up Denver omelets, calmed by the sound of the circular saw. She was thinking they would do well to get into town to buy groceries.

Mason was trying to remember what the deductible was on the insurance policy. $350? $500? $1,000? "Good grief, I think I left the policy back in the city," he muttered.

Sinkiewicz put his head in the kitchen door. "You want the same opener as before? Your electrical is OK; I need to rig a new connector. Thanks, I don' mind if I do," he added, as Miranda handed him a cup of coffee. Mason nodded distractedly, wondering if the winch was insured as part of the boat or as part of the trailer.

"I've got a long grocery list," said Miranda. "We can stop at the Co-op after you finish with the boat people."

Mason patted his pockets, checking for wallet, checkbook, and car keys. He looked again at the newly attached safety chains on the boat trailer.

"Mason," said Miranda.

"Coming, coming."

Mason Thrip put the van in gear and swung down the velvety asphalt drive. "Should take this slower," he said and braked at the drive's only right-angle curve.

"Thong!" sang the winch, taking the braking as a signal to launch. Humming, the cable quickly uncoiled, releasing its burden, and the Rolling Boil slid backwards off its trailer. It missed the driveway entirely and hurtled into a stand of blueberry scrub and bracken fern. A small flock of crows rose instantly, enraged and shrieking, flying straight up into the tall pines to caw furiously down at the driveway. Mason gave a terrible cry that silenced them. One attempted a final statement, but it was nothing to Mason's, and the bird subsided, embarrassed.

"Well, that beats all," said Miranda, shading her eyes and squinting into the sun-struck crash site.

"I do *not* believe this," Mason yelled. "This is *not* fair!" Ted Sinkiewicz wandered up.

"Sounded like a stuck pig," he said, and spotted the boat. "Whoa, now there's a fix." But Mason was already scrabbling down the little ravine to the boat. The winch cable, still taut, shone in the afternoon sun.

"Randi," Mason hollered hoarsely, "Call . . ."

"Dockworks'ud be good," Sinkiewicz said. "746-5505. Tell 'em to bring the big truck."

"My god," said Miranda. "Listen. Could you do me a favor? Are you quitting at 4:30?"

"Well . . ." said Sinkiewicz, who was planning to knock off at four but hadn't wanted to admit it. Mason was crashing around in the underbrush, uttering terrible cries as he discovered each new gouge and scrape.

"Give me a lift into town, as far as the Co-op. Mason will pick me up. Or," she finished lamely, "I'll find the town cab somewhere."

"It's the Chrysler dealership."

"What is?"

"The town cab. They just slap this cab sign on whichever used car's got gas in it. Call 'em. They do airport runs, mostly."

"Jeez," said Miranda, starting in to call Dockworks. In the dense shrubbery, Mason made a particularly rending sound as he discovered that the propeller blades on the inboard motor had been badly twisted, and in the wrong direction.

"Merciful heavens," said someone in the driveway. "I was going to ask if you could help us with a petition, but maybe not right now." She looked at Mason in the weeds with the Rolling Boil. "Is there anything I can do? I'm a neighbor," she trailed off, fascinated by the scene at hand.

"Yes," said Miranda, "Yes, yes, there is. Is that your car near the road? Would you please run me into town? I'm a little desperate."

"Absolutely. I'm Maureen Hendrickson, by the way," she said, mentally trading the ride for help with the petition. And she'd have a captive audience; she could explain the details. On the other hand, Mrs. Thrip (identified at this address on her lake map) did look a little desperate.

"One fast phone call," said Miranda, "and I'll be right with you. Thanks so much. Mason," she said into the ravine, "I'll be back in an hour; I'll get a cab."

"That's ok," said Maureen. "If it's not too long I'll wait, unless you want to hang out at the Chrysler dealership."

* * *

Dutifully waiting for Gertrude to finish with her customer in the County Collector's office, Sydnor examined pamphlets describing local hiking trails and indulged in some creative eavesdropping. Gertrude and the gentleman who had just carefully spelled his name seemed to be engaged in a mild wrangle over some sort of permit—business, signage—along with a state tax registration form.

"Is that required?' he was asking.

"If you want to do business in this state it is," Gertrude replied. "You can take it with you, return it here, or mail it to that address on the bottom. I'll fill out the top part of the permit form; you can fill in the signage details when you're ready to install. Who's the employer?"

"Random. . ." The man stopped. Sydnor went into high alert. "Ah, I'm actually self-employed. That doesn't change the form or anything does it?" Gertrude looked at him appraisingly for a moment.

"Not if all the information is accurate and factual," she said, pulling a couple of lines of assessor-speak out of her head.

"Well, heh, heh," said the man. "I'm sure it'll be all ok and above board."

Gertrude stamped several papers, hard, and took a check. He thanked her and left. "Excuse me," he said to Sydnor who was regarding him as one would a particularly messy piece of road kill.

She stepped up to the counter. "That man," she began. "He was going to say Random, wasn't he?"

"Sounded like it," Gertrude said. "Wouldn't be surprised. Stranger here."

"Well," Sydnor mused, then remembered business. "We've got up a petition here, but thought we'd check if we need a permit or something before we go ahead and circulate it." She handed Gertrude a sample.

"Let's see. Sponsoring organization, persons responsible . . . we determine you're not inciting to riot, no fee, and leave a copy. But," she added, glancing at Sydnor, "riot might not be such a bad idea, considering." And stamped it.

Sydnor thanked her and headed back to the lake to tell everybody about the Random Mining Company mole spotted in the county office. But because she stopped at the Co-Op for tonic and limes, she ran into Mrs. Press, which shortened her communications run. "

"Tell the judge please," she said, "it's some man named Mactate with the mining company and he's setting up in town, god knows as what." Sydnor had a clear, decisive voice, so Larry Running Bear had no difficulty hearing the conversation from the next aisle where a more stable applesauce display was under construction, nor did Minnie Rosenheim who had run out of baking powder and was stocking up in the flour and sugar aisle.

* * *

The Washington County Woods Gazette had published the Riverbend mining photos through some sort of professional courtesy (one editor called the other and asked if there really was a photo morgue—there was). The tricky part of the transaction was figuring out who the photographers had been for photo credits. "Some of these were taken, oh, I guess you could say under adverse conditions," said the Riverbend editor.

"Threatened?" Buster inquired.

"Yeah, well, chased into the woods. We had to get the sheriff to walk around some."

"Boy," Buster breathed, anticipating Sturm und Drang.

The photographs and the first batch of letters provoked an immediate response: equal parts rage, horror, and threats to those who favored environmental destruction plus some political 'I told you so' harangues. And one from a reader who said the offer could prove very profitable for some lucky people. "There's a hornet's nest," Buster thought. It had to be a stranger. The writer made no reference to the photos.

The mail brought a letter to the editor from a representative of the Sierra Club. It detailed some of the Random Mining Company's more egregious operations across previously pristine countryside and welcomed community efforts to protect, et cetera, and offered assistance. The organization's representative looked forward to attending the forthcoming meetings between mining company people and the town's governing council.

Which meant that we are going to have some, thought Township Council Chairman Maxwell Skyler, who read it, and Gerald Mactate, who read it and shot off a message to Ross at headquarters. Judge Press read it and sent off a letter to the Sierra Club welcoming its interest (and enclosed copies of some Riverbend photos); he also sent copies to the Natural Resources Dept. at the state capitol for the hell of it.

Energized from his evening with the Native Americans and Arthur Rosenheim, Judge Press called Maxwell Skyler and filled up a good part of Skyler's answering machine tape. This whole thing was beginning to get unwieldy, he thought, though Nelson Two Snakes had turned out to be a pleasant surprise. The guy was a sharp as a samurai sword and—if pushed—could get impressively mean. He smiled. It was as good as Chicago politics, practically.

Skyler called back, intrigued. He kept missing Press at meetings. "Hell yes, let's by all means get together," he said. "And with anybody else who wants to—the Sierra people and the Monkey Wrench Gang and Save the Whales. I've just had the most stupid conversation with some nut named Mactate!"

"I'll bet he's the mining company mole, right?"

"He's a lunatic is what he is," Skyler growled. "He had the temerity—the *temerity*—to suggest he be appointed—*appointed*—to the Town Council as some kind of intermediary between the township and the mining company. Of all the tom fool notions!"

"I take it you declined his offer?"

"Declined! I told him that this is a voting democracy! Nobody gets appointed because we like the color of their eyes! I told him that these kinds of overtures were not welcome; it may be the way his company does business, but it's not the way it's done here. I told him a bunch of other stuff too; good thing nobody was taking notes." Skyler seemed to remember suddenly who he was talking to.

"Well, good of you to call," he said. "I've been hearing about you. Small town, news travels. You know Nelson and his people. We need to rig up a preliminary meeting, all parties."

"I think you need Larry Bear too; Nelson's the Big Guns. I'd save him for later," Judge Press cautioned.

"We need to talk," Skyler said. "Where are you? Yellow Perch?"

"East side."

"Are you free now? My wife's got bridge tonight."

"You're welcome to join us: hamburgers, potato salad, pie and ice cream," Press said raising an eyebrow toward his wife Adeline, who nodded.

"Sounds wonderful. Fifteen minutes, and I'll bring notes I made on some of the township's land ownership documents. By the way, a Chippewa lawsuit against the National Resources Department is a first, I think."

"Attention-getting," said Judge Press.

* * *

From headquarters around the Tintinger's dining room table, Sophie and Sydnor meanwhile, had distributed petition forms to a cadre of volunteers assigned to canvass on foot, in boats, and in various vehicles. After some calculation, it was clear that there were no more than forty to one hundred families on any given lake, and that the group should concentrate on the more densely populated Upper Chain and Lower Chain of Lakes.

Maureen Hendrickson had spread out a rather battered surveyor's map of the territory, divided it into squares, and assigned volunteers to appropriate units.

"This is a good time," Sydnor said cautiously, "to bring up the Big Dog Problem."

"What?" said Evangeline Juska's sister-in-law, clutching her petitions.

"It's why people stopped walking around the lake. This lake, anyway. Big, barking dogs. Territorial and all that. Very intimidating, sometimes."

She briefly contemplated telling them about a great slavering beast, barely manageable by its owner. It answered to "Fluffy." The people had left the lake several years ago, fortunately. The sheriff had said quietly, after Fluffy had cornered Kurt Wraddle in his own garage, "Just shoot it."

"Check before leaving the car," Sydnor said. "Announce yourselves. Ditto for approach by lake. You're armed (or oared) after all. Leave walking to areas you're familiar with. Ask Mr. Bleu about local owners' livestock. He must have been menaced all across the county delivering mail. And don't waste time hunting impossible-to-find people. We're going to put our best feet forward and cover the town as well. Shop owners, restaurants, people hanging clothes out."

"Here's the town's street grid," Sophie said, "all divided into zones. "We'll meet back here in three days to plan the town canvas." She sounded far more optimistic than she felt. "And if you find someone who's willing to ask friends and fellow workers to help, give him or her a couple of forms that have already been started. Otherwise, I think we have to stay out of places of business."

"What about at church?"

"There's an interesting idea. Get the minister to work it into his sermon." Lightening will strike us, Sophie thought. And then thought, oh, let it.

Out they went, armed with determination, many ballpoint pens, and into adventure.

11 DRY RUN

Township Council President Maxwell Skyler and some officers were meeting more or less informally with representatives from the Random Mining Company. Skyler called it a preliminary meeting; both sides considered it an opportunity to feel out the opposition. Larry Bear was representing the tribe, Arthur Rosenheim stepped in to cover technical expertise, Judge Press was on hand for legal questions, several local business owners sat in for bulk, Charlie Haney served as secretary. The stated objective was "meaningful dialog."

The mining company's interests were represented by a mining engineer, the company's in-the-field lawyer, an irritated-looking man named Wicker, the two on-site supervisors in plaid shirts, an extremely uncomfortable Rev. Weathersill, presumably in the role of a happy customer, and Gerald Mactate. Random Mining's on-site plaid shirt people had names like Shist and Doppler. Haney, who did not know shorthand, abbreviated the two as SHT and DRP for the full 15 pages of his report.

The gathering in the community room of the Old Town Hall did not begin auspiciously. Several of the Random Mining principals had got lost and had to be led out of the township's recycle center and pointed in the right direction. It made for a certain testiness as the group settled. And, while someone had thoughtfully provided coffee, the Old Town Hall plumbing was in the process of reassembly—a slow, loving reassembly with appreciative comments about 75-year-old angle joins—and was not functioning. This was not a problem in the woods, so naturally, no one had cancelled the plumbers. (There was also an ancient outhouse overrun with large furry brown spiders. That *was* a problem, as they were fearless.)

Gnarled old plumbers were working on the gnarled old plumbing and throughout the meeting, their comments from the crawl space beneath the floor were audible: "Need some breaker fluid here," and "Lookit! Part of an old grease trap!" These ejaculations frequently arose as someone was attempting to make an important point—usually the mining people. The locals sort of rolled with it and didn't drink the coffee.

Once introductions were over, Random Mining suggested, as a thesis, that its efforts were economically altruistic: jobs for the community, metal for industry. Judge Press noted that no more than 85 positions were likely; they would disappear when the ore —shipped to processors out of the county—ran out. He distributed documentation from Riverbend and other mines. "Speaking of jobs, you'll note that observers comment on the minuscule cleanup crews that you had assigned to other played out sites."

Arthur Rosenheim interrupted to ask, "What, specifically, is the toxin management program that your company has for this project?" The mining engineer, SHT, and DRP all spoke at once citing modern methods of detoxification and tailings management.

"If you can keep the sludge moving," said one of the plumbers from under the floor, "you can pump 'er into a 600-gallon holding tank."

"Have to pump 'er pretty regular," said his colleague. "Or she'll plug up and blow."

Mactate looked apprehensive. He had been oddly quiet, and was staying out of Maxwell Skyler's range.

"But you've got this dirty water problem," Arthur said, nudging his metaphorical knight diagonally across the board to menace the mining company's rook.

"That, folks," Skyler said, "is what's got the environmental people interested. "We're at least as interested as they are," he added.

"We can assure you . . ." said Wicker, wondering which environmental people they'd missed.

"But can you prove it?" Arthur inquired. "I think the subject may come up." Charlie wrote furiously. Wicker glanced at his mining engineer who was carefully examining the ceiling.

"Reverend Weathersill," said Larry Running Bear. Weathersill started. "What survey maps have you been using as baselines for the church camp boundaries?"

"Well, the old ones. I mean, the ones we've always had."

"1965? 1928? 1893?"

"I'd have to look," Weathersill said uneasily.

"We'd like to see them too, if you don't mind. The tribe keeps records from way back; there's been some concern about boundary accuracy. We'll stop by tomorrow, about lunchtime. Or earlier, if that's better." Weathersill flashed on old movie scenes of mounted Indians whooping through the woods, then snapped out of it.

"Lunch time. Fine," he said.

"Now really," Wicker said, "what has this to do with the matter at hand?"

"Just move it a bit to the left," instructed one of the plumbers. "That way we can tap into the pump for the outside faucet." Wicker looked furious.

"Well," Larry replied, "speaking for the tribe, if our land is your land, your sludge may be our sludge. We don't want to be landed with a bunch of indestructible sludge, do we?"

There was more verbal scrimmaging; Shist expounded on breakthrough technologies to handle mine wastes. Arthur Rosenheim quoted some figures on typical amounts of mine waste and suggested that Random's estimates were for amounts that were trivial or worse. Doppler defended land recovery methods; Larry Bear asked if the recovered territory would grow wild rice, a significant cash crop dependent on wetlands. The "meaningful dialog" served to strengthen each side's mutual antipathy.

"Mr. Mactate," said Maxwell Skyler abruptly, "What is it exactly that you do?"

"I'm sort of an advance man," Mactate said.

"And what does that entail?"

"Well, it's sort of like public relations. I guess you could say I make friends."

"You're an lobbyist, in other words." Mactate winced slightly.

"You could put it that way, I suppose."

"Mr. Mactate, the Random Mining Company will have to have a great many friends to operate here. And so far, I don't see much of a cheering section. So expect a great deal more interest than you may have met with up till now.

"On the 27th," Skyler continued, "there's an important Township Council meeting open to the public at the high school. We expect a large crowd. There will be tribal representatives, environmental people, and various experts that have been invited. And the press. There has been a lot of interest from the press. I assume you'll be there as well. Seven p.m. sharp. There will be an opportunity for everyone to speak, and I might mention that important decisions are made in these meetings. I think we've accomplished all that we're going to today. It has been very informative. Thank you."

There was a loud clanging noise from underneath the floor, over toward a corner. "Sounds like vapor lock," a plumber said clearly.

"Well," his colleague replied, "I suppose it's some kind of progress. Hand me that blow bag."

* * *

Charlie Haney was excited and energized by the Old Town Hall session with Random Mining. He was also thirsty and yearned terribly for a cold beer, but first he wanted an audience. He swung by Minnie Rosenheim's to find Walter, and described the meeting to both of them.

"Why that skunk Mactate," said Walter. "Cosying up around town, a spy for the mining company. I'll bet he's weaseled right into Rotary. We should be warning people," he said. "We should organize a resistance network or something."

"Well, this prelim meeting has pretty much blown his cover. I don't know that there's a lot more than we can do, short of putting a notice in the paper," Charlie replied.

"If you two are going out for beer, for heaven's sake go out," Minnie said. "Or we'll be up to all hours."

Minnie was not a hot-tempered person—people who watch bread dough rise are frequently calm—but she had a tendency to reconsider events and, over time, stoke up little simmering pockets of rage.

On Saturday, Minnie Rosenheim's pastry shop was thronged. Customers were picking at pastry samples from a tray above the lemon squares. Four or five people, nibbling cheesecake wedges and armed with paper cups of coffee, were slipping into sugar shock. The café corner with little tables and chairs had been an inspired idea. Eyes glazed, customers with bits of graham cracker crust stuck to their T-shirts, ordered more of whatever they were eating and sat down to distribute butter and cream cheese onto the family midsections.

Minnie was not happy, however. Brooding, and oblivious to booming business out front, she ground her teeth. The nerve. The unspeakable *gall* of that man. Mactate, who people were being friendly to—was an asp, a viper, a spy for the mining company.

No raspberry cheesecake had been more viciously glazed. Great gobs of thickened berry filling rose into ridges and hummocks. One of the cashiers looked in and, startled, fled back to a customer holding a quartet of brownies. Minnie continued to steam. Were they all so naïve, so, so unworldly that they could be taken in by some big city slime ball? A squirt of raspberry filling landed on the table top. A mining spy from Minneapolis or where ever he was really from?

She reached for the bowl of whipped cream and slung evenly spaced dollops, edging the pie, and marched it out to the display case.

Now, the odds for Gerald Mactate's sweet tooth acting up this Saturday would ordinarily have been low to moderate. He was working. Armed with the names of town council members, he had sought out the most available of them to "say hello." This was a euphemism for shaking hands and beaming and saying what a great job they were doing. And, oh, as a new resident, he'd be really enthusiastic about helping the town in some way. Wasn't that Random Mining something? So how does a person go about . . . which, after several days, began to sound odd, even to him. Something wasn't . . . right, somehow. The atmosphere was not percolating properly. The pitch wasn't coming together.

The business people smiled, said hello, and went right back to helping customers. One man had a small machine shop, and while polite, was involved in attaching a fitting to something. "Hand me that Allen wrench," he'd asked Mactate at one point. Gerald Mactate could not have identified an Allen wrench if one had dropped on his head, so that interview was a washout. And it made him feel as if he'd failed fourth grade.

At the lumberyard, he'd been forced to wander around in an enormous shed, surrounded by stacks of prefabricated trusses. He'd been peering through piles of boards or beams or something, looking for his contact, when somebody yelled, "Watch out!" And about a half ton of lumber landed on a metal shelf a yard above his head, where a sign read "THIS IS A HARD HAT AREA." A lumberman was approaching him at a brisk clip to (he guessed) ask his business, tell him he was an idiot, or throw him out bodily. He made up a silly question, said he was new in town, apologized, and got out of there. It was either that or buy window frames.

Back in town, he decompressed by pretending to look at some vacant office space just off the main street, quietly, not wanting to have to bond with a rental agent. Awkward, really. A whiff of caramel corn from the candy shop next reminded him that he'd missed lunch. Well, that was easily remedied; a nice piece of coffeecake at the pastry shop would hold him till later.

And so it was that, as Minnie Rosenheim was moving a tray of walnut-caramel drop cookies, Gerald Mactate bounced into "Remember When" pastries, smiling and ravenous. It was a hunger doomed from the start.

"Hello!" he beamed at Minnie, admiring the red flush creeping up her cheeks. "I'll have . . ."

"You quisling!" she said loudly.

"Ahhh . . ."

"You skunk!"

Conversations stopped. Coffee cups froze at chin level.

"Ahhh . . ?" Mactate attempted.

"You are a mining company spy!" Minnie yelled. The cashier cringed behind her register. Customers stood transfixed.

"Now, I can . . ." Mactate began. People were beginning to stare at him. "Heh, heh," he tried.

"You came to infiltrate!" Minnie cried. "To take advantage of people who welcomed you!" She had almost reached a full head of steam. "You want to ruin our woods with a mine! You work for *them*!"

There were disapproving murmurs from some customers.

"It's just . . ." Mactate began, edging away from the counter. And Minnie threw a walnut cookie at him—hard.

"Ow!"

"I wouldn't sell you a toothpick," she shouted, and pitched two more cookies at his head. Customers dodged, and several took refuge behind the café corner's ice cream chairs. A small boy cheered and his mother grabbed his arm.

"Spy! Assassin!" Minnie shrieked, and Mactate fled, stumbling out the door in a hail of walnut cookies.

A great quiet settled over the pastry shop—its customers suspended between awe and shock. Minnie looked around. "Well," she said. " Free coffee for everybody." And much relieved, she returned to the back room, switched off the oven, took out six graham cracker pie crusts, and began mentally organizing a further offensive against Gerald Mactate and all his works.

An astonished murmur rose from the shop. And the sound of coffee being poured.

12 SOME PROPERTIES

At the Constantini's, the deal was that Sal (and the business) paid for everything and Lucia ran everything. It was a highly satisfactory arrangement; Lucia got to grandmother Sal's children at fairly predictable intervals. Sal, for his part, got secondary summer camp services and all the comforts of the house on the lake, which ran with the precision of a Swiss timepiece. Occasionally a summer storm took down trees and the power, but residents simply plugged their refrigerators into gasoline generators, broke out charcoal grills, lit kerosene lamps, and carried on. Lucia's grandsons were enchanted; it was camping out.

It was one thing to operate under lake radar, but Sal knew his mother's was not to be messed with. He meditated—and had been for some time—on how to bring up the subject of Victoria. A love affair in the privacy of his city apartment was not an issue; at Yellow Perch Lake, disappearing at 6 p.m. and returning the following 10 a.m. was. Plus there were the boys to consider. And he wanted Victoria around. A lot. It was all very problematic.

Now, Lucia was more sensitive to emotional atmospherics than her son imagined. She had observed that he'd been generating some kind of free-form static electricity for the last several weeks. She'd idly considered tapping him with the metal vacuum cleaner extension to see if the contact threw a spark. And she was quite patient about some things. Whatever this was could turn out to be interesting. She looked forward to it.

Sal initiated the campaign in the other camp.

It was Thursday; Victoria's seminar was ending and she had packed the jeep for a quick getaway to beat the weekend traffic up to the north woods. They had managed considerable time at the apartment—Sal and Victoria took turns cooking simple meals to clear the evenings of anything so time-consuming as dining out. Victoria adjusted her wardrobe to include "sneaking in" clothes, as she called them, and in the mornings swept around Sal's bathroom in a lush terry cloth robe with "Plaza Athénée" embroidered on a pocket.

They were good together, knew it, and were getting better. Victoria, who had a deep understanding of hubris, was pretending that this was a normal state of affairs.

"Very nice," said Sal, examining the robe. "Very Victoria. Needs to be shorter, though."

She unhitched the towel he'd wrapped around his waist. "Very nice," she said. "Terrific resilience, entirely appropriate sizing."

"Oh yes? And so early too," and Sal expertly popped Victoria into the shower, robeless, and stepped in after her. Remarkably there wasn't much splashing.

Later, he dropped her off quietly at the Staff Only entrance in the museum wing, and asked, "You're leaving when?"

"As soon as I can escape the wrap-up luncheon."

"You have to meet my mother," said Sal, holding Victoria's door shut so he could kiss her.

"What?"

"Up north. I'm coming up Saturday morning."

"Sal . . ."

"I'll see you Saturday. Victoria?"

She'd gone rather white around the mouth. "Your mother?"

"You'd have to sooner or later. You're going to be late."

"Oh my god, your mother?"

"It'll be fine. Saturday."

And Victoria's morning was ruined. Why would he do that? This was frightening. Was he crazy? Well, yes, that was a given, but she wasn't rushing around to introduce *her* parents. She felt a little faint at the thought. No, she felt a little faint at the thought of Lucia Constantini, a genuine Italian matriarch.

Was he nuts? "This is Victoria Caruso, we're sleeping together at every available opportunity." Or "Victoria and I are having a passionate affair." Or maybe, "I'll be spending the nights with Victoria at Tamarack Lake Lodge." Oh, that's charming. He'd lost his mind. Had she missed some sort of ethnic marker? Would it require special clothes?

Victoria put her hand to her head and went to beg some Alka-Seltzer from the department secretary. She suddenly felt a little queasy.

* * *

Sal, facing a daylong cooling off period before Saturday, felt guiltier than he'd expected. Victoria was going to think about this sudden introduction to the family and she was going to be pissed. In fact, Sal acknowledged to himself that he hadn't quite worked out how this conjunction was going to be accomplished. It had not occurred to him that it might be so awkward as to be painful—for Victoria, anyway. People who give orders and expect them to be followed, proceed briskly on their appointed rounds tending to ignore spots of blood and angry cries. It came to him that the current situation was different. Very different.

He drove into his parking place, turned the key in the ignition, and thought. He'd bring the boys. They didn't understand why they couldn't be up north all the time. (Sal understood, but he wasn't going to get into custody explanations with an 8- and 10-year old). They'd love it; it was the solution, or part of the solution, anyway. The boys could deflect almost any kind of awkward situation. Hell, they *were* awkward situations: small buzz bombs waiting to happen. He still had no idea as to how to manage the event, but felt a lot better about it. He'd need some very strong coffee to negotiate with their mother; extracting the children from their busy summer schedule required patience and diplomacy. Sal took a deep breath and went to muster these attributes. And to wonder how Victoria was feeling. She would have had enough time to get—what—angry? Appalled? Alarmed? But not pleased. Probably not pleased.

Sal began to suspect that all this time he had been enjoying what was called The Unexamined Life. And that it was about to be examined very carefully indeed. Ah, Victoria.

※ ※ ※

Saturday morning was warm and windy with great puffy clouds casting fast-moving shadows through the woods. Victoria, at the table in her cottage and surrounded by texts and notebooks, was disconsolately listening to a tape recording of heron sounds: "frahnk frahnk, frahnk," it squawked. She rewound the tape and played it again, frowning. "Frahnk, frahnk" was a heron warning call. All the heron calls were unlovely and most seemed interchangeable. The sounds were mostly territorial: my eggs, my nest, my fish, my feeding area. Considering that one heron rarely got close enough to another heron even to determine the other's sex, this degree of commentary was remarkable. It made mating an exercise in what-the-hell optimism. Brave heron, Victoria thought.

She said, "Frahnk," softly to herself, and rested her forehead in her hand. Something had to be done. She shouldn't be this uneasy. She'd lost her appetite but was getting a hunger headache. When she raised her head, Sal was at the screen door watching her, concerned.

"Are you all right?"

"I don't think so. Did you just get here?" Sal came in and perched on the chair across from her. "You're scaring me," Victoria said without preamble. "This whole thing is flapping out of control. Is there some sort of ceremony associated with meeting your mother? What are you going to say to her? Do you realize

I've known you for—what—a little more than two weeks? What are we doing? Is this some kind of blood-mingling event? Sal? What am I missing?"

"You want to know my intentions?"

"I want to know what seems so critical to you. I mean, if I were struck down by a speeding car tomorrow, what would all this formality have achieved? I'm not making any sense." She paused and took a breath. "But if you have intentions, that's even scarier than meeting your mother." She looked near tears.

"Oh Victoria," Sal said, dismayed. " Please. I'm sorry. I've done this all wrong. Are you going to cry? Please don't. I mean, do if you're going to, but I don't cope very well." He reached across the table, touched her wet cheek, and his heart plummeted toward his shoes, taking his stomach with it. He tried again.

"I'm trying to hammer out some kind of life or relationship or something around us—you and me—because I'm terrified you might disappear and you are wonderful and gorgeous and funny and smart and—I know how this sounds—no one I can remember has ever made me this happy." He took a breath. "So ok, I moved too fast, but listen." He felt a little ill, an unfamiliar sensation. He leaned forward and took her hand.

"Please be part of my life, your terms. I want to be able to argue with you over dinners and make love to you and take you fishing and skiing and traveling and—you know—but there's no need to sneak around. We're grown up. I hope. Please, come over this afternoon. Say hello. My mother is no fool; she knows I've been up to something and Victoria, I can't tell you how pleased she'll be to find out that you're what I've been up to. She's very wise and funny. This sounds idiotic, but you get the idea. Will you consider it? Please?"

He threw himself back in the chair, spent. "I never wanted a drink this early in the day before," he remarked to the fireplace. "Maybe an aspirin would be better."

Victoria studied him for a bit. "I'm astonished you can be so eloquent at 10 o'clock in the morning," she said. "I wish we had gotten some of this aired out before.

"You're still scaring me, but I think I can handle it, what with your codicil and all. I'm still considering our—I guess—attachment, and what a surprise it's been—wonderful, mostly. But I've got to say, Sal, if you push too hard, I'll push back. Or I'll evaporate right out of here." He was paying close attention. "We've got something splendid going, I know, and it's a good thing that you're madly attractive on all fronts, to me anyway, because after being corralled into your plan—*your* plan—I should not give you so much as the time of day."

Sal rose, said, "Don't move," leaned across the table, and carefully kissed her on the forehead, nose, and mouth.

"You are a mushy, sentimental person," Victoria said, blotting her nose on a piece of notebook paper. "Now tell me how you've arranged this ever-so-casual household introduction."

***

They agreed to rendezvous at the Constantini house at 3:30. Meanwhile, Lucia was making a scorched earth run through the Co-op, Sal chauffeuring; he needed to pick up a knife sharpener. He wondered if anyone at the hardware store had found the one in the wheelbarrow of socket wrenches.

Victoria would drive over at the appointed time. There would be food. ("There's always food," said Sal, resigned. "It gives us something to do with our hands I think.") Victoria began to twitch at about noon. She had eaten a hard-boiled egg, washed it down with a glass of milk to settle her stomach, and checked the first aid kit to see if any seasick pills might be left from a European trip a year and a half ago.

This is ridiculous, she thought. She was working herself into a state. The Constantinis were in town. The thing to do was to reconnoiter, take the edge off the strangeness. She would simply drive over, park somewhere inconspicuous, and wander down to the lake and check the place out. Much relieved, she tossed her bag, a sweater and an emergency wrap skirt in the back seat, slid behind the wheel and drove—as quietly as possible in a rattling jeep—to the east side of Yellow Perch Lake. There was the mailbox, there was the driveway. She casually drove a little beyond these markers, then found a space for a U-turn and doubled back past the driveway and edged the jeep into the entrance of an old fire lane she'd spotted fifty yards or so further down.

She cursed her shorts, checked the weeds for nettles and briars, and set off toward the lake, trying to drift toward the Constantini driveway. And so was a little flummoxed when she stumbled onto an asphalt boat launch. It ran parallel to the driveway, apparently, but at a steeper incline and it plunged right into the water.

Glancing around—it was very quiet—she cautiously followed it down to the edge of the water and a view of the property's lakefront. It took awhile to absorb the panorama. Well. These were creature comforts, indeed. Besides the boathouse, there was a deck big enough for dances, a screened gazebo, a long dock-like pier, something large moored at the end under canvas, and a gaggle of rowboats. All for one family, she thought pensively.

Victoria sat down next to a small cedar and took it all in. Maybe, she thought, I can just sneak back up to the jeep and drive away. And then something hopped, close by.

She turned slowly and there, tentatively emerging from the leaf litter, was a fine and attractive mud-colored toad. She slowly reached out and lifted it up, careful not to startle it. It was a beauty —rounded, well fed, and self-satisfied looking. Its throat made steady fluttery movements. "Hello Bufonidae," she said, barely touching the top of its head with one finger. The toad closed its eyes.

"How do you know its name?" demanded a child's voice very close by. Victoria froze, being careful not to squeeze the toad.

"It's the toad family name," she managed, calmly. "The frog family name is Ranidae; it's different." Damn, she thought. Trapped.

"What are you going to do with it?"

"I'm going to put it right back under these leaves. Toads don't move very fast and they try to stay out of sight. A lot of critters want to eat them."

An eight-year-old boy in a striped T-shirt emerged from the underbrush and studied her and the camouflaged toad. "What kind of critters?"

"Bigger critters. Snakes, foxes, badgers, gulls, big water birds."

"There's a big water bird on the other side of the pier," the child volunteered. Apparently a stranger in the woods holding a toad was to be trusted.

"What color?" Victoria was alert.

"Blue sort of."

"Can you show me?"

"Sure," said the boy and trotted off toward the pier. Victoria picked herself out of the leaf litter and followed.

"Wait," she said, quietly. The boy turned and looked at her. "I want to sneak up. Can we fit under the pier?" she whispered. He nodded importantly, and together Victoria and Tommy Constantini dropped to their knees and crept through sand and pebbles and leaf muck for a proper view.

"There!" whispered the boy. It was a large blue heron.

"Beautiful!" Victoria whispered back. "Look. He's caught a fish and he's banging on that stone so he can eat it."

"Why?"

"So it doesn't wiggle when it's going down."

"Wow. Would it eat the toad?"

"Yes. That's why we put it back under the leaves."

"Will it be ok?"

"I think so. Look, it's hunting for another fish."

"What kind is it?"

"It's a blue heron." The heron, partially camouflaged by an overhanging branch, made fast beaky stabs into the water.

"Are they nice?"

"No. But they're interesting. Watch." Victoria gave a little whistle. And with a loud pneumatic flap, the heron took off.

"Wow!" said the boy.

"Good work," said Victoria, smiling at their small nature adventure. "Can we get out on the other side?"

From a small balcony just off a living room high above the pier, Lucia Constantini watched, fascinated. She went back to the kitchen where Sal was mounting a knife sharpener. "Sal, Tommy and a young woman are under the pier getting absolutely filthy and stalking a blue heron." She was much amused.

"Oh hell," he said, dropping a screwdriver. "She's early! Where's Nick? I'll get them. Under the pier?"

"Take towels."

He dashed down to the lake and his youngest son barreled into him explaining at full tilt. "There was this toad and we put it back into the leaves so the blue heron wouldn't eat it and then we snuck up on the heron and watched it knock out a fish so it wouldn't wiggle and we're going to hunt for more toads and herons are not friendly."

"Good work," said Sal. "Dry off; you're dripping."

"That's what she said too. I have to tell Nick. Nick!" he yelled, dragging the towel up the stairs.

"Is this what's known as a finesse?" Sal inquired, handing Victoria a towel. "Did you and Tommy just stumble into each other or is it some kind of plot?"

"It was the toad. A really fine toad." She beamed at him. "What a nice kid that is. Is there another one somewhere nearby? I can only whip up one toad at a time, though." She was futilely blotting her knees. "I have something dry in the jeep; I'll be right back."

"Meet me upstairs," said Sal. "Just turn into the driveway. I want you to know that getting a stamp of approval from that eight-year-old is worth hard currency in this family."

"Any friend of Bufonidae is a friend of mine," she said, returned the towel, and sprinted back up the launch track to the jeep.

"Just when you think you're not going to be surprised, you're surprised," Lucia said to Sal back in the kitchen. "I thought she'd be taller."

"What?" he said, astonished. "Why? How?"

"Just a feeling I had," said Lucia, pulling a tray of puff pastry out of the oven. "And you don't need to introduce her to Nicholas, because Tommy is taking care of it," she added, looking out the kitchen window. "With due respect, your young woman comes highly recommended."

"Mother," said Sal.

"Yes?"

"Nothing. Never mind. I should have spent a lot more time with toads, I guess." Lucia laughed and outside, Victoria approached the house, under escort.

* * *

"That must be Victoria," Sydnor said, handing Sophie the binoculars. They were in low slung lawn chairs at Sydnor's lake edge and were unabashedly spying. "Thank goodness, she's a real person. Can you see what they're doing?"

"Standing on the dock with Tommy. Sal's giving her a towel," Sophie said, squinting. "She's pretty, or at least from this distance. Dark hair; she kind of matches the Constantini color scheme." She passed the binoculars back to Sydnor.

"We shouldn't be doing this," Sydnor said, adjusting the focus. "But she gets points for hanging out with Tommy. What's that she's wearing?"

"Short Bermudas or something," Sophie said. "I don't think she's been to the lake before. Do you suppose this is some special event?"

"Goodness knows, but she's there and that's pretty significant. I don't think Sal ever brought any love interest to the lake. What he does at home is another story, of course. I've got to get better binoculars," Sydnor said, putting them down.

"You are a pair of shameless hussies," said Webb severely from behind them.

"No question," Sophie replied, "and since you're going to be prim about it, we won't burden you with any new information."

"And," Sydnor added, "we won't utter a word about the half hour you spent watching Milt Hendrickson to see where he was catching Walleyes."

"Yeah, yeah," said Webb. "Actually, I came over to beg and plead with Sydnor to find the dratted survey of the property. The plat."

"Though my fault, through my most grievous fault," she said. "I know, I promised."

"And tell me again," Sophie asked. "It's desperate that we have this right now because?"

"Because it shows exactly the location of our property lines and we can figure out who pays what percent when we resurface the driveway," said Webb patiently. "And it had better be soon, because large pieces of old asphalt are washing downhill when it rains."

"Well, that sounds a little more critical," Sophie admitted. "Should I help you look?" she asked Sydnor.

"No, no, it's either in the attic or the garage. It means tearing the place apart. I'll do it."

"Judging from the first go 'round with the mining people," Webb warned, "I'd say we were going to be busy and distracted pretty soon. I wanted to get my pitch in before then."

"Did you hear about the cookie-throwing incident in the pastry shop?" Sophie asked. "I would love to have been there. Three cheers for Minnie Rosenheim."

Webb had picked up the binoculars and was idly scanning the shoreline opposite. He paused. "Who is that on the Constantini dock?"

"Description?" Sophie inquired.

"A real dish with dirty knees," he said.

"True love," Sydnor said, "makes dirty knees beautiful and an occasion of great joy."

"So it would seem," said Webb, lowering the binoculars.

13 LOVES' LABORS

Nicholas, the ten-year-old, assumed that his brother was making up the toad-heron story, but Tommy seized Victoria's wrist, tugged her over and said, "See?" as if that explained everything. Nicholas looked impressed and grubbily shook her hand. Victoria, charmed, allowed as how she could use some extra ballast when she did her heron-spotting canoe tour. Nicholas understood her value immediately and was starting to figure out when they could do this when Sal opened the kitchen screen door and brought the trio inside.

Lucia Constantini considered that, close up, Victoria seemed quite all right. A little mussed from running through the woods and romping with elementary school children, but her nails were short, her hair was under control, and her apprehensive air was rather winning. She was nicely spoken. The grandsons liked her immediately. A good sign. And of course, Sal was looking at her as if she were made of rare porcelain.

How wonderful to be young, Lucia thought. All that possibility and time. "Are you at Tamarack Lake for the summer?" she asked Victoria, genuinely wondering if Sal would be tearing up here weekends through Thanksgiving and Christmas.

"Just until after Labor Day; the kids I'm tutoring will go back to school. I will too, to finish up."

"Doing?"

"Ph.D. work for a biological sciences degree, specialty in large water birds. I'll teach or do research or it may lead to something completely different. A year following a flock from summer territory to wintering grounds in South America would make a good science book, for instance." Sal had stopped slicing a tomato and was listening. Ah, Lucia thought. Unshared information.

"Victoria says there's a heron nesting site in the Nicolet Forest that's going to be part of her research," said Sal who had resumed slicing.

"Isn't it right across the road?" Victoria inquired.

"Gracious!" Lucia said, alarmed. "You can hardly get in; the roads are only trails. We used to pick raspberries in there somewhere. Nobody can find the patch any more. That forest goes on forever."

"I suppose the herons figured out that there's safety in impossible places." Victoria looked thoughtful; she found she was holding a plate of radishes. Sal gently took it from her and put it on the counter.

Healthy young people, full of juices, Lucia thought. She had decided to be blind, deaf, and dumb to the sexual aspects of this burgeoning romance, and that would be a neat acting job, because the physical connection between the two hung over them like a shared halo. What a difference, Lucia thought, from the first go 'round. Everything from the hair . . .well, that was history, and we all have to live with our history; that's tricky enough. Still, there were wonderful things to be had from wreckage, sometimes. She smiled at the grandsons who'd raced each other up from downstairs.

A carillon of cooking timers erupted, and Lucia snatched a loaf of bread out of the oven, admired Nick's band aid, tested a tomato sauce, sent Sal downstairs to the second freezer for ice, and —with her chin—indicated to Victoria that the plates and napkins could be usefully placed on the low table next to the living room balcony.

That was how it went. Victoria was not cross-examined, questioned, or studied—or not obviously, anyway. After a what was either high tea or an early supper, she was handed a pole, assigned a cushion marked "leave in boat" and clambered into an aluminum row boat with Sal and the boys for some late afternoon fishing.

"Can you stick a worm on a hook?" Nick challenged.

"Yes, and I can clean fish too."

"Blech," said Tommy.

"It's pretty messy," Victoria said, "but you have to do it if you want to eat them."

Sal was arming the fishing poles. "Something for everyone," he said. "You get to pick: worms, minnows, or one of these lures that look like chewed bubble gum."

It was all terrifically normal. The boys got a bucket of panfish, something grabbed Sal's lure, ran it 300 feet while his reel screamed, then stopped. Something else neatly removed Victoria's bait without a twitch, and finally an evening cloud of mosquitoes dive-bombed and drove them in.

So, with periodic adjustments, a pattern developed. Victoria researched, wrote, and dealt with various obligations during the week. These involved tutoring the two shirttail cousins ("the Tamarack Lodge relatives," she explained to Sal) who were having a bad time with math.

"They began to lose it by about algebra," she said. "It's taking a lot of effort to get them back on their feet, mathematically speaking. I'm afraid algorithms are going to be out of the question."

"Teach them to diagram football plays," Sal offered. "Then they can make some kind of living in sports bars. When did you get into this higher math, anyway?"

"Oh, you know, you have to for a science major. And it wasn't that hard—I was always interested in scientific stuff—curious, anyway. You should have seen my diagrams of amphibian circulatory systems. They were beautiful but looked like maps of the Paris subway. At least I never fainted over a dissection table like one guy in class."

Sal was in the north woods by 4:00 or 4:30 p.m. on Friday afternoons. He'd decided the business could take care of itself after noon on Fridays. In fact, he suspected that it could run itself without human intervention for weeks before anyone noticed and put a hand in. It was a noticeable modification of his previous position as captain lashed to the helm of the ship.

And, after all, several generations of Constantini skills had pounded the operation into a sturdy functionality. Sal explained, "It's not one of those situations where the first generation builds it, the second generation expands it, and the third generation spends it. But you have to keep control of the inventory, which is incredible, and watch the market. It needs a steady hand and periodic nudging. Hell, I'll bet my mother could run it; she's a brilliant organizer."

"She certainly is," said Victoria. She considered that there was a lot to be learned from Lucia Constantini just by watching from a safe distance.

When they were around, the children took priority. "Horseback riding," Sal would say, and off they'd go, the boys to pound around dirt trails on surly-looking ponies. Later everyone would swim if it was warm enough. Plenty of hard exercise seemed to be the goal, so that around an evening bonfire with nicely charred marshmallows, Tommy usually fell asleep and had to be carried up to bed. Nick staggered a little, but made it without aid.

"How can you do this?" Victoria asked much later when it was quiet. Lucia had been asleep for hours. "I'm exhausted."

"You have to train, but it's worth it. It's good for you, too. I'll run you back to Tamarack unless you'd like to curl up in the boat house for a while."

"Tempting, but I'd still be there in the morning. It was insane to get on those horses," Victoria moaned.

"Just wait. You'll feel muscles you never knew you had."

"Take me back to the cottage, please. Our carnal pleasures can wait while I rebuild my energy stockpile."

"I wish you'd drive back to the city with us."

"Bad form," said Victoria. "To Tommy and Nick I'm an up north person. Let's not confuse them. And I have work to do."

"Right. We can confuse them later. Summer isn't going to last forever. Have you thought about that?" Sal asked seriously. "September? Fall?"

"Yes. No. I don't know. Not in any useful way. Is next Friday a childless weekend?"

"You're changing the subject," he said, accusingly.

"Right. I hope you're planning some heavy necking at my cottage. I might be able to absorb some of this sizzle you keep generating. Is there a dynamo in there?"

Sal's return trips from Tamarack Lodge were highly variable. On the children's weekends, he was always back for breakfast with Tommy and Nick, and usually in time to deal with the bacon.

The boys added Victoria to their schedule of northwoods adventures. She could not have escaped even if she'd wanted to. Lucia Constantini, relieved of some of the responsibility for entertaining two young savages, appreciated Victoria's social skills. They could, apparently, be retooled instantly to accommodate special interests, ages 8 to 10. "Look, a snakeskin," Victoria would say, holding the tattered thing up for everyone to admire.

"Let's see, let's see," and all three would huddle to examine the artifact.

"Do you ever feel left out?" Lucia asked Sal, who was watching this piece of nature study from the kitchen window. "And do you ever think for a minute that she might be smarter than you are?" she ventured.

"I'm counting on it," Sal replied tranquilly, holding a sweating glass of iced tea. He flourishes, Lucia thought, studying her son. He looked, well, sleek. Sort of like a large cat that's been thoroughly and appreciatively licked. Lucia, mildly scandalized, caught herself. What an odd thing to think of. It was far too early for a glass of wine, but she poured one anyway, then put it down on an end table, and considered her own—courtship, she supposed it was—and pulled a chair around to gaze at the lake and indulge in some reminiscence. How time does fly, she thought.

*　*　*

The childless weekends were much looser. Victoria worked like a demon during the week to free the weekends for Sal. Sal worked like a demon all the time, she supposed. Sometimes Sal and Lucia cooked, or Sal and Victoria dined out or made grilled cheese and tomato sandwiches. They wandered through the occasional craft fair, dozed on cushions on the pier, hiked in the woods, or lazed on his boat in the middle of the lake, drifting with the wind. And they enjoyed each other.

"We can't make love all the time," Victoria said from under a large straw hat. They were on Sal's boat and bobbing around the point just out of sight of the Constantini house.

"Yes we can, but it's pretty public on the lake."

"I refuse to be sanded to a high gloss by runaway passion on your hull or top or whatever you call it."

"No no no," Sal coaxed, "it's like this." He eased over the side into the lake and slid her from the deck into deep water, holding a judiciously placed tie-bar.

"You are insane," Victoria said. He was supporting her under her arm with one hand, and doing scandalous things around bits of her bathing suit with the other. The operation, fully functional, required some pressure against the hull that generated an alarming bobbing sequence, alarming to any interested watchers, anyway.

Victoria, to keep from frightening the loons, ducked her head into the water and expelled a strangled cry and about 800 bubbles before coming up for air.

"My treat," said Sal, looking wickedly pleased.

"Holy shit," Victoria said, trying to inhale. "You will pay for that, but on dry land and when you least expect it. Am I still wearing the bottom half of my bathing suit? No, no touching. A simple yes or no."

"More or less: you'll need to adjust a little. Can I help you climb back in?"

14 PUBLIC RELATIONS

Random Mining's pressure to schedule town meetings at inconvenient times and in out-of-the-way places met polite, firm, and then solid resistance. The company would have preferred not to expose itself to public scrutiny at all. But civic groups—inexplicably growing more interested—wanted to hear all about the mining company's plans.

The local people pointed out that school auditoriums were the ideal size for the meetings, but were free only after school and practice hours. Therefore meetings would be in the evenings. Ross and Wicker also learned that there were no out-of-the-way places. The entire area was out of the way.

Shist and Doppler thought of the Old Town Hall and admitted that they, at least, wouldn't be able to find it again without a local guide or marks chopped into the sides of trees. So there were public meetings and there were many of them. Gerald Mactate discovered that the audiences were not yokels. Some had done mining research, others knew about Riverbend; sometimes a professional geologist or biologist or environmentalist was invited to speak. Their comments were knowledgeable and skeptical and the audience listened carefully. Discussions were often contentious and picketers enlivened some of the meetings with Random Mining personnel.

"Outsiders," said Wicker dismissively at a local coffee shop after one of the noisier gatherings that included not only picketers, but marching, chanting picketers.

"Cream and sugar?" asked the waitress who was wearing an orange T-shirt emblazoned, "Stop the Mine. Save Our Waters."

"Are you going to leave a tip?" asked Mactate innocently.

The local papers faithfully reported the topics under discussion at the meetings, and included quotes and arguments. Equally important, although not reported, were small private get-togethers in stores, church lobbies, over bridge, and in offices. If the Random Mining people were surprised that local interest hadn't died down or at least leveled off, they would have been alarmed at the nature of the some of the private conversations and judgements that were underway. One anti-mining group that had formed immediately was the resort owners association. They were the ones that got in touch with the U.S. Bureau of Mines.

*   *   *

The Yellow Perch Lake canvassers, somewhat tattered, reconvened at the Tintinger cottage at the appointed time. They had done well, considering. There had been Big Dog Problems; several were solved by just sitting in the car and letting the animal slaver against the door until the owners came out to see what the ruckus was. One dog had inadvertently flushed a deer, and ran baying into the woods, leaving the coast clear for signatures.

Dieter Vilnus had gathered signatures representing a good cross section of various Balkan countries. For whole lines, scarcely a vowel was visible. "Where did you find these people?" Sydnor asked, confounded.

"Oh, I check out some fishing clubs, some people we know, a picnic, then I just row around."

Evangeline Juska's sister-in-law had sprung into a canoe with her husband, and they darted madly into coves, along the sides of pontoon boats, and insinuated themselves next to piers and docks, surprising a large number of signatures out of dampish boaters and bathers. After all, canoe is basically nonthreatening.

Evangeline herself went to the Rotary and Women's Club antique show, planted herself at the entrance, and did well. Though, she said, she'd had to admire some pretty awful stuff—kewpie dolls and rusty andirons and godawful tea cozies. She said it involved real effort, because the show was on for all of Friday and Saturday.

Sophie, in a floppy straw hat, worked the addresses closest to the excavations at the church camp and did a land office business. Everybody hated what was happening, and Sophie was hard-pressed to extract herself from some highly emotional conversations. She said it was the hat; it made her look sympathetic.

Al Gustave simply got into his all-terrain vehicle, and followed Mr. Bleu for several days on the more out-of-the-way mail routes. They both had a good time, and there was only one incident involving a tethered pet llama with a terrific spitting range. Gustave considered that his names should be worth more because they were in such dangerous places.

And Sydnor took her map and added all the rural gas stations and convenience stores she could locate. Then, in a burst of inspiration, she remembered the trailer camps. Some had been around for years. These were, goodness knows, well-established residents, summer and otherwise, and all neatly lined up. All in all, canvassing was a real slog, but other than a mild case of poison oak and the sudden hatching of the season's black flies, it had gone pretty well.

The canvassers and helpers managed to gather slightly fewer than 1,000 signatures. "No congratulations yet," Sophie said. "The town is next." Webb said he'd help do the town. He'd been buying supplies and paying Association bills, courtesy of Sal's contribution check—which was amazingly, embarrassingly generous. They were assembled around the Tintinger's porch table, summing up.

"Are we going to return the unused balance?" Sydnor asked.

"Never give money back," said Webb. "Sets a bad precedent."

Of course, the canvassers turned up some people who were completely unaware of the mining situation, and who had to be educated very quickly. "What is wrong with these people?" Sydnor demanded. "Have they been living in caves?"

"Some people do," said Webb. "Look at the country's voting record. Can anybody think of an event that would coax out the local TV station?"

Sophie rolled her eyes, surprising Al Gustave who had walked over.

"Well, it would help get to the cave people," Webb said.

"How much of Sal's money do we have left?" Sydnor asked him.

"Several of us could fly to San Francisco and back after dining very well."

"Is that enough to rent a hot air balloon? A balloon carrying a message? We could land it within easy distance of the local television studio. Wow, the publicity!" Sydnor said enthusiastically.

"Hold on, hold on," Gustave interrupted. "Seems to me you got a hold of the wrong circus. Everybody'd get all excited about your balloon, and you'll drive the mining fight right out of their heads. It's human nature."

They all stopped and regarded Al Gustave.

"That's probably right," Sophie admitted.

"We need a splash," Sydnor said, dejectedly.

"How 'bout one of them planes with banners," Gustave asked. "Take a page out of the company's book. Have 'em tow some kind of message—'kill the mine' or something."

"Not bad," Webb said.

"But the point is to get some local news coverage," Sydnor persisted.

"Buzz the station. That'll get their attention. Not sure it's legal, though."

"We'll think of something," Webb said, and reached for the phone book.

High, Wide, and Handsome Flights (FAA approved) agreed to tow a message banner for a three-hour run. The banner would simply say, "No Mining."

"I had no idea this was so expensive," Sophie said later, stunned at the numbers on the flight company's estimate.

"Making a new banner and fuel, I guess," Webb said, "plus the hourly rate, insurance, overhead, incidentals."

"They must be making the banner out of titanium," Sophie said.

"It's nylon; I asked. We can have it afterwards since it's paid for."

"Oh good," Sydnor said. "A two-block long hammock. Now all we have to do is get the TV station to pay attention."

"Let's bribe them" Sophie suggested.

"Good idea," said Sydnor.

"Very professional," said Judge Press who had stopped by to check on the petition progress.

"It's public relations!" Sydnor cried. "Anyway, we can't hold a candle to the mining company's dirty work. And I've got a good idea. I write a 'no mining' press release about the terrific petition project, stick it on top of a chocolate cake, and we deliver it to the station.

"They get the cake, the press release, the message plane is buzzing their area, presto! Instant story. But we have to get the pilot to match our timing. And we offer Nelson Two Snakes or professional-looking Judge Press here for a follow-up interview.

"Hey," Sydnor said, exasperated, "we're offering *news*. This is the north woods; the TV station considers a fish over 24 inches feature material."

"It's so idiotic that it'll probably work," the Judge said.

"It'll work," Sydnor said, confidently. "We could offer some news type a free plane ride, but I think that's going too far."

"You bet; all kinds of liability problems there," said the Judge.

Coordinating cake delivery with the airplane schedule fell to Webb, who attempted to suck Judge Press into the project and failed.

"I've got more than enough on my plate," the Judge said, "what with the mining people that keep turning up, the agencies, and Nelson. They're all arguing and they all want to do presentations. If Skyler can't impose some priorities, we'll all be at the township meeting for two days. And we're not finished with the preliminary work, not by a long shot."

"Offense rests," said Webb. He took Al Gustave and went to talk to the airplane people. Webb realized that he'd have to trust them to get the message banner right; on the ground it looked just like piles of rope.

"We do this a lot," said the High, Wide, and Handsome pilot reassuringly. He was about five feet, seven inches tall and weighed perhaps 138 pounds soaking wet. "Usually we do stuff like 'Geraldine will you marry me?' Once we did a 'Congratulations on 25 years,' while the wife was serving surprise divorce papers; she threatened to shoot us down. It gets pretty lively sometimes. Yours is a piece of cake."

"Funny you should mention that," Webb said, and unfurled a map to work out the flight path.

"Can you sneak down and buzz 'em?" Gustave asked.

"Absolutely illegal," said the pilot. "Which is not to say it's never happened. But you don't want to dive and hook the banner on a water tower or something. There's an automatic release, but still. You'd have to climb up and chop the thing off. Gets people upset."

"Oh boy," Gustave said, delighted at the possibilities.

Minnie Rosenheim made a large chocolate sheet cake with raspberry jelly filling for the event. She decorated the top with an outline of a plane in white icing pulling a "No Mining" banner.

"Oh, nice," Sydnor said.

"This is free," said Minnie. "It's the least I can do. How about 'Keep it Clean' along the sides?'

There are many people and things that are turned away at radio and television reception desks. A 14- by 18-inch sheet cake that smells like a raspberry-chocolate parfait is not one of them. The staff bore it away.

Unaccountably, the operation went well. The weather was clear. The plane was a novelty. People in town and on lakes stared up at the message banner and, as they always do, read it out loud—and the timing was perfect for the Yellow Perch Lake canvassers, clipboards in hand, who went, literally, to town.

*　*　*

The resistance group met much later that evening to assess the action.

"The banner thing was wonderful," said Sophie, radiating satisfaction. The station had used a shot of it to fill out the story. Unexpectedly, the news anchor described a "massive" canvassing effort. "He made it sound like the good little guys were fighting the big bad guys," Sophie added.

"We're still out there with the sign-up sheets," Sydnor said. "It feels massive all right, but mostly it's hard work." She'd ordered 300 "Stop the Mine" buttons to distribute and was wearing one.

Judge Press had met with some township movers and shakers who had been part of a terse exchange with one of the mining people. "Not expected," he said, "but there's been a setback."

"That being?" Webb inquired.

"A judge threw out the Chippewa lawsuit against the Natural Resources Dept."

"Damn," said Webb.

"What? Sydnor cried. "What suit? How do I miss these things?"

"The tribe was charging the department with bias and collusion with the mining company," said the Judge.

"Did he say why he threw it out?" Sophie asked.

"Something about procedures and legal intent," said the Judge. "My guess is that he just didn't want to see the department breached, so to speak. The land rights issue is still viable, I think. We'll refile on that."

"Dunderheaded jerk," said Gustave.

"Seconded," said Webb.

※ ※ ※

"Let me get this straight," said Ross to Gerald Mactate, on Ross's private line. "This woman threw cookies at you?"

"Somebody told her that I was with Random, I guess. I was in her bakery. It was full of people and she yelled at me. Called me a Quisling. I know it sounds funny."

"It sounds ridiculous," said Ross, considering the remarkable quality of education in these hinterlands. Quisling. "So we can assume that whatever feeble cover you had is blown, I believe is the term?"

"Well, it started when the township council chairman asked me what I did."

"And did you tell him?"

"I pretty much had to. He caught me off guard."

"And this is as close as you've gotten to the township council."

"He didn't welcome me with open arms, if that's what you're asking," said Mactate crossly.

"Gerald, unless you have some compelling reason to remain in the area that you've not shared with me, I think you should fold your tent, so to speak, and quietly steal away. As soon as possible, before you generate more hostility. The company is as well represented as it needs to be at the moment. You can fill me in on the other details back in the office. I will attend the town's meeting with Wicker."

"Right," said Gerald Mactate. He was mightily relieved.

15 AFTER THE MOUSE

There was a hastily-called gathering at Judge and Adeline Press's cottage. It was the first time that Webb, Sophie and Sydnor had met Max Skyler. He looked like a township council chairman, Sophie thought, but a chairman who spent his spare time single-handedly moving boulders from inconvenient locations.

"This is Natural Resources' final draft copy of its Environmental Impact Statement," Skyler said. "I was just showing the Judge. What they've done is dismiss all the evidence that questions or contradicts any of their 'clean mining' claims. Or the evidence has been omitted or countered by some phony expert hand-carried in by the Commerce and Industry Association or the mining company."

"Christ on a crutch," said Judge Press, holding a section of the document. "It cites a law that permits contamination in rivers, and then applies it to ground water."

"There's more," said Skyler, who had read every word. "Basically, these idiots are saying that the toxins and the acids draining from the mine would be contained in this giant underground silo thing and would never ever get loose and seep into the water system."

"Where's their evidence?" asked Webb.

"There isn't any," said Judge Press, studying parts of the text. "It's all conjecture. Assumptions. Whoever put the fix into the Natural Resources Department 'experts' fixed them good."

"They're going to submit this as gospel?" Webb asked.

"Looks like it," Skyler said.

"Can't we get this to somebody scientific? And real? And important?' Sydnor asked, and stifled a yawn.

"And fast. I wonder if Arthur Rosenheim if knows anybody at Interior," said Judge Press thoughtfully. Webb handed him the phone.

"Tell me if I can help with something," Sydnor said, starting to leave.

"What's wrong?" Sophie asked her. "You've been yawning all evening."

"Not enough sleep," Sydnor said. "It's this mouse."

In the midst of the anti-mining campaign, the canvassing, roughing out press releases, demystifying the Natural Resources' Environmental Impact Statement, and racing back to her real job at the end of long weekends, Sydnor's life was being made miserable by a mouse.

The first noise at 2 a.m. brought her bolt upright. It was a banging sound coming from the kitchen and, barefoot, she stormed in and turned on the light to see was it was. The noise stopped. The next night, what sounded like a small pile driver started just after midnight. Sydnor crept into the kitchen without turning on the lights. She shouted and slammed a cupboard door for emphasis. The noise stopped again. Sydnor kept the kitchen light on and went back to bed, fuming.

It was a mouse, the noisiest mouse in the world. In the morning, she discovered an Oreo cookie beneath the kitchen stove top, half-chewed, with the surface texture of a well-used hockey puck. She threw it away and vacuumed out the crumbs, remembering that her mother once had taken a toothpick and carefully cleaned all the gray goo out of a kitchen stove vent pipe, only to learn that the stuff was a sealer designed to keep gas from leaking out and asphyxiating the household. Sydnor felt the same kind of cleaning mania building, so she knew the mouse would drive her crazy.

This was serious. She needed to concentrate, to focus, and the creature was ruining her sleep. She needed weaponry, and during her next grocery run into town, bought two mousetraps from the hardware store.

Webb walked over while she was setting one of the mousetraps for practice. She placed it carefully on the porch steps. Webb regarded it doubtfully.

"Built-in plastic cheese?"

"Isn't it weird?" she said. "The print on the back says it carries an irresistible cheese odor that lasts and lasts. It's a bigger target for the mouse to hit or something."

"It must smell wonderful," he said. "No mouse in its right mind would mistake that for cheese."

"I'm surprised that mice would even eat the stuff. Sometimes the orange dye comes right off on your fingers," Sydnor said, examining her hands critically.

"Looks like they work just like regular mouse traps, though."

"I'll find out," said Sydnor grimly, "probably at about two in the morning.

The mousetrap went off around 4 a.m. Sydnor jerked awake, and with a reflex backhand motion swept a box of tissues and her wristwatch from the nightstand onto the floor. She stalked into the kitchen and lifted the stove top. The sprung trap had taken a chip out of the enamel; there was no sign of the mouse.

Damn and blast, she thought. Try again. Let's think scientifically. Thinking what might be the best way to think scientifically, she poured a large glass of orange juice, drank it, reset the trap, and retreated to the bedroom. After half an hour she rose, pulled on a robe, found a particularly English murder mystery and curled up under a heavy quilt and the warmth of a reading lamp on the living room couch. There was no other sound from the kitchen.

At about 5:30 a.m., the loons began their pre-dawn gabbling and pale apricot light brightened the mist on the lake. Sydnor quietly opened the front door and stepped onto the porch, immediately soaking her slippers in heavy dew. The air smelled heavenly. From a rich damp base of cedar and broken pinecones rose the fragrance of trod-upon wintergreen and fern. A hint of late lilacs feathered the air, or maybe it was Sophie's morning glories.

She stepped into the yard and an eagle, with a great flapping, lifted out of a nearby tree, startling her. It flew across the lake, occasionally dipping, an eye out for fish. "Think mice," she murmured to its retreating form, and went back in to put the coffee on.

At 4 p.m. Sydnor was crouched on the kitchen floor with a flashlight, peering under her appliances. Behind the stove were some scattered mouse droppings, but in a corner of the cupboard under the sink, screened by water pipes and an old glass gallon milk jug filled with ancient wooden clothespins, was a recently occupied mouse nest.

Collectors' items all, thought Sydnor, and carefully slid a mousetrap in amid the cardboard fluff, stray peanut shells, and bits of shredded mop and dishcloth.

At 9 p.m., Sydnor, Sophie and Lucia Constantini drove into town for the second show at the local shoebox size theater.

"I loved the part where you could see the waiter in the background carrying the woman, kicking and screaming, out of the restaurant," said Lucia Constantini with satisfaction.

"Yes," said Sophie, "but what was that mortar fire during the big musical number?"

"That was no mortar fire," said Sydnor, "that was the bowling alley in the basement."

"Let's see," said Lucia Constantini. "This is, what, Saturday? It's Knights of Columbus team night. Father Peter bowls with the B-team, usually."

"Oh," said Sophie, "Is that why . . ."

"Eight-thirty mass is so rocky? Yes. A lot of beer flows and sometimes it's hard to get it all transubstantiated by morning," Lucia cackled. "One Sunday last June, Father Peter was such a terrible color that one of his servers ran home and mixed him a pitcher of bloody marys to get him through the 10 o'clock service."

"The right drink for a Sunday."

"In some ways, it's a very realistic religion," said Lucia.

At 11:45, Sydnor checked the mousetrap and went to bed.

Hours later, the trap clacked shut. At last, thought Sydnor in the morning half-light. She burrowed into her pillow. Sleep drifted back.

There was a rattle. Last twitch, she thought. Sleep drifted back again. After a silence, another rattle. Sydnor squeezed her eyes shut. A small determined banging ensued. She gripped her pillow. There was a little clang and more banging.

"Christ," said Sydnor aloud. She had an undead mouse, a very active undead mouse, and worse, perhaps a wounded one. She sat up and stared out the window. A mauvish sky. Her watch read 5 a.m. Scuffling sounds continued from under the kitchen sink.

I hate this, she thought, stepping into slippers, I hate this, I hate this. Pulling on her robe, she took the garage key from its hook in the kitchen, refusing even to confront the situation under the sink without a shovel or broom or something at hand. She was quite aware of being listened to; that was enough.

Outside, drops of dew had spattered onto ferns and raspberry leaves. New toads the size of dimes hopped in all directions. The air smelled as if the world had just recently begun, but the garage was icy cold and Sydnor held her breath to conserve body heat. She gathered a flashlight, a spade, and considering a moment, added a garden hoe. You never know, she thought.

In the kitchen, she steeled herself. "I hate this," she said again, then opened the cupboard door and stooped with the flashlight to look.

The mouse stared up at her, silent. It was very much alive; the trap had closed around its neck but apparently not snapped and the mouse was wearing it like the extended platform of a guillotine. In mouse terms, wearing the trap was like wearing a door. It made escape into crevices impossible.

"Some trap," Sydnor said, and the mouse started but didn't blink. They regarded each other for a bit. It was small and gray with black eyes like tiny jellybeans. It had placed itself in the open, facing the cupboard door and—Sydnor would have sworn—was watching expectantly.

She sighed, rose, rummaged in the kitchen junk drawer and found the pickle fork. Gingerly she reached toward the trap. The mouse tensed but stayed still.

Delicately and with an odd seizing in her stomach, she hooked the fork into the soft wood of the mousetrap and gently lifted it, mouse and all. The mouse was airborne, its feet churning madly. Sydnor eased it out the back door, down the stairs, and put it down on the ground. The mouse gripped the leaf litter with its tiny paws, but it didn't stir. Sydnor studied it briefly; it studied her back.

"Hang on," she said, and trudged back into the garage, returning with a small screwdriver. She knelt next to the trap, and carefully working around the mouse, inserted the screwdriver next to the trap spring and pried it up. There wasn't much resistance. The mouse backed out of the trap and shook itself. It was chubby, with a fat little ruff like a miniature lion. It stretched experimentally, did two complete neck rolls, curled itself into a ball and uncurled, and then tested all of its legs, diagonally and in tandem. Sydnor rocked back on her heels and watched, fascinated.

The sky was turning rosy and abruptly through the trees came the raucous hawking sound of crows. The mouse froze in mid-flex. And swiveling on the spot, it dashed off and disappeared back under the cottage to safety.

Sydnor leaned against a tree for a moment, then finally collected pickle fork, screwdriver, hoe, shovel, the trap, and then threw them into a heap. Less than 30 minutes had passed; it felt like two days. Stepping out of her saturated slippers, she walked barefoot through the kitchen, turned out the lights, fell back into bed and slept like the dead.

"And with a clear conscience," Sophie said later.

"Or something. I mean, it's one thing to knock off an anonymous mouse, but it's another thing entirely to meet one under your sink and rescue it from your mousetrap and discover meanwhile that this mouse is fairly bright and, doesn't seem to be afraid of you at all. And it was so damn cute, which is also annoying. Plus I keep getting the feeling that it's better at its essential mouseness than we are at our essential peopleness." She stopped. "Actually, mouseness is probably a hell of a lot less complicated." She looked at Sophie. "Just ignore all that. I must be punchy."

"I think you're going round the bend. Come have a cup of coffee. Do you think you should get a cat?"

16 INTO THE WOODS

"Field work," Victoria called it. She was assembling supplies—lanterns, insect repellent, packaged food, blankets, tarp, water, along with various recorders, notebooks, and camera, briskly checking items off a long list. It was late on Sunday afternoon.

"And you're doing this when?" Sal inquired, wondering how a box of firecrackers qualified as field supplies. "Is this an honest-to-god requirement for the degree?"

"This week sometime; the weather looks good. There's no point observing a heron habitat if it's pouring rain. And yes, it's required, and I'm looking forward to it."

"Couldn't you do this a little closer to civilization? The Nicolet Forest is pretty impenetrable."

"That's the whole point. If people could just ramble in, any sensible heron wouldn't nest there. Don't worry; I've done this kind of stakeout before. I'll probably leave midweek sometime, and when you're back for the weekend, I'll most likely be finished. You can help me pick bits of bark out of my hair."

"Victoria . . ."

"Look Sal, don't worry. I'm *Victoria* Caruso, not Robinson. The actual rookery site is no more than five miles in. I'll only be about four and a half miles off any paved road."

"Animals?" Sal ventured. "Bear, skunk, wolverine?"

"I'm more likely to be sniffed to death by deer. We really need more wolves. Lots more wolves." She zipped some matches into a waterproof packet.

"I'd feel better if you weren't doing this by yourself," Sal said cautiously. There was a fine line here—he could feel it—between his genuine concern and something that could be read as a no confidence vote. Victoria, as part of her personal rules, brooked no protective fussing. She had made it plain that she did what she did, that her independence in these matters was sacred, she could take care of herself, and that she believed that otherwise Sal (or some Sal equivalent, he suspected) would safeguard her right into the ground, and what use was that?

"This is the primary piece of my thesis work. It's very important; a lot of the committee's decision rides on it. Don't worry. I can always send up flares or something." Sal, who would have organized a team of beaters to drive out the local wildlife and doubtless the herons as well, smiled fiercely, hugged her, and bit back seven or eight cautions that he'd been going to make.

"Ok. Good luck. I'll find you on the weekend." So each, with spoken and unspoken apprehensions, proceeded according to plan.

Victoria, with a Forest Service map of the Nicolet taped to her dashboard, had reconnoitered a week earlier. The road, which petered out to a gravel trail, had a three-digit number and that was all. It was, according to a colleague, the closest approach to the heron rookery. He was studying a kind of nighthawk called a Bull Bat which had a cry that chilled the blood, and he had no interest in large water birds.

The road was maneuverable in broad daylight, and she drove until there was just enough room to turn the jeep around. A steady breeze from the northwest carried a zoo-like scent. She picked her way through the woods, carefully marking a trail, and located the rookery area. There was enough breeze to keep the leaves rustling and to muffle her approach as she crept close enough to look at the site. Victoria clutched a tree in surprise. It was quite incredible and it stunk to high heaven.

A large spindle of tall spiky trees, many dead, wore thatched heron nests stuck onto treetops like crazed hats. Dozens more were slotted onto branches. The nests of brush and twigs were cemented into place by layers of whitish birdshit, which had drizzled down the limbs and trunks over years and gave the rookery the look of a vast surrealistic painting. The smell was intense. Victoria was able to identify the composting mess of aromas as a combination of heron guano, broken eggs, and dead . . . things that had dropped out of nests during feeding, or maybe while being fed. The *Ardea Herodias'* nesting site was considerably nastier than she had expected. She cursed herself for not carrying a camera, although it was plain that a longer lens was essential. Would it be useful to get some shots of that crud on the trees and on the ground? God, she hoped she wouldn't have to walk through that. No, the entire rookery population would rise up, shrieking. Or maybe attack. An interesting possibility; she would look into it and bring rubber boots just in case.

Squinting through small binoculars, she made some estimates of hatchling numbers. The chicks—it was hard to call them chicks—were so ugly as to be nearly hilarious. Mostly beak and eyes with insane-looking tufts of feathers sticking up at odd angles.

Ok, she thought, in the interest of maintaining an undisturbed habitat, she'd come back and creep around the periphery in late evening and again at the crack of dawn, both times when the herons were active. In a perfect world, she considered wistfully, she would drive in, make her observations, leave, and come back the next day. But you couldn't just blow into these places. Crashing through the woods in second gear was akin to sending ahead a pack of baying dogs. Bad analogy, she thought. A menaced heron would attack a dog. The beak was like a pneumatic drill and it could be deadly.

Victoria withdrew quietly back along her trail. She was screened from the herons by underbrush and a downwind observation point; yet some of the big birds seemed uneasy. She was really going to have to put in a couple of overnights. Oh well. She'd sleep in the jeep. None of this sleeping bag on the ground nonsense. She gave herself a little pep talk on the value of first-hand observations and on the relative safety of a proper camp. Victoria eased through the trees and brush to the jeep. Yes, she'd bring flares. Very definitely, flares and rubber boots.

* * *

Sal had mastered two kinds of patience: the first was a function of business management, the second his children imposed. He wasn't able to apply either variety to the Victoria situation. He was alternately bemused and angry. Both emotions shortly merged into a gnawing worry.

Monday and Tuesday were all right; on Wednesday during a meeting, he slipped into the adjoining kitchen, poured himself a cup of coffee, and returned to find his managers staring at him. He raised an eyebrow at the production head.

"You were up next," Williamson said. They had been waiting for some sensible description of an international deal, and he had simply left the room.

"Sorry," he said. "Different drummer." The treasurer regarded him as if he were mad; he took a quick gulp of coffee and launched into the financial ramifications, stressing the benefits involved if a Canadian distributor were brought in to run some interference. Everyone scribbled notes. That was more like it.

On Thursday he busied himself at a potential site for a new store, interesting because it was a teardown situation. Later he picked up the boys and drove them to a sailing lesson. Nick and Tommy had a wonderful time; Sal slid steadily into a funk. On Friday morning he signed a stack of correspondence, left a list of instructions for an extremely eager summer intern who was practicing to be an administrative assistant, threw his pen across the desk, leaped into a van and drove north as if all the devils in hell were after him.

She wasn't at her cottage. He took the key from its hiding place, unlocked the door and looked inside. It was swept, tidy, and empty. The rooms felt abandoned—as if they'd been empty for a long time. His imagination, he knew, but it added a layer of worry to the sturdy base he'd already created. Sal walked up to the office in the lodge and asked the manager if anyone knew when Victoria had left.

"Oh gosh," said the manager. "I think she was around on Wednesday morning; you know, people come and go, so I can't say for sure. I'm pretty sure she wasn't around Wednesday afternoon." Sal smiled his thanks. In certain major metropolitan areas, a recipient of that kind of smile would automatically reach under the bar to make sure a weapon was within reach. But this was the north woods, so Ralph the manager took a small step backward and said, "She'll be on her way back by now, probably."

Sal, nerves neatly bundled, returned to Victoria's cottage to wait. And wait. She hadn't returned by 10. Or by midnight. He stretched out on a couch and fell asleep, had terrible dreams, and woke at six. There was no sign of Victoria. He felt a fool; that was immediately overridden by a surge of anger, and then by a grinding sense of disaster. What had happened to her? He'd have to find her himself. In the Nicolet National Forest? Somewhere close to a heron rookery?

Sal controlled his urge to storm into unknown territory without direction or preparation. He thought for a moment, standing in Victoria's empty cottage and did the first rational thing he had in 24 hours. He called Larry Running Bear.

* * *

"You're kidding," said Larry Bear. "You think she's lost in the Nicolet National Forest?"

"Yes. No. I don't know. She's observing a heron rookery in there somewhere and she was supposed to be back by now. I don't know the site, I don't know where she drove in, I don't know where the roads go. I thought . . ."

"Sal, how long have you known this woman? You're dating someone who camps in wilderness to look at herons?"

"Larry, don't make it worse. Just . . . can you get us in there while it's daylight? This is driving me nuts."

"You want trusty Indian scout to guide foolish white man into the national forest and find a heron rookery? Man, you really believe those old Indian tracker legends. It would be easier to hire a helicopter."

"Look, Victoria—her name is Victoria—considers any kind of messing around with her research—it's for her thesis—the worst kind of interference. I shouldn't do this. She'll hate it if we find her, but she should have been back by now. She's not. Maybe it's stupid, but I can be stupid; you can be the expert. Will you do it?"

"Buddy, you're going to owe me big, big time."

"Anything. Can you get away?"

There was a little silence. "Well, it's this or research ways to deep-six the mining company," Larry said. He was considering escapes and approaches. Sal held his breath. He was doing that a lot lately.

"Ok. We'll take my truck. Meet me at the grocery store—the one that closed—that's about six miles east of your lake road turn-off. Half a hour, say."

"Should I bring anything?"

"A fine Burgundy, if Victoria drinks wine. Maybe it'll help if she's going to be as pissed off as you say she is."

"You think you can find the rookery?"

"Hell, yes. Finding heron rookeries is part of an old Chippewa tradition. It's like when you guys go to summer camp and learn to tie knots. We go into dense forests and find heron rookeries."

"I never went to summer camp," said Sal, distracted.

"Well, I never learned to find heron rookeries," said Larry, "but I've got one of the great and legendary Army Corps. of

Engineers maps of the Nicolet National Forest. Let's go. I'll meet you."

* * *

They bumped into a gravel road marked by a number. "So this is why you don't show up for basketball any more," Larry said. "Sorry about the shocks," he added.

"You don't have any shocks in this thing," Sal gritted, hanging onto the door as Larry maneuvered around a muddy depression.

"That's what I mean," Larry said. "But this explains why nobody's seen you around much lately." They hit a root; the truck swerved. "Stan Wolf saw you with someone in the Porsche. You were headed out of town."

"So we've been spotted."

"Just by your friends," Larry said. "Are you and this Victoria serious?"

"You think I'd drag us out here for some dippy summer romance? I'm pretty sure I'm serious. God knows what Victoria's thinking. Besides about her dissertation, I mean. Did we want to take that trail?"

"No. It goes to County Road X—I think it goes to County Road X—after about eight miles. You have to drive through a stream. Here. Unfold the bottom half of this map and hold it on the dash."

"Would you have been able to follow this trail in the dark?" asked Sal.

"Probably with an industrial strength spotlight mounted on the roof. But then we'd have deer jumping back and forth in front of us."

* * *

The drive seemed long, but mostly it was slow. After a few more miles, the track narrowed and branches slapped the sides of the truck. The sunlight dimmed under the forest canopy. Larry downshifted and looked at the map.

"This track is going to get too tight to squeeze out of pretty soon. How about hiking the last mile or so."

"You think we're that close?"

"Best guess. Your Victoria's left some tire tracks to follow. What's she driving, anyway?"

"A jeep. A tan jeep," Sal sighed. "Are the tracks going in or coming out?"

"They're just tracks. Nobody could have passed us though. You game?"

"Lead," said Sal, resolutely. He had developed some mixed feelings that he would have been hard pressed to describe. They trekked along the gravel track, startling squirrels, deer, and something long and furry that whisked into the woods.

"Why are we being so quiet?" Sal asked.

"It's the Chippewa way. You want to talk about something?"

"I guess not."

The track veered to the west, into the wind and an unpleasant swamp-like smell. There was the sudden annoyed racket of crows and then the trees thinned and the sun hit them full in the face. That was why they didn't see Victoria immediately. She had pulled the jeep back onto the trail from a small clearing and was stacking camping gear, the tan tarp and a shovel, into the jeep. There was a canvas bag on the ground.

"Oops," said Larry as Sal walked into him. Victoria froze in the middle of rewinding some film. She was in scruffy Levi's and some sort of faded shirt with the sleeves rolled up. It had a new-looking tear on one arm. Her hair was wrapped in a khaki cotton scarf. Victoria, in fact, looked like a World War II refugee that had just escaped across the Pyrenees. Worse, Sal realized, she knew it.

"What . . . ?" she began, then said "Oh," as she spotted Sal.

Warning bells went off in his head. Mistake, mistake, mistake. Victoria's "Oh," resonated deep in his masculine unconscious; it was the kind of "Oh," that women have said to men over countless years. One hears it during holidays when men present women with handy tire inflaters or a small electric drill. Perhaps Athena or Hera said it when Paris chose Aphrodite as the fairest goddess of the three and ultimately kicked off the Trojan War. Sal registered the drop in temperature immediately.

Larry subtly retreated a step. "This is Larry Bear, Victoria," Sal said. "I got worried and asked him to . . ."

"I get the picture," Victoria said, cooly. "You assumed I was hopelessly lost, frightened, and weeping somewhere in the woods. How do you do," she said to Larry Bear. "You're the guide?"

"Old friend. Basketball team," Larry said, rather obscurely.

"Well," she said. "It's interesting to see you intrepid explorers—not especially flattering, but interesting. Now, if there's enough fresh water in your canteens, you can mosey on out, and I wish you would, because I can't drive out until you do."

"Victoria," Sal said helplessly, "I waited all night . . ."

"And panicked," she said. "Look. I'm finished here. I want to get out of these woods and, more than anything in the world, to take a shower and clean my nails. Meet me at the cottage in three hours. I don't want to seem ungrateful, but I didn't need rescuing and I don't now. We'll talk about this. And," with a small smile at Larry Bear, "I'll know who to call if I want to traverse a bog or something."

She picked up a Coleman lantern and put it into the jeep. Larry, acknowledging Victoria's dismissal, had started back along the track. Sal caught up to him. "Man," Larry said, "Instant sunburn. She's really something, isn't she? I don't think Burgundy is going to do it for you. What's your plan?"

"My plan," said Sal. "My plan is to go quietly and listen. I thought about opening a vein and bleeding all over her kitchen in repentance, but she would just stitch it up with fishing line and throw me out. Do you ever get the feeling that whatever you decide to do, it's going to be wrong?"

Larry looked at him sympathetically. "Love is hell," he said.

"Is that an old Chippewa saying?"

Larry considered a moment. "Actually, the genuine old Chippewa saying goes something like 'When the cold comes and the fire is good and there is much game, the warrior must have a woman who will make the food and dress the hides.'"

Sal pondered this. "Love is hell," he said.

"But you get a bunch of clean hides."

* * *

Victoria, scrubbed and serious, was waiting at her kitchen table. Sal stopped at the screen door and looked in.

"Come inside," Victoria said, "so we can have a civilized fight. You slept on the couch, didn't you."

"Are you going to yell at me or let me explain."

"You deserve to be yelled at. How many women do you know who welcome interlopers when first, they're working in a sensitive area; second, haven't showered in four days; and third, generally look like hell and probably smell like it too. And oh yes, get to be introduced to an absolute stranger who is an old friend of yours who thinks I'm eccentric or nuts or both."

"Larry doesn't . . ."

"Yes he does; I can just imagine your conversation when you hauled him into your rescue mission."

This was alarmingly accurate, and to forestall a possible word-by-word playback, Sal said, "Wait. Truce. Please."

"All right. Your turn."

"Remember," he said, "I'm new at this. I have never known a woman who disappeared—alone—into the wilderness for days at a time. Who doesn't worry whether she's a day or so late getting back. And nobody knows where she is, really. It scares me. I get crazy. Give me some credit, Victoria. It wasn't the National Guard, it was Larry Running Bear and I do respect your independence, but I needed to know where you were and that you were safe. Is that so strange?"

"Not if I were 12 years old, But I'm a grownup—we keep coming back to that, do you notice? Sal," she said, stopped, and looked at him. "Sal, do you understand what I've been doing for the last few years?"

"The thesis. Your thesis," he said, frowning at the digression.

"That's just part," Victoria said, firmly. "It's the course work, it's negotiating with an advisor—who is nuts sometimes, then meeting with a dissertation committee that reviews the prospectus. And they can disagree on what you think you're doing and kill it.

"But if they like the prospectus, you do the work and write the dissertation—the thesis. Got that?" Victoria made an effort to keep her voice steady. "The advisor comments, the committee reads it, they ask questions, you defend it, and then—only then and if you don't have to rewrite the damn thing—it's accepted, you're stamped approved and get your degree.

"I'm three steps back there in the process, and my point, my long and messy point is that anybody who has labored through years of graduate work doesn't depend on or need permission to operate at her own pace in order to get the dratted job done. We didn't populate this backwater planet to be cute, Sal. You do good work. I do good work. Mine will never make me rich, but by god it's a worthy enterprise and I'm entitled to do it."

"Oh, low blow, Victoria."

She took a breath. "Yes, I guess it was. I'm sorry, I know that's not what you're working for. But do you understand?"

"I get your point, but it doesn't put my mind at ease for some reason. You're going to do this all over again sometime, aren't you."

"Maybe, but not soon. Why?"

"I think it would help if I knew."

"Sal, you can't keep charging into wilderness areas after me. It's unprofessional and terribly embarrassing."

"Victoria, I'm trying to get my head around this. There's a whole bunch of unknowns that I need to factor in. Do you plan to parachute out of planes onto mountainsides or desert islands . . . ?"

"You certainly didn't think you had found somebody who wears polka dot dresses and little ruffly aprons, did you?"

"I don't know if I worked out that what you do is a permanent pattern and if it means there's a whole other personality in there that's going to go off to South America for six months at a time to study wading birds."

"Ah," Victoria said. "Is that what this is about?"

"Shit," said Sal. "I don't know. Maybe." He was angry and unhappy.

Victoria studied him. "I think we should take a vacation from each other for a little bit," she said.

Sal snapped to attention. "Hold it," he said. "I thought we had plans."

"We do have plans. They can be postponed for a while."

"Victoria, the boys are counting on the canoe tour."

"Tell them I have to study for a test and I'm sorry. It's true, only more so. Their summer is not going to collapse without me."

"That takes care of the children," said Sal evenly.

"This isn't about the children though, is it," Victoria said quietly.

"Right. There's us. You're putting us on ice?"

"Sal," she began, then stopped. "I don't think you should call it that. A brief vacation. This is critical work. I can't be distracted or muck it up. Sal," she said, her knuckles whitening on the table edge, "this is going to be my livelihood. I'm not asking permission."

Sal gazed at her with an unreadable expression. He leaned over, stroked the back of her hand, and without a word, walked out of the cabin. When she heard the car door slam, Victoria put her head down, permitted herself some unwelcome tears, then resolutely turned to gather her things.

The next day Sal swung by to negotiate visitation rights or something, but Victoria had packed up early, cleared out the cottage, put a cardboard box marked "Tommy and Nick" on the porch, and left for the city.

17 PASSING FOR NORMAL

Nothing happens in total isolation. Victoria and Sal had retreated to neutral corners and privacy, and avoided the curious, the interested, and worse, the sympathetic. They were fortunate, for privacy is a relatively recent luxury. A generation ago, it was nigh impossible to suffer alone. Extended families, neighbors, small houses, and shared bedrooms and bathrooms kept the victim miserable in the bosom of the family. Someone was always asking if you were "all right." This is still true to some extent. One school of thought maintains that this is all to the good, that support at such times is necessary. They are wrong.

Sal and Victoria had a small audience of sympathetic watchers—silent sympathetic watchers. At Tamarack Lodge, the manager, Ralph, marked Victoria's departure. She had left her key at the desk with a note, and later Sal drove in, picked up a cardboard box from her porch and left. Ralph made an educated guess about the situation, and kept his opinion to himself.

Back at the lake, Lucia registered Sal's deep seismic disturbance immediately. She scrupulously avoided comment and took her grandsons to an absolutely ridiculous movie in town, a later show than usual. Sal was out on the lake when they returned, and Lucia sent the boys to bed.

That evening, Sydnor was sitting on her pier with binoculars and a large glass of wine, watching a loon make a series of dives just as the sun began to dip behind the trees across the lake. To the right and beyond the loon, a set of running lights switched on. It was Sal in his boat, not fishing, not moving. Not a good sign. She watched for a time. Oh, please don't either of you screw this up, she thought.

The whole Victoria-Sal operation seemed madly romantic and absolutely appropriate and very sexy and she didn't want to see it spoiled. Sydnor knew she was a little jealous of how available Sal and Victoria were to each other. It made her ache. It would be wonderful, she thought, to have that. She carefully placed the binoculars lens down on the pier so they wouldn't reflect a flash from the setting sun.

Victoria had returned to the university early, bought a few groceries, gathered her mail, and unpacked. It was an uninspiring task, and she knew that if she thought about it at all, it would begin to take on some kind of emotional resonance that she didn't have time to deal with. She called her advisor's office, left a message, and then arranged all her thesis materials on her desk.

What a lot of work, she thought. Victoria brooded about Sal for a moment and made herself stop. Get to work, she told herself. Get to work and get this thing written and then you can get on with your life.

* * *

Tommy and Nick loved the box of stuff. With the exception of Larry Bear, few people could have assembled such a peculiar and interesting collection. "Where did she get the deer hoof?" Lucia asked. Sal examined it.

"I think in the Nicolet. It's more a deer foot, see? There's this short attached bone with hide."

"Eeeooouu," Tommy said.

"Hunters?" Lucia wondered.

"Wolves?" Nick asked, fascinated.

"I hope not," said Sal. "Watch out for the moth; it's dry and it'll tear."

"Does Victoria want it back?" Tommy asked.

"No, I think it's all yours," said Sal, who was washing his hands, literally, of the moth.

"Take everything to the porch," Lucia commanded, and the boys went off, debating about tying a cord around the deer foot for something. Lucia had extracted only the barest summary of the hunt through the woods. "Where is she now?" she asked. "Wasn't there going to be a canoe thing?"

"She's taking a leave of absence," Sal replied carefully. "She's in the middle of writing her dissertation and maybe she's punishing me a little too. She said she'll be gone until she finishes, whatever that means." He was studiously neutral.

"Hm." said Lucia. "Must have been interesting for Larry Bear. What's he up to?"

"He's talking about starting law school," said Sal. "I'm filling in for somebody on his basketball team next weekend; I have to get into shape."

"Sal, that reminds me, I'm doing a last picnic for the neighbors at least, as long as Tommy and Nick are still here and you'll be around. And I want to introduce the Thrips to some more people. There will be about 14 of us. You will be here, won't you?"

"People are going to ask about Victoria, mother. It's going to be awkward."

"Only for you, dear," Lucia said. "It builds character. She's finishing her dissertation; that's quite impressive."

"I should start back to the city," said Sal. "Let me know if there's anything you want me to bring back."

"Sal," Lucia said quietly. "She has to do her work." He sighed, hugged his mother and went to say goodbye to the boys.

* * *

Tucked into a tiny university apartment, Victoria was writing furiously. She had done the research, she had gathered her primary sources, her secondary sources, and she was incorporating her fieldwork. Charts and diagrams were roughed out. They required a particular typeface, separate numbering, and a specific position in the document.

A Manual for Writers of Theses and Dissertations (Fourth Edition)—the graduate student's bible—lay face down next to her, open to the chapter on proper formatting of footnotes. Everything had a rule. There were formats for exceptions to the rule, and formats for exceptions to the exceptions. There were two pages of scholarly abbreviations.

The whole dissertation process represented a mini-industry, involving professional typists, supervising faculty members, and the university's dissertation director and secretary. Their gimlet eyes could spot improper margins and pagination at 20 paces and reject the entire effort until the submitter achieved nit-picked perfection or went mad and was committed to an institution for the temporarily insane.

Some candidates spent years on their dissertations; some could never pull the process together at all, and grew old rambling around university campuses, frightening undergraduates and growing long gray hair. Victoria's dissertation trajectory, however, had the geometric precision of a precisely aimed weapon.

She was working flat out and, as long as she could remember to eat, she was confident that she would make her personal deadline. She unplugged the phone.

*   *   *

Because Sal had foolishly brought up the subject, Lucia had, at the last minute, handed him a short and puzzling list of grocery items, condiments, and odd necessities for the picnic. "What's filé powder," he asked, frowning at the list.

"Powdered sassafras," said Lucia, checking off items on a kitchen clipboard.

"Is that even legal?"

"You're thinking of wormwood," Lucia said, "that's what's in absinthe. Call the Cajun restaurant on Third Street; they must get theirs somewhere in town."

In fact, Sal had been thinking of how much activity he could generate to fill a Victoria-less time and space that loomed endlessly long, so he was happy to hunt down filé powder. Periodically he checked on the anti-mining campaign up north; Lucia had that front covered and a good thing too. He couldn't do much more with so little time and this far away.

There was no answer at Victoria's university number. She had probably unplugged her phone. At his office, he caught a glimpse of the summer intern wandering around; he obviously needed more to do. Maybe they both needed more to do. "Ronnie," he called, and the kid leaped into the office as if on springs. "When do you leave for school?"

"September 10. There's a day for early registration, but . . ."

"Good," Sal said. "We have an overdue project that will need all your time and attention till then. It's the Constantini Awards Dinner and here's how it works. Take notes." Ten-, 15-, 20-, and 25-year employees (and the ones with even more service years at Constantini's) would be identified, invited, fêted, and nicely rewarded. Dinner would be at the new Arts Center and Pavilion. "Get a list of available dates. We'll pick one," Sal instructed. "And they owe us, so no need to beg."

"I want a list of everybody," Sal added. "I'll call Personnel and get you cleared. Plus they'll help and suggest nice take-away gifts. Nothing cheesy. Now, some of those people—awardees—will get special surprises for efforts above and beyond the call and so forth. That's one of the things I need the list for. And when you call the Pavilion, get menus. This is going to take a lot of organizing. So get started and report back."

And Ronnie, who all but saluted, nodded vigorously and rushed away. Sal had—just for a second—thought of sending him after filé powder, but dismissed it as unprofessional.

"You're doing an Awards Recognition Dinner?" yelped Shirley in Personnel. "We haven't had one of those in five years!"

"High time," said Sal. "We're overdue. And Shirley, you're probably in one of the higher number categories yourself. Listen, the summer intern—Ronnie—is going to assemble the basics for me, for us actually, so load him up."

"The read-headed kid with the energy?"

"That's the one."

"He's pressing his nose against my window right now. I just had that washed."

"The take-away gifts. Think what you'd like to have, since you're probably going to get one. Get me some samples. Thanks." And, having engaged a strategic corner of the company in intense planning and phoning and arguing, Sal went off to the urban Cajun restaurant on Third Street for lunch and to sample the mysteries of filé powder.

* * *

"*Ibid.*," said Victoria, deep into footnoting. "*Ibid. Ibid.*" She had cast aside *op. cit.* and *loc. cit.* after checking the *Manual*. *Ibid.* would do it, except in a same-author, two-reference situation . . . Ok, but then there was *idem*, " . . . sometimes abbreviated as *id*." Good god.

She was thinking simultaneously about the need to create a bibliography and to eat something. Where had she put that information about stick transfer rituals as related to nest building? No, it would be—she riffled through numerous pages—it would be after the courtship thing, raising and lowering the head. Let's see, "a low moan continues . . ." Whose? Clarify. The males choose where to build the nest. Really, how weird, but maybe after all that bobbing and weaving . . . . Victoria pushed away from her desk and went to open a can of sardines, unconscious of how much they resembled a typical heron's diet.

18 PICNIC

The following Saturday, Sal arrived early with a bag of supplies, handed it over, and Lucia rummaged up the container of filé. She measured a level tablespoonful, and dumped it into a vat of gumbo. "You must have left terribly early," she said, stirring briskly.

"Five," said Sal. "That stuff is expensive."

"You want to powder a bunch of sassafras, go right ahead. I'm glad you're here. Kick-off is noon, and I could use some help."

"Where are the boys?"

"Sydnor and Sophie took them on a bicycle tour around the lake. They just left, so there's almost an hour of quiet. It was very nice of Sydnor, especially, since her correspondent person has turned up in that way he has." Sophie and Sydnor could be counted on for odd services; Sal met Magnus Quinn, Sydnor's correspondent person once, and liked him. Come to think of it, he'd be a perfect center for Larry's pick-up basketball team. A real coup, but Sydnor would probably kill him for suggesting it.

"Now," said Lucia, "how many chairs are there in the boathouse? Do you remember?"

"You're not going to cart all that food down to the lake," Sal protested.

"No, no," Lucia exclaimed, stacking napkins and tablecloths, "we'll eat up here on the deck, but dessert is at the boathouse with lemonade and more wine. It keeps the sticky stuff close to the water."

"What's dessert?"

"Blackberry sorbet or that lemon Bavarian crème with that nice raspberry sauce that's full of Grand Marnier," Lucia said with satisfaction.

"We'll be arrested for purveying without a liquor license."

"Piffle," Lucia said. "It's the calories that are the killers. And you might want to take it easy if you're serious about basketball this evening." Lucia mixed and stirred; Sal fetched, carried, and counted chairs. At noon, there was the sound of an aquatic snarl from the lake.

"Ah! That's Mason and Miranda's boat," Lucia said. "See if you can get them tied up, Sal, so Mason doesn't fall in like he did at the Juska's." Smiling at the image, Sal jogged down to the dock. Several neighbors had kindly suggested that Mason's natural habitat was land, not water. Still testing fate, Mason was standing up in the boat, waving a bottle of champagne and a canoe paddle.

"Man's a menace," said Al Gustave, who'd cut through the woods and was waiting to see the impact of Mason's approach. "Don't see how Miranda puts up with him. Hang on a second," he bellowed at Mason, who was jabbing ineffectually at the dock with the paddle. Miranda tossed a line to Gustave and said, "Mason, if you drop that champagne overboard, I'm making you dive for it. Mumm's," she explained to Sal, "good Mumm's, extra brut. There's more in the cooler."

"We're starting the main course upstairs," said Sal, as the group sorted out rope, paddle and champagne. He snagged Gustave to help haul out more chairs and some camp tables from the boathouse.

Though Maureen and Milt Hendrickson arrived simultaneously, one came by land and one came by sea. Milt rowed in as Maureen pulled into the driveway, careful not to jostle a platter of deviled eggs on the on the back seat of her station wagon. Sophie and Webb Tintinger arrived next and released Nick and Tommy, who shot out of the back seat like cannon balls.

"We couldn't fit the bikes in," said Nick breathlessly, "so Sydnor and Quinn are rowing them back!"

"They're rowing them?" Sal asked.

"Only after considering riding them," Sophie said. "Have you ever seen a six foot, four-inch man on a bicycle designed for a 10-year-old?"

"No, but I would have liked to," said Sal. He was cheering up. The boys were hopping up and down on the dock as an antique green rowboat bearing bicycles made a dignified approach from across the cove.

"Hard right," Sydnor said, peering around her oarsman as they coasted in.

"Got it," said Sal, as the boat thumped alongside the dock. Sydnor clambered out, sat on the dock, and swung her legs back into the rowboat to steady it. She lifted out the smaller bike and Quinn handed the other one to Sal.

"Deliveries made anywhere in all weather," said Quinn, examining the surroundings. "This is quite an operation you have here, Sal. Was that real champagne I saw?"

"Being poured as we speak. Are you up for a little basketball later this evening, by any chance?"

"Sal, he's only here for about 72 more hours," Sydnor protested.

"Well, it'd be a change from all this love, affection, and appreciation I've had to put up with for the last day or so," Quinn said, smiling, and with a calculating eye on Sydnor.

"Sal, you crumb," she said, and turned to Quinn. "I'll meet you up on the deck in a minute, and would you please pour me a glass of champagne?"

"Sydnor, it's only a basketball game with Larry Bear," Sal protested.

"Not that," she said. "Your Victoria. Is she here?"

"Ah," said Sal. "And so it starts. Come upstairs; I'll fill you in."

More lake people arrived, sunburned, carrying various edibles and primed for a long, gossipy afternoon. Sydnor winked at Quinn across a mound of potato salad and turned to Sal in a quiet corner of the deck.

"What happens when she emerges from seclusion, Sal," Sydnor asked. "I mean, she's finishing up, summer's finishing up, do you have plans? Or," seeing Sal's stricken look, "a plan?"

"Jesus Syd, I don't know. I mean, I know what I want to do, but Victoria could jump in any direction. If I say what I want to, she could leave immediately for Peru or someplace. Or she could throw her arms around me, swear undying devotion, and then leave for Peru or someplace."

"Peru; some people have all the luck," said Sydnor pensively.

"No, it's awful, said Sal desperately. "And everybody else loves her too. Sorry, I didn't mean to dump all this on you."

"Nonsense," Sydnor replied, "this is what friends are for. And anyway, you taught me how to water-ski. It's a lifelong bond. You want me to drift over to Tamarack and see if I can learn anything useful?"

"How?"

"Well," she said, "I could pretend to deliver something to find out if she's coming back there."

"What are you two plotting?" asked Quinn, approaching with two glasses of champagne along with some cheese-filled crunchy pastries.

"Nice grip," said Sal, eyeing the victuals. "Sydnor is offering to help my difficult romance. It's called on account of dissertation and it's driving me nuts."

"Objective?" Quinn queried.

"To have and to hold," said Sal, seriously.

"You can consider this and still play basketball?" Quinn asked, handing a glass to Sydnor, who was watching Sal with interest.

"About the only thing I can do to stay sane is play basketball," Sal replied somewhat bitterly. "Come on, Judge Press has a great supply of fairly dirty jokes. It'll be fun and you guys can drift off if it gets too rancid."

"Oh, spare me," said Quinn. "I bet I can match him, and in dialects, too."

"You boys," said Sydnor, fondly. "Won't Larry Bear be sorry he missed this warm-up session?"

"Actually, he's here somewhere," said Sal, glancing around. "It seemed better if we were all starting from an overfed position."

Guests and neighbors milled around with plates of gumbo and fried chicken and potato salad, forming little groups to discuss the mining company, fish, the petition, fish, the PR campaign, and more fish. Dieter and Mrs. Vilnus were absent; that eliminated speculation about this year's crappie sizes.

Sophie congratulated Miranda Thrip, almost a stranger, on her petition signature gathering method. She had walked a three and a half-mile stretch of road repairs south of town and got every flagger, every driver, every asphalt spreader and group hanger-on to sign. Mason was amazed. Miranda, who was being casual about it, was even more amazed.

There were nice lubricated-sounding conversations coming from the deck and the boathouse. Quinn had wandered off to talk sports with Larry Bear and they were wandering back. Sal was sitting on the stairs to the boathouse watching Nick and Tommy launching a rowboat; Sydnor sat down next to him.

"Listen Sal," Sydnor said abruptly, "we're struggling to get more anti-mining support. I've been meaning to ask. Do you know anybody? I mean, you know everybody, but what about in the Commerce and Industry Association. We're being steamrolled by them."

"Yeah, they're the major players in the state; I know all kinds of people," Sal said. "Steamrolled how?"

"Some loopy spokesman keeps telling the papers that a polluting sulfide mine would be a wonderful thing up here. Somebody named Craven or Cramer. He's got to be a plant. He can't be independent; he's too gung-ho."

"I think I know who you mean," said Sal. "Let me check around. It's nuts; there are a couple of dozen members I know of with family places up here. They can't be investing in hot and cold running mining pollution. I'll tell you what I find out. Did you get any gumbo, by the way? It's terrific. Hey!" he said, standing up suddenly. "Those kids are going to capsize that boat!" and took the stairs two at a time down to the dock.

Quinn, who'd absorbed much of this, took Sal's place on the stairs and said, "Haven't you been the energetic agitator. I wondered how you kept busy up here besides painting the porch. Where are you now in this struggle? Are we talking demonstrations and fire bombs yet?"

"Once I thought the worst word in the language was 'developer,'" Sydnor said. "Now I think there are two: 'mining company.' We have some fingers in the dike. We need some more. We're being screwed over—is that the term?—by our elected officials who don't give a damn about ripping this territory apart and then poisoning it, just for good measure."

"Your hands are beginning to shake," Quinn said. "I admire your determination, but have some gumbo. You need to keep up your strength. Another glass of champagne?"

"Quinn, did you ever want to kill somebody?" Sydnor asked.

"Sweetheart, my primary objectives are getting the story and staying intact; it tends to dilute specific hatreds. And let's not hang around here till late, I'd like to have something to reminiscence about the next time I'm pinned down in a flooded field or somewhere."

"You have that basketball game," Sydnor said.

"Hell. I do. Wait up?"

"Of course."

Later that night, after Sydnor made Quinn walk around in the lake to rinse off the basketball sweat, they lounged on quilts and blankets in front of the fireplace. The blaze from tinder dry birch and oak sent out a wave of heat like a bow-shock. The bottle of red wine was well beyond room temperature.

"Either I put this into the lake to cool or we drink gin and tonic," said Quinn, opening the refrigerator. "Is there any tonic?"

"Pass me a cold beer please," Sydnor said. "It's less trouble."

"You've got stout!" Quinn exclaimed. "Now I can get drunk and resupply my dwindling iron content all at the same time."

"Quinn, did you ever write any mining stories for the paper before they shipped you off-continent?"

"Does that question connect to stout in some way?" he inquired. "No. It would have been the business section or environment reporter. When we had an environment reporter."

"The governor of this state," Sydnor said, opening her beer, "was known for nattering on about fawns and snake tail dragonflies and it got him elected. He was lying through his teeth."

"Syd, find out who's shipping him cash and how much," Quinn said reasonably. "Follow the lobby money. I know a guy who keeps track of every penny from lobbyists all around the country. He's probably in hiding from the current administration, but he'd love this. I'll give you his number. Who knows? Maybe he's a fan of the snake tail dragonfly. Are you making that up, by the way?"

"How could I make that up? Tell me about this guy. What a treasure: you cook, you write, you tie a reef knot practically one-handed, you have mysterious contacts . . ."

"Full disclosure," he said. "Those contributions are public record, or are supposed to be. But he's got some incredible sources and you don't want to examine his methods too closely. And since

I'm a momentarily a hero, did I mention that there's been a rumor that I might be reassigned back to the mother house? To the infighting that passes for our national desk?"

Sydnor sat back and regarded him. "What kind of rumor? A corporate rumor or a gossip-around-the-coffee-machine-in-the-news-room rumor?"

"As a matter of fact," Quinn said, "the newsroom rumors are almost always true and management rumors are usually idiotic. This one's new, so it's both. Something's happened in the corporate chain of command that's nudged me into a strategic position. I don't know what it is. You don't seem to be overwhelmed with excitement; could we have a little enthusiasm here?"

"I'm under control," she said. "It's my survival mechanism. Come on Quinn, the paper hauled you all the way back here to suggest a career change?"

"They hauled me back, at enormous expense, to make some not-very-subtle-suggestions about career options at the paper."

"Might I just mention," Sydnor said, stabbing at the fire, "that you're having the time of your life and it's dangerous as hell and that's why you're having the time of your life? I don't think you could decompress into a situation that didn't have bombs going off in the distance. At least, not without coaching by Buddhist monks."

He pulled Sydnor and her quilt closer to him and said, "Think big picture. You now have a collection of some of the most exotic postcards and stamps in the world from places that may not even exist in another year or two. All that would vanish. Could you handle it?"

"Be serious," she said. "Let me explain what it comes down to. This romantic adventure works because it teeters on an edge made of excitement and geography. Suddenly you're here and suddenly you're gone again. It's thrilling, it's exotic, it's got fever pitch anticipation and relentless deadlines built in, which is great for sex. On the other hand, you could be dead next week. Now, subtract all that—ok, leave the sex—and tell me: would you be happy working boring normal hours and barking at baby reporters?"

"You have the most disarming way of putting things," he said. "It worked wonderfully before I shipped out; I don't see why it wouldn't again."

"Let me try once more," Sydnor said. "You are not a domestic animal, if you ever were. It all burned away in the jungle or the foothills or wherever. You've had high adventure and great escapes. It's narcotic, I can read it in your letters. And, ok, full disclosure, I don't want to see this relationship—god, how I hate that word—deflate like a leaky balloon because the paper has coaxed you back into a desk job."

"What are you drinking?" Quinn asked her, amazed. "I know that, or most of it, and I plan to jigger my arrangements so life doesn't get boring. That's off the record, by the way. And I look forward to sleeping without the sound of gunfire. And with you, which should more than make up for the gunfire."

"Well then, saints be praised and all of that, if that's what you really want," she said, but it sounded like a question.

"Two things," said Quinn. "First, it still may not amount to squat. But this particular war is ending fast, so there isn't going to be anything to cover for much longer." Quinn spun the empty stout bottle. It stopped, pointing at Sydnor.

"Timing really is everything," he said. "On one hand, I want to get back there and be in at the finish. On the other, I don't particularly want to get killed. The unofficial position is that it's time to get the hell out with whatever scraps of glory, honor and red, white, and blue bunting we have left, which doesn't answer your question."

"Yes it does," she said, rising. "We'd be in the same city; the thought makes me giddy. Come to bed. We'll examine all angles."

"Indeed we shall," he said.

And then he was gone again.

19 GAINS AND LOSSES

The Yellow Perch Lake resistance group hoped and prayed for Random Mining to blunder and when it did, it was a beauty. In a well-attended Rotary meeting, the company's waste and toxins expert, defending the safety of its underground holding silo, said confidently that it was designed to last for 9,000 years. The public's hoots of laughter and disbelief rang throughout the region and beyond. Fortunately, a reporter had been there.

"Mining Toxins to live Longer than the Pyramids!" read one headline. "Who Needs Tut? We're Saving Our Tailings," read another. Random's mine-versus-town fracas had begun to interest some of the larger news media. The flap also brought otherwise disinterested geologists, geo-chemists, and hydrologists out of their laboratories and into the public forum, with scathing comments about clay and plastic lining materials, corporate disdain for the environment, and misrepresentation of science in a quest for profit.

"You nitwit," said Ross to his head of public relations. "You always, always, always clear this kind of thing with R. and D. or with me. Even I know better than to air this kind of claim."

"In a month no one will remember," the PR man protested.

"On the contrary," said Ross through gritted teeth, "this is the kind of thing people will remember for a long, long time."

It turned out that Arthur Rosenheim knew several of the geologists who had turned up; they had impressive credentials, were well regarded and were not on any political payroll. In a public television round table, a geologist from the state university pointed out that despite the mining company's assurances about the impermeability of its underground waste silo, a fairly common acid leachate ("lechate?" Gustave asked) would chew right through the clay liner.

"Random's simulated their test of the thing," the geologist added. "It's not a real world situation." He seemed ready to speak endlessly on calcium concentration damage, but the mining company's expert countered immediately that any seepage would be monitored or spotted in the drainage pipes. The geologist replied that was all very jolly in theory, but nobody he knew in the industry had heard how the mining company could do that.

This exchange brought a stern letter to a state capitol newspaper from a university hydrologist. "No waste system of the kind that Random Mining is proposing has been in use anywhere for more than a decade," he wrote. "So 9,000 years in the Egyptian desert possibly, but certainly not here. We live on land separated by 27,000 lakes. Now that's accurate. You can count them."

Back in the city, Sydnor met Quinn's contact in a seedy bar some blocks away from her office. It was a neighborhood best traveled by car, with the windows rolled up.

"I wouldn't do this for anybody," said Doug, the contact. "But Quinn saved my ass a couple of times and he said this was a good cause. How do you know him, by the way."

"Work," Sydnor said, figuring that was close enough. "He said yours was rather special information, but he didn't say exactly why."

"Exactly why," Doug repeated, ruminating. "He probably meant that some of my information on lobbyists' contributions doesn't appear on the public record."

"Doesn't appear?" Sydnor asked, interested. "Because?"

"The usual reasons. It's in the form of travel and entertainment payoffs, gifts of apartments in Aspen, mortgage deals, simple graft, that sort of thing. Sometimes escort services, maybe a new gym for the local college; it gets more exotic in the medical area. A new clinic exchanged for a passing grade on a new drug, funding laundered through a corporate development office. And sometimes a gift of estate, you know, when someone dies? Except sometimes no relatives had ever heard that that's what the deceased had in mind."

"Jeez," said Sydnor. "It makes the mining companies almost seem tame."

"That's a cold hard cash area," Doug said, handing over a folder. "But there's some dirty stuff too—it's all in here."

"What a great investigative reporter you'd make," Sydnor said, thanking him.

'Well, actually, I was once," he said. "Ask Quinn sometime. He'll tell you."

* * *

Webb and Sophie's usual cocktail hour had taken on a vaguely depressed air. The Tintingers had produced beer, iced tea, and potato chips and handed them around. Al Gustave and Judge Press were drinking something with a higher octane rating and Lucia, a surprise guest, contributed a bottle of pinot noir.

"What's the score?" Gustave asked.

"Little slippage," said Webb, eyeing Judge Press.

"The ass in the governor's mansion has eliminated the Public Intervenor's office," the Judge said. "The Intervenor's job was to make sure other government agencies were following the law."

"Doomed," said Gustave.

"What?" Lucia cried. "The Public Intervenor is a wonderful woman. She was the speaker at our retreat last year. She's smart and really knows her stuff; she couldn't be bulldozed by some bureaucrat."

"Apparently that was pretty clear to the boys in the state capitol," said Webb. "So they eliminated the office and folded it into Natural Resources where it can be molded, like putty, into any shape the governor and his cronies find most useful."

"Open that," Lucia said, handing Sophie the pinot noir. "Maybe it will make me feel better."

"A glass of wine. What a wonderful idea," said Sydnor arriving with a mass of newspapers. "Bad news, but I think it means the opposition is getting angry, impatient, and maybe careless again."

"Oh goody, more bad news," Sophie said, pouring several glasses of wine.

"What," demanded the Judge.

"Somebody in high places has mounted a smear campaign against the three or four Natural Resources managers who didn't fall right into line behind the higher powers and the mining companies. Who were actually defending the environment. Details in the papers," she said, tossing them on the table.

"I'm just going to get me a gun and go down there and shoot 'em," said Gustave, pink with fury.

"Have some wine," Lucia said.

"Ok," said Judge Press. "Time to dig some dirt. Sydnor, where's that lobbyist list that your lunatic friend . . ."

"Quinn's lunatic friend, thank you," said Sydnor. "In the cottage. I'll get it."

"Good. And have you got that list of the names of the editorial page writers?"

"How about a wire service or two?" Sydnor asked. "What are you going to do?"

"You, Sydnor, are going to quote me, a fine legal mind, in a statement. I am outraged at the hundreds of thousands of dollars being spent to subvert the governor's office and the once-respected Natural Resources Service by greedy, immoral mining companies. We are going to lay it on thick. And we are going to identify the big-gun recipients of several hundreds of thousands of dollars."

"I know some good lawyers," Lucia said, off on another tangent entirely. "Do you think it's worth calling in one or two to defend the people who are in trouble? Are they scientists?"

"Pro bono?" Webb inquired. Lucia wrinkled her brow.

"Well, it's not a question of money if we—the business—contribute the legal services," she said, as if it were all taken care of. "We won't need to pay everything; we have some favors owed," Lucia added demurely.

"My god, good for you," said the Judge, making a note never to pick a fight with anyone named Constantini in this state.

The gathering ended quickly. Sydnor and the Judge would work up a fast draft. Lucia would make some calls. Tomorrow Webb would drive down to the capitol with Judge Press to find out what useful information the loyal opposition party might like to part with. Sophie would sit tight, worry, and count names. Petitions were still straggling in.

20 THE MONEY TRAIL

Part of the money trail, as the Washington County Woods Gazette dubbed it, began at the door of the state's Commerce and Industry Association. Both the official and Doug's unofficial records showed that the Association spent some $175,000 lobbying state representatives and opinion leaders. This largess, applied like a mustard plaster where it was judged to do the most good, was designed to overturn laws that would have made it difficult for Random and other mining companies to operate. It seemed to be working.

The Woods Gazette editors had plugged smiling photos of some Association executives into the article. The Association president quickly scheduled a news conference to present "the business point of view" then promptly cancelled it when it became clear that some of the membership hadn't realized that they supported efforts to eliminate protection for lakes and waters. They were angry and very vocal about it.

Public records also showed that Random Mining had distributed slightly more than $100,000 to local officials and administrators and certain persons in the Natural Resources office who might help neutralize the environmental safeguards in the state's existing mining regulations. "I suppose we have that investment to thank for killing off the Intervenors's office," Webb said, reading the papers' gratifyingly rapid response to Sydnor's incendiary press memo; it had named the recipients of the largest amounts of Random Mining's cash contributions. She had whipped up an impressive looking letterhead with contact numbers and listed the lake association as the board of directors in very small type along the bottom of the page.

Getting into the spirit, several reporters who belonged to a duck-hunting group calling themselves "Mallards Forever," dug up names of several mining company lobbyists who previously had been executives in the same companies that they were now lobbying. It made several interesting feature stories.

"What could be more convenient," Sydnor marveled to Sophie. "Just cash in your stock options and slide right into another insanely profitable position, probably in the same building." The principals identified in this little exposé protested loud and long that what they were doing was not illegal, and indeed, had been done since time immemorial.

"Shit floats," said Al Gustave.

The articles were picked up by a wire service, reprinted, and several morphed into television news. The Yellow Perch Lake group and friends (with some help from Max Skyler) scrambled to keep information coming. They chatted up various editorial writers and reporters, some of whom took up strong anti-mining positions; several began calling the lobby money payoffs and bribes despite angry huffing noises from the recipients.

Another $114,000 (Doug's list again) had been forwarded from somewhere unspecified directly to Random Mining for that company's own lobbying purposes. This was odd since the money usually flowed in the opposite direction. Judge Press and four student volunteers from the Boundary Waters Young Independents League did some quiet and persistent research that tracked the "contributions," designated as educational funding and seminar expenses, back to the state's executive offices, specifically, to the Department of Special Programs.

"What does it do?" Sophie asked.

"Nobody knows," said Webb.

"The current secretary of that department is the governor's chief political advisor," said Max Skyler.

"Ah," said Judge Press. "Where are they getting the cash?" he demanded. "Is it our tax dollars at work?"

"Slush funds, real and phony special programs underwriting, outright gifts," said Skyler. "Harder to trace."

"Hell," said Sydnor, "Now we have to do a backgrounder on how the mining industry channels secret funds into the pockets of the instruments of evil."

"That's not bad," said Skyler. "Mixed metaphor, but not bad."

"It takes too long," Sydnor complained. "We have to keep the heat on."

One of the Young Independents who had dreams of a hot career in investigative reporting offered to infiltrate Random Mining's local headquarters and try to find the $114,000's recipients, influential or otherwise. Judge Press considered the bespectacled and earnest young woman who fairly reeked of honesty.

"A good thought," he said, "But I'm afraid not. There's no way you could examine files and pretend to interview people at the same time. It might be a single sheet of paper. It might be a stack of three by five cards. It may not be at the local office at all. No, we're out of luck on this one."

About a week later, Judge Press found a smudged manila envelope stuffed into his mailbox. He opened it immediately and found a list—a machine-made copy of a list—of some 30-odd names that someone efficient had marked on the original with little numbers and dollar signs. The original had had puncture marks in all four corners as if it had been thumbtacked to a wall for easy reference. There was nothing else in the envelope.

"My, my," Judge Press said. "A mole, and perhaps on our side. Only one way to check," and he handed the list to Sophie.

"Please, sound as imperial as you possibly can," he said. Sophie divided the list with Sydnor, and using their most important-sounding voices, they called each of the names to confirm that the amounts received were accurate. The recipients were cooperative, anticipating that another gift might be forthcoming.

Moving fast, the Yellow Perch Lake Association bought advertising space in the state capitol's major newspapers and listed the names of the rest of Random Mining's gift recipients along with the dollar amount that each received.

This investment paid remarkable dividends, considering that the persons listed were strictly grass roots types whose perceived folksiness must have appealed to the mining lobby. Thus, people whose pockets had been lined, people with businesses and constituencies and respectable positions, were suddenly lit from above. Customers, strangers, and voters stopped them on the street and asked awkward questions. Interested and persistent columnists called. Friends grew frosty. There were arguments at dinner tables and in offices. One newly minted representative was loudly denounced in church by his 83-year-old aunt who accused him of desecrating God's creation. Another neophyte politician said to a wire services reporter that if the money was good enough for the administration, it was good enough for him. He would come to bitterly regret the comment.

The Yellow Perch Lake group watched the fallout, stayed alert, and wondered if it would get worse before it got better. If it got better. No one in or out of the resistance movement admitted to being the mole.

21 VICTORIA ASCENDANT

The Governor's Dinner, an annual celebration and payback for the important, the loyal, and the foot soldiers, was a highly glossy formal dinner and party. The Constantinis were always invited and Sal always escorted his mother because Lucia knew everybody and had he arrived with a date, the speculation would have drowned out normal conversation. Conversation wasn't the spirit of the evening though, backslapping was.

The Constantinis rambled around, working the room, hailing friends and being hailed in turn. Sal wondered if Victoria, who was still incommunicado, would put up with this sort of thing. He dismissed the thought for later consideration. The dinner guests did impromptu business over drinks and hors d'oeuvres; it added to the evening's luster. Deals were confirmed, loyalties were renewed, votes were promised. Just off a little lobby the Constantins ran into the Governor's party.

"Sal!" boomed that worthy. "Wonderful to see you here. And we can count on your support as usual?"

"I understand you're getting quite a bit from Random Mining," Sal said, with his dangerous political smile. "The folks with plans for our ground water? Up north?" The Governor's cadre went suddenly quiet, waiting for a signal telling them how to react. The Governor's bonhomie slipped a bit; what was this? He'd missed a signal somewhere. The Constantinis had clout. They were important; they made things happen. He needed to—? Breaking the silence, Lucia swiveled toward a party at a nearby table.

"Stephen Cramer!" she said in her best, clearest chivvying-the-builders voice. "Why are you pushing for that awful sulfide mine right in our back yard?" She bore down on the table like a small bulldozer and announced to the stunned table of eight, "I can say that kind of thing to him because I was one of his confirmation sponsors." The Stephen in question was bright scarlet and the center of interested attention, not all of it friendly.

"Remember your Father Baltimore Catechism on moral correctness," Lucia admonished, placing her index finger firmly on his chest in emphasis. Sal, who had learned to look disinterested during similar but less contentious exchanges, took her arm and calmly led her away.

The scene ended further conversation; waiters carrying salads appeared and the governor's party dispersed to various tables. Sal guided Lucia toward the Constantini enclave. "We should have arranged to have someone taste our food," he said.

"Don't be silly dear," Lucia replied. "We have just made this dinner a more interesting event than anybody anticipated. I think it'll turn out to be very useful. And we're on the side of the angels."

Sal, who ordinarily kept his profile so low as to be nearly submerged, sighed. He was aware of the buzz from the corner Press table and saw that he wouldn't be able to escape the room unquoted. Well, at least neither would anyone else. What had possessed them? Could it have been Victoria and her blue heron? He concentrated on working up some sensible comment before the main course was served. While interested diners swiveled to look at the Constantini table, Lucia smiled graciously and passed the Thousand Island dressing.

* * *

Victoria Caruso, somewhat thinner than she had been earlier in the month, dazedly accepted congratulations from her thesis advisor, from members of her committee, various museum colleagues, and the Bull Bat expert. "Nice job, Victoria," he was saying, thumping her on the back. "You made *Ardea Herodias* seem almost interesting."

"Stop that," her advisor said, detaching him. "It was a very, very fine defense and I'm sure you've learned something from Victoria's methodology."

"Miss Caruso," interrupted one of her thesis committee members, "an excellent piece of work and again, our thanks for agreeing to do your oral defense early. You know Bradshaw leaves tomorrow for Madrid, and we wouldn't have been able to meet again until November. Oh, and Miss Caruso, I did like the heron calls; I don't believe anyone has ever included that kind of material in any of the *Ardea Herodias* papers that I've juried. Most, most, satisfactory."

"Thank you," Victoria said faintly.

"Lunch," said her advisor, who was a matronly woman, an expert on sandhill cranes and, more privately, on methods of preparing spaetzel. "A celebratory lunch," she announced, gesturing to the group. "On the department."

"I didn't . . ." Victoria began.

"Nonsense! It's traditional," trumpeted her advisor, and the crew bore Victoria away to a local eatery and beer garden, where everyone raised glasses, proposed toasts, and she was forced to be enthusiastic and gracious. However, she subtly tipped several beers into an enormous pot of dark green mother-in-law's tongue placed (suggestively, she thought) near a corner of the table. The plant was thriving.

Finally, after the first dessert, she caught her advisor's eye, mouthed "Family celebration," and stood, nodding to everyone like a short-circuited wind-up toy, and finally slid away. Good grief, she thought, they're here for the rest of the afternoon. What a lucky escape! She considered leaving taxi money for anyone tipsy and befuddled, but remembered that lunch was on the department, and bolted for her jeep.

There was still time, she thought. It was about three in the afternoon. Victoria, to her surprise, realized she was shaking. She took a deep breath, held it, exhaled. That was better. She knew where she was going, more or less; she hadn't worked out what might happen when she got there. She was excited but a little ill from the food, which she hadn't wanted.

It took about 20 minutes to get to her destination. She pulled into a parking slot marked Visitors and considered how best to proceed. Let's see, she thought. Avoid the reception desk, keep the element of surprise. She got out and edged around the building until she came to a loading dock in the rear. Glancing around, she nipped up a short flight of steps and tried the door to the building. It was open.

Victoria closed the door quietly, checking that it wouldn't lock, extracted a comb and lipstick from her bag, and—without a mirror—made approximate repairs. She really felt a little lightheaded, but squared her shoulders, opened the door and went inside.

She marched confidently down a hallway, made a quick right into a stairway, and took another deep breath. Bearings, she thought, get your bearings. Second floor, northeast corner; the sun is now in the west. She turned right again.

At the end of the hall, as it had been described to her, were the executive offices; both doors were open. Victoria approached, smiled sweetly at a secretary who raised her eyebrows in query, and looked into a large room occupied by Sal, a kid with red hair, and the very personification of a Head of Personnel. They were taking clocks and some sort of leather goods out of boxes. Sal looked up then and so did everyone else.

"Take a break," he said to the others. "Better yet, we'll finish tomorrow." Without taking his eyes off Victoria, who hadn't moved, he rose, said, "No calls. Go home, Maria," and taking Victoria's hand, drew her into the office and closed the door.

"I made it," she said to him, "I got the . . ." and keeled over like a sack of ill-balanced potatoes. Sal caught her before she hit the desk.

"Maria," Sal yelled to the back of the retreating secretary. "Get me a cold wet cloth of some kind. Quick."

"Oh. God." Victoria was saying fuzzily. "Sorry."

Sal settled Victoria on the office couch and propped her with a cushion.

"Thanks," he said to the secretary, now all agog. He closed the door again, and pressed the towel to her forehead and then to the back of her neck.

"Are you back?" he asked. "Does this mean you're back?"

"Yes, but this isn't the entrance I had in mind," Victoria said wanly. "I missed you. The committee loved the paper and I had to go to lunch, but I missed you. I wanted to tell you . . ."

Sal had filled a small glass with some dark liquid he'd fished out of the credenza. "Try some of this if you can," he said, holding it for her.

"Um," said Victoria. "That's wonderful. Is it about 100 years old?"

"About," said Sal. "Let me get you a throw. You feel cold."

"I think it's the shock or something," Victoria said. "They moved up the orals date and I haven't had much sleep."

"Or food," said Sal, touching Victoria's cheekbone. "You look like a 'Send This Kid to Camp' poster."

"I'm so glad you were here," Victoria said, attempting to sit up.

"Hold it, love," said Sal. "Remember, Constantini cares. We're making special arrangements." He made two fast phone calls, one to security to keep an eye on a jeep parked in Visitors overnight, another to have a van brought around to the loading dock. He gave a note to the secretary and, still agog, she made a third.

"Service elevator," said Sal to Victoria, and scooped her up and took her downstairs.

"Where. . . ?" Victoria began.

"Mother's," said Sal. "It's closer. Applications of hot soup, warm bed, cool sheets, and I will tell you bedtime stories."

"Heaven," said Victoria. "I want to kiss you right now, but the adrenaline rush would probably put me over the edge again."

"Doze," said Sal. "It's only a few minutes." Later, what Victoria remembered was something wonderful tasting and being tucked in. She was aware of Sal and Lucia's quiet conversation, and then she slept for 12 hours.

"I don't usually give this kind of advice," Lucia said to Victoria later the following morning over masses of scrambled eggs and toast. "But I think you should stay here or at Sal's for the next few days. You need to convalesce and recharge. Can you do that?" Victoria was wrapped in one of Lucia's robes and felt wonderful and coddled.

"I could do that," said Victoria, smiling at Sal who was spooning off some cappuccino froth. The gleaming machine, adorned with golden flags and eagles, occupied a large pantry and looked as if it could be pressed into service for national defense.

"I can't thank you enough," Victoria said to Lucia. "I've never had this kind of thing happen to me before."

"My dear," Lucia said, "if this is the worst that you've ever had happen, you can count yourself among the most fortunate of creatures."

"Dibs on Victoria," said Sal, depositing a line of milk foam on his mother's cheek. "We have to get the jeep, I have to get to work, Victoria has to get her stuff. The cleaning people were in yesterday, but there's almost no food in the apartment."

"I'll send over some groceries about five," said Lucia. "I hope you can get through the day," she added, eyeing Victoria dubiously.

"I'm fine. I feel terrific, said Victoria. "I even managed to hang onto my bag." She hugged Lucia, and as Sal drove out to the street, she turned back to see where she had been staying. A large white Queen Anne Victorian with a turret and an impressive porte-cochère amid a sweeping lawn retreated through the rear window.

"Sheep may safely graze," said Victoria, watching the house disappear around a curve in the driveway.

"I think we have that," said Sal, whose mind was on other things. "Take the apartment key."

"How will you get in?"

"You'll be there," said Sal confidently, "otherwise I'll call missing persons. Victoria, listen. You need some recovery time and I finally get a chance to take care of you. Do you know how much I've wanted to take care of you?"

"Yes, I believe I do," she said. "But you have to disguise it somehow so you don't make me feel feeble. I hate feeble."

Sal pulled her to him and the van jiggled a bit. "You're the least feeble person I know," he said. "Let me wait on you hand and foot anyway. Curl up on the living room couch and I'll shower you with dinner and candy and flowers and silks and satins." Victoria looked astonished.

"I just threw in that last part to see if you were paying attention," he said. As they climbed out of the van in Sal's parking slot, he glanced up and eight or so faces immediately disappeared from the windows. "Oh, this is going to be a hot topic of conversation at Constantini," he said wryly.

"What will you say if anyone asks you about our goings-on yesterday," Victoria asked curiously.

"'That was Victoria. She just got her Ph.D.,' said Sal. "If anyone asks, which I doubt. There's probably a lot of fainting going on in corporate America."

"I am really sorry, Sal," Victoria said. "Stopping in like that seems so stupid today, but it didn't yesterday. What I can remember about yesterday."

"Well," said Sal briskly, "you'd have to come out of my closet sooner or later. I'm taking you to our awards dinner, for instance. Do you have anything formal?"

"Sal," she cried. "I'll relapse!"

"Relapse on the couch," he said. This was sounding more like Victoria. "There's melon in the refrigerator and I guarantee that dinner will be good. I'll see you later, but if you start feeling rocky, call me right away." Several new faces backed away from the windows. Sal hugged Victoria carefully, put her into the jeep, and marched in to reaffirm his leadership position.

Lucia had outdone herself (or maybe this was normal procedure, Victoria thought) and had sent over a modest crown roast with extra wild rice and a clutch of baby vegetables. There was a lush bunch of Almeria grapes.

"Well, that's mother's interpretation of food for the convalescent," said Sal, unwrapping a dish of snow peas and julienned carrots.

"Right," Victoria said. "And I want to eat it all. I'm starving. Plus I have to get my strength back for sex."

"Victoria, yesterday you could barely stay in an upright position," said Sal. "I'm planning on a quiet, celibate evening just holding on to you. Can we handle that?"

"Yes we can," she said. "You tell me about this awards dinner thing. And I'll tell you how thinking about you and herons made me a little crazy. But let's eat."

22 CONDITIONAL CLAUSES

Victoria recovered to full fighting form quickly. She busied herself shuttling between the university offices, pausing at bulletin boards offering placements and positions, and transferring her belongings to Sal's apartment. He had begun referring to it as "ours," which gave her a odd feeling that she hadn't yet integrated. Sex, which had been sleeping with its head under its wing, reawakened gloriously refreshed and with feathers twitching.

They may have overdone it a bit.

One morning, while they were still working out breakfast schedules and closet space, Sal, to his surprise, staggered a little when he got up. It was a first. He felt as if he had run a mile, exhausted but giddy. He watched Victoria out of the corner of his eye; she was stacking manuscript paper into a three-hole punch and humming a little under her breath. So pretty, so harmless looking. He was not certain he'd been on the receiving end of anything so . . . . aggressive, so creative, so . . . good. Words failed him, again.

Sal poured a cup of tepid coffee, mostly so he had something to hold on to. "Victoria," he said. She looked up.

"You're dashing when the blood drains out of your face," she said, smiling. "Are you going to lecture me?"

"When you finish that," Sal said, nodding toward the stack of paper—a copy of her thesis, "we have to have that serious talk we keep planning but not having. You can maybe go on like this forever, but if the sex gets any better, we're both going to have heart attacks," he said. "Or maybe just me," he added. "I want to put in a bid for something a little more steady-state. Victoria? Do you read me?"

She sat down in front of the three-hole punch and looked at him carefully. "You said on my terms."

"Yes I did. What are they?" He abandoned the coffee. "I mean, I'm going to be a twitchy wreck with no powers of concentration and with shaking hands. It's probably not the sex. It's the indecision. What do you want to do with this? Can we weave something like a long-term—ok, call it a life—into your terms? Somehow?"

She examined him clearly, appraisingly. "Do not," she said, "ever think that I don't take this seriously. I'd hate to be responsible for the shaking hand thing, unless you're just exaggerating." She took a breath. "I'm not going to run off and leave you. I'm not going to go away. I may seem a little scrambled at the moment, but my primary passion is real. You still take my breath away. Am I messing that up somehow?"

"Let's talk about best of all possible options," Sal said, reaching for her hand.

"'Come live with me and be my love and we will all the pleasures prove?'" Victoria ventured.

"Exactly."

"Christopher Marlowe. You might like him. Sal, could you hold off life-planning for a day or two while I confer with an expert on this sort of thing?"

"An expert? Who?"

"Someone with a great deal of information on the particular aspects of the subject at hand," she said.

"Who is?"

"Your mother."

"Oh god," Sal cried, clutching his head. "By all means. Do. I'll leave the country until it's over. Are you serious?"

"You said this summer it was important that we meet, and you were right. Your mother comes equipped for all kinds of crises. This would be just a chat. Probably a three on a scale of one to ten," Victoria said reasonably.

"I know a wonderful personnel manager. Maybe we could bring her in—you know, for balance."

"You're getting defensive. Lucia's a very wise woman. You said so yourself. Would you like a little something with that cold coffee? Scrambled eggs? An aspirin? You look like you could use a shot of brandy."

As it turned out, Victoria simply called Lucia and asked if she could talk to her about some things. Lucia, who'd considered that she had discharged her primary duty toward maligned biologists, was back at the lake and invited Victoria up for the weekend.

"It's just the two of you, right?" Sal asked, carefully.

"Yup," Victoria said. "But if you want to talk to *my* mother, feel free." Sal looked stricken. "Relax, Lucia's on your side," said Victoria hugging him.

"Two strong women both thinking about us is scary, Victoria, especially if one of them is you. I'm going to feel the vibrations through the soles of my feet."

"In fact, we're mostly going to bake," Victoria said. "There's a bread made with prosciutto and onion your mother said she would teach me. I'll bring some back for us."

"Better than nothing," said Sal gloomily. "I have a weird feeling about this whole female weekend thing." Victoria smiled.

* * *

"We are going to bake two kinds of bread," Lucia said, "and, I'm guessing, discuss the care and feeding of Constantini men."

"How many of them are there?" Victoria asked, surprised.

"Only one for you," said Lucia, "but from a family with some patterns that keep turning up each generation. Better forewarned. I'm delighted you could come up here. You look better, too."

"I really want to do the bread," said Victoria, "but I wanted to ask some things about Sal."

"I can guess," Lucia said, "and by the way, this conversation is not chipped into stone tablets, it's just us exchanging interesting information."

"Thank goodness," said Victoria. And throughout the next two days, while the yeast rose and fell, Lucia told Victoria about Sal's father, who had the great good sense to leave the business alone, and about the pitfalls involved when hired relatives quickly reached their level of incompetence.

"Sal's responsible for most of our growth," Lucia said, "but it doesn't get talked about much, and that's just fine for everybody. It saves feelings, and so nobody cares about jumping into some imaginary limelight."

Over a giant mixing bowl, Victoria, in garlic powder, salt and flour to her elbows, said, "Sal was wonderful when I collapsed in his office. Almost like he'd had practice."

"Yes, the care-taking thing," Lucia said. "As long as it doesn't turn overbearing, but I think you've passed the danger point. Knead the dough harder; use the heel of your palm. That's better. Let him take care of you sometimes; he needs to. He does it very well, by the way."

Victoria turned the dough into a shallow bowl. Lucia announced a one-hour rising time for the dough to double in bulk, rustled up some lunch and also prepared the filling for the bread. "Has Sal said anything about the divorce?" Lucia inquired as they finished lunch. "Just punch that dough down. We need to roll it."

"I haven't dared ask," said Victoria.

"I think you should," Lucia replied. "That was an awful year and there were wounds that took a long time to heal. All right, the oven is preheated, time to spread the filling."

"Where were the children during all this?"

"In very high quality grandmother care largely, and it wasn't easy," said Lucia crisply. "You'd think it would be because they were small."

"Did it all . . . just get resolved?" Victoria asked.

"Yes, because of the money," Lucia said. "Now we pinch the dough together and make some diagonal slices that bake open."

"The money," Victoria repeated a little blankly.

"There's a great deal of it. Sal's attorney worked out a very good settlement that incorporated plans for wonderful schooling and a generous shared custody arrangement. Cost the earth and worth every penny. Pop that right into the oven," Lucia added, checking the temperature.

"And?" Victoria asked carefully, feeling that there was more. Lucia glanced at her and made a decision.

"The arrangement is so comfortable that I can't see Sal's ex ever marrying anybody else and giving any part of it up."

"My god," said Victoria. "Does that happen often in these situations?"

"No," said Lucia, "but that's how it turned out." There was a little silence.

"In some circles," Victoria ventured, "it's called the Law of Unintended Consequences."

"Well, like death and taxes, we have her, possibly forever, attached to Nick and Tommy. Now," Lucia continued thoughtfully, "what do you suppose will happen when and if you and Sal set up more permanent housekeeping?"

"Oh man," said Victoria, slowly sitting down in a kitchen chair.

"Tomorrow," said Lucia, "we do a bread flavored with olives, rosemary, and some other things."

"Lucia," Victoria said, "why wouldn't he tell me about this?"

"Because men don't, usually, and it was terrible for everybody. But he will, you know, because you're here and, I'm pretty sure, you love each other and you let him swoop down and save you. And he's very proud of you."

"He is? He never said."

"He will. We're a very possessive family. And at the moment, you've got the lead for the position of our first Ph.D." Victoria looked stunned. "I have some wonderful stories about the Constantini temper for tomorrow," Lucia said. "They sort of go with the olive bread."

23 MORE GAINS AND LOSSES

The political and mining interests, angry at the local resistance, fought back. The Commerce and Industry Association began a serious assault on the previously sacrosanct status of the steams and rivers in what Random Mining considered its sphere of influence. Under the Federal Clean Water Act, the waterways had always been protected from mining. The Association sharpened its campaign to have the Federal Clean Water designations repealed.

"What are they claiming?" asked Sydnor who had just raced back from her real job four hours to the south.

"Some nonsense about fluctuating later levels voiding the outstanding waters designation," said Webb. "But I think they've hit a nerve, because Nelson Two Snakes has organized practically every tribe and town in the northern part of the state that has clean water running through it. They're demonstrating."

"Wow," said Sydnor. "Can he do that?"

"Do you mean can he, or does he have that much influence. Yes to both, I think. The Native Americans don't want their rivers and trout streams downgraded to so that Random Mining can dump its wastewater in them."

About the same time as this conversation, an enormous gathering of tribes and friends of Native Americans began picketing the state capitol building. The Native Americans were in full paint, carrying signs, chanting and dancing. They also distributed remarkably professional position statements.

Editorial writers came out on the side of the Indians, recapped what was being called a disgraceful land grab, and lowered the governor's approval rating by about nine points.

The Natural Resources Department, like obedient hand puppets, immediately announced that more study was necessary and quickly assembled an advisory committee to take up the question of what was or should be outstanding waters. Remarkably, instead of applauding the motives of the hastily-assembled advisory committee, the public, plus environmental groups of all stripes and colors, sportsmen's clubs, and an impressive number of legislators, rose up furious and ready to do battle with mining and the enemies of clean water.

"'The only thing necessary for the triumph of evil is for good men to do nothing,'" said Judge Press, pleased.

"Who said that?" Sophie asked.

"Edmund Burke," said the Judge. "It's the only statement of his that anybody ever quotes and just as well, since the man never shut up, but it looks as though we've got good men . . ."

"And women," said Sydnor.

". . . doing something," he finished.

"Especially since Natural Resources named some guy from Random Mining to be on this supposedly neutral Advisory Committee. That really got 'em," said Webb.

"Ok," said Sydnor. "Does anyone have a can of tuna to lend me? I'm starving and there's nothing in the cottage. And any ideas what we do next?"

※ ※ ※

Back in the city, one of Lucia's pro bono attorneys was explaining the intricacies of libel law to his new client. "A libel must be written," he said, "otherwise it's only slander. So it's fortunate that the guy actually put it into a document. What a dodo," said the attorney, pleased.

The client, a biologist who never expected to be surrounded by such high-powered legal expertise, said uncertainly, "That's good?"

"Yes," said the attorney. "If it had been merely slander, we wouldn't have anything tangible. We can claim retribution for your scientific, um, stand, I suppose. What actually was it?"

"I pointed out that the indigenous paper floater mussel would be destroyed by mining residues in its fresh water habitat. And so would some other . . .oh, fish and dragonflies and things. It would have screwed up their Environmental Impact Statement."

The attorney studied him. "Could you get a bunch of other scientific people to back you up?"

"Oh yes, no problem," said the client. "It's common knowledge. The Department can't libel all of them, can they?"

Interesting question, the attorney thought, but said, "I think we'll go for an apology and public retraction and perhaps something in damages."

"Damages?"

"For injury to reputation, malicious intent, that sort of thing," said the attorney, warming up. "Unless in a situation of absolute privilege, which this is not. Yes, I think the prospect of awarded damages would be perceived as highly embarrassing."

"Well, go ahead then," said the client. "Because they've really embarrassed me." Dammit, he thought grimly, he would fight for the paper floater mussel. It was a tough little creature, but it couldn't survive mining residue.

Reinforcements began arriving. Statements or people from the U.S. Bureau of Mines, the National Academy of Sciences, and the U.S. Dept. of the Interior appeared. The Bureau of Mines quoted its own study, stating simply that most if not all new mining operations were guaranteed to pollute associated rivers and waters with dispersal acids and toxins. The resort owners association rejoiced, made hundreds of copies, and sent them everywhere.

"It's like watching wolves eat their young," said Webb. "Why are they on our side?"

"I think," said Judge Press, "it's either because Random Mining's not big enough to defend, or because it's screwed up so badly in this state that the Fed doesn't want to share the taint."

"You believe that?" Webb asked.

"For the moment," said the Judge.

That weekend, one of Arthur Rosenheim's buddies at the National Academy of Sciences appeared on a Sunday morning press panel. After a circular argument with a mining executive, he lost patience and addressed the camera directly.

"Bottom line," he said, "despite the water contamination levels Congress specified in the Safe Drinking Waters Act, Congress certainly didn't intend water to be actually degraded to that level. It's a worst case scenario. Frankly, those levels are dangerous; you wouldn't want to touch that stuff, and man, you should see what it does to the perch."

The mining executive opened his mouth and closed it, apparently flummoxed by how to organize a rebuttal in the two minutes remaining. The program preceded Sunday football, so its large audience was left to contemplate images of sick perch. Arthur called Max Skyler later and said his buddy would be willing to talk about bad water and sick perch anytime.

Finally, the Department of the Interior responded to Judge Press's request for comments on the Natural Resources Department's draft Environmental Impact Statement. "This is wonderful," Sydnor said, reading it. Her fingers twitched toward a notepad.

"Just summarize please," said Sophie, who had decided to feed everyone and was mixing a salad. "I'm the only one who hasn't had a chance to read it."

"Ok," said Sydnor. "It says the Environmental Impact Statement failed to adequately assess risks involved. It says there's a reoccurring pattern of failure to deal with the mine's impact on the area's national resources—all kinds. It says (and this is wonderful) that the statement indicates no plans for restoring the environment beyond just getting the mine up and running."

"Hot damn," said Al Gustave, who was leaning on the porch.

"Press conference," said Sydnor.

"No," said Judge Press, who was right behind Gustave. "But perhaps yes if we can get an Interior Department spokesperson in on some pretext to say this again. The Forest Service agrees with the Bureau of Mines, and Sierra Club is planning to join in. And I think we should ask Nelson Two Snakes too. But before we get all celebratory, remember, there's the upcoming Council vote that will determine this, one way or another."

"That's a dash of cold water," Sydnor said. "We have to keep going right down to the wire."

"I'm sure Max Skyler agrees," said the Judge.

"Gather the troops," said Webb, tossing vinegar and oil on some salad. "And let's find out what Lucia's lawyers are up to. Plus does she know anybody who's got a suitable press conference space for hire? Somebody fearless?"

* * *

Lucia had had a call from a very competent-sounding lawyer and was pleased with herself and her myriad works. She was reporting some of these works to Sal who rang to make sure that Victoria was on her way back. "Anthony at Brown, Brown, and something says the opposition is discussing our terms," Lucia said. "He thinks they'll accept." Sal realized that he had drifted dangerously far out of the loop.

"Our terms?" Sal asked. "Terms about what?"

"We've been doing some pro bono—is that right?—work saving some nice state biologists from a smear campaign," said Lucia, sounding profoundly satisfied.

"We?" said Sal.

"The company. If you have a few minutes," Lucia said, "I can fill you in."

"Yes, do," he said to his mother cautiously. Now that Victoria was back, he really needed to pay more attention.

24 ELSEWHERE

It was one o'clock in the morning, and the shelling wasn't any louder at least. It was constant though, as if all the munitions in Southeast Asia had been carried here to pound the city and everybody in it into dust.

Saigon was humid and disintegrating, but somehow parts of it still managed to attract. The surviving colonial hotels hinted of charm and fizzy drinks on verandas. Magnus Quinn and Carson Doyle, the Reuters correspondent, were on one, risking an evening meal. Carson, a Brit, was fearless, funny, good company. "It's amazing that they can keep supplies coming in," he said, dipping a chunk of fish into the sauce. The lights flickered periodically; their waiter seemed unconcerned.

"They take turns," said Quinn. "Today serving stuffed shrimp, tomorrow manning the mortars in the hills."

"Bitter, bitter. You've been here long enough," said Carson. "You're beginning to sound like the guys from AP . . . twitchy, paranoid."

"And they're right," said Quinn with less humor than he'd exhibited in the past weeks. "I hear that all this background shelling is supposed to lull us into complacency just before the big push into the city. Are you staying?"

"Hell, no," said Carson. "I'm shipping out in three days with anything or anybody friendly—I've been bonding with the

Aussie medics. The sun never sets on the Union Jack and all that. Canberra, Auckland, it's all the same to me. The objective is out of here and far away. Quinn my man, the prognosis is not good. Speaking of which, I hear one of your colleagues got himself shot up."

"Randall. He'll be ok when they figure out whether to save the toes or lose the toes. He says he's telling everyone it was terrible frostbite. A stupid, freaky thing. He's lucky to be alive."

"Ah, that's what we all say."

"The advantage of being under siege," said Quinn, "is that the enemy is too busy to slip in and plant more land mines."

Something exploded closer than before. Several dishes broke in the kitchen and it seemed a good time to get back to the hotel where the press was billeted. It was near the center of the city, possibly on the theory that if communications went down, all the news services could talk to each other.

Carson wandered down the hall for a nightcap. Quinn let himself into his room.

Was the shelling closer? It was hard to tell. He collapsed onto the bed and thought about getting out early and filing something about the mood in the streets.

He rolled off the bed, and was crouching to get the small travel case from underneath when he was surrounded by metallic shrieking. He flattened instinctively as the window blew in with a roar, and the walls of the room rippled from impact. Glass was suddenly everywhere, and shards had landed on his back and shoulders. There was roaring in his ears, then he heard someone shouting in the hallway, so at least he wasn't deaf.

Turning carefully onto his right side, he glanced up. A 15-inch piece of shrapnel was embedded in the plaster wall at pillow level. It would have taken his head off. There's a lead, he thought. Journalist misses death by inches. No witnesses.

He raised his hand and held it in front of his face and focussed. He registered that it wasn't shaking. Maybe later:

delayed shock? The hell with it, he thought. Moving slowly and keeping low, he calculated the distance—over glass—to the door.

25 UNCONDITIONAL CLAUSES

Victoria tore back to the city late Sunday afternoon with two loaves of great-smelling bread and burning curiosity. It was a fairly long drive and she had a lot of time to think while negotiating traffic. She had made certain decisions. They would change her life, and she didn't want to change her life to the point where she would lose her grip on it. Selfish, she thought. No, not selfish, democratic, balanced. I am a complete person. I am multitudes, she thought, ricocheting off a half-remembered Walt Whitman line. What an adventure. Over the weekend she had learned a great deal and maybe a little too much.

She found Sal in a quiet but obviously highly charged state, one unfamiliar to her; Lucia would have known it. There was static electricity in the air. She kissed the top of his head, setting off a small spark, deposited the bread on the kitchen counter, and waded in, chatting about the weekend.

"It was sort of like," she said, "spending time with an older version of Glinda the Good, you know, from 'The Wizard of Oz.'"

"Lots of information?" Sal asked, neutrally.

"Oh yes." She studied him. "I hope you're not annoyed about my time with your mother," Victoria said. Sal raised an eyebrow at her. "But," she continued, testing the ice, "if we're going to share a roof and a bed and god knows what else, we needed—I needed—to see what's lurking in your emotional shrubbery, so we don't wind up yelling at each other."

"What an interesting choice of words, Victoria," he said, pulling his chair closer. "Mother unloaded the divorce story, right?"

"She said I should ask you about it," Victoria said quietly. "I've never known what to ask. Or if." Or how you might react, she thought.

Sal regarded her grimly and then pushed his chair several inches back.

"Let me tell you what I know about yelling," he said. "Yelling was just the beginning. It was just warming up. We broke furniture: she threw a lamp at me, I pitched a vase into the living room mirror. I'd storm out; she locked the door, I broke the lock. Once I broke the door. Tommy heard us one night, he woke up screaming; he was little; he thought the house was falling down.

"After that we moved our disagreements to a counselor's office. He looked like Bela Lugosi. What a farce. I had a cut on my ear where I'd been clipped by a piece of glass and she'd pulled something trying to open a locked drawer. Maybe there were knives in it. The counselor decided we should to go back and examine our deepest childhood traumas. She threw a briefcase at him; better him than me, but it got us finally divorced. Irreconcilable differences. That's the short version. But it took a long time." He seemed tired. "Consider it background."

It was very quiet in the kitchen. "Oh Sal," Victoria said, tearing up a bit.

"I try not to think about it. Do you want a tissue?"

"I guess," she said, but instead rose, walked around the table, put her arms around him, and dripped salt tears into his curls. "There will be no yelling. I promise." She hugged him a little closer and rubbed her face in his hair. "And here I've been sashaying around, assuming your life was all sweetness and light."

"Anything's possible," he said, reaching around for her. "That's where you come in. Stay with me, Victoria. Stay with me, with us, and everything."

"I am. I will," she said. "How could you think I wouldn't? Well, I know how you'd think I wouldn't, but this will work, Sal," Victoria said. "You'll be amazed." She seemed to be dripping again. Sal gave her the tissue.

"Yeah?" he said. "Do I have to travel with you to weird places with bad plumbing while you stare at big old beaky birds?"

"Yes, but not always," she said, "and in exchange I will dress up in horrible ruffles and smile lovingly during corporate functions."

"The Constantini Awards dinner," Sal offered.

"The Friends of the Earth Mountain Hike," she countered.

"My god, Victoria, I love you so much," he said unexpectedly, and enveloped her with slightly more force than she was ready for.

"Don't stop now," she said.

Later, much later, Victoria rose quietly to close a window; it was cold. Wrapped in a blanket, she looked at Sal, who'd entangled himself in a sheet and was safely asleep.

Given her interests and experience, Victoria often ruminated on theory versus whatever reality she happened to be dealing with. She studied Sal. This was reality, all right. He was, even in repose, quite something, she thought, less corsair, more second baseman for the White Sox. She smiled and watched him breathe.

Remarkable. Here was represented—what—maybe 150,000 years of hominid development because, after fiddling around with evolution for eons, nature had decided that this version was probably good enough. He turned a little onto his right side and Victoria studied the component parts: nose, good shoulder, deep chest, splendid leg, dark and curly hair; how well it was assembled. Not an extra ounce of fat, she thought, leaning forward and gloating a little. She wondered idly what his sons might inherit from this gene pool.

But he was awake and watching her watching him.

"What are you doing?" he said. "What time is it?" She leaned forward and put her hand on his chest.

"I want to crawl right into your skin with you," she whispered, unwinding the sheet. "I want to swim up and down your veins and arteries and make love until I lose consciousness."

He reached for her silently. Victoria opened the blanket, spread it like a bat's wings, covered them both, and slowly nuzzled her way down his sternum. "You're serious," he said, catching his breath.

"I do love you, I do." Victoria said into his chest, tasting salt, nibbling a tiny curl of hair. She stroked him lightly once, twice, and found what she was looking for. Sal inhaled hard and grabbed the edge of the mattress. "Hands across the sea," she said.

26 THE STORM FRONT

All the principal players in the township meeting on the 27th met at different times and places to polish their battle plans. Ross and Wicker had filled briefcases with statistics, testimonials, masses of technical briefs, and copies of the Environmental Impact Statement. Maxwell Skyler and some of the council members had been closeted for hours the previous day. They were armed with notes, statements, charts, and photos. Judge Press had joined them briefly, as had Nelson Two Snakes. Later, Skyler met with several newcomers over dinner; Arthur Rosenheim stopped by, shook hands all around, and left. The Yellow Perch Lake contingent delivered boxes of signed petitions to the council and kept out of the way.

Early on the evening of the meeting, heavy-looking clouds moved in and the air grew cool. By 6:30 the sky in the northwest had darkened alarmingly, and thunder muttered. The air smelled of wet and ozone. Sydnor, Sophie and Webb left early for the high school; the gym was the only place large enough to accommodate the crowd. Sal and Victoria drove up from the city for the event and stopped at the lake house. Lucia Constantini's intense canvassing and entertainment schedule had finally caught up to her; she had collapsed onto the daybed on her sun porch and begged off.

"Tell me all about it in the morning," she said. "I'm almost asleep already."

"It's like missing the first half of a movie," Victoria said in the car. "How can you tell what's going on?"

"Believe me," Sal said, "it will be crystal clear in about ten minutes, but I can give you the plot outline. You know what my mother has been doing, right? Well, everybody else—you don't know them now but you'll meet most of these people eventually—everybody else has pitched in and done some incredible stuff."

Sal's overview got them all the way to the high school and a parking place at the edge of the rapidly filling lot; they joined the throng. Inside, Maureen Hendrickson waved from across a thicket of folding chairs. Webb was chatting with Max Skyler, Larry Running Bear, and a stranger. "Coffee," Sal announced, and Victoria slung her jacket over his chair next to her. Sydnor had spotted them and intercepted Sal at the coffee machine.

"And that's Victoria?" she asked. "Emerged from her tower? Do you plan on making introductions?"

"I'm hand-carrying her around the lake," said Sal with satisfaction, "but she doesn't know that yet."

"Good," said Sydnor. "This coffee's always vile, by the way. You're forewarned."

Al Gustave and Judge Press were seated near the coffee service. There were other familiar faces. Minnie Rosenheim was saving a seat in front. Walter Hansen was fishing around for more coffee creamer. Lake people and townspeople filled the auditorium. Each side was surprised to discover how many people they knew from the other side. Estelle Malmaison nodded a greeting to Sophie, Gertrude from the County Clerk's office hoisted a coffee cup to Sydnor, Charlie Haney nearly fell off his chair staring at Sal and Victoria, and one of asphalt truck drivers gave a little wave to Miranda Thrip and Mason glared at him.

Some council members were setting up their chairs on one side of the small stage and talking with hangers-on. A Rotary member was retrieving more chairs from another room; the crowd was large and people were still arriving. It seemed to be turning into a big deal. There were two TV crews, an unfamiliar reporter, and the local reporter who doubled as photographer. The air in the auditorium grew warm and thick.

Sydnor caught the subtle but pervasive odor rising from the wrestling mats on the north wall. The smell was a sort of unifier, like a perfect white sauce that binds lobster into thermidore. She realized her clothes would carry the fumes right up to the cotton/sturdy cycle, also that the nasty coffee was making her hungry. Why were there never donuts at these things?

"Walter!" said Sal. Hansen jumped.

"My word, Sal. Surprised to see you. How's your mother?"

"She's fine. Listen, Walt, who's the guy Max Skyler's talking to?"

"Couldn't say; he came in just before the Random Mining people—the two tall ones and the short guy in the tan jacket." Harassed-looking Rotary members were setting up yet another row of chairs in the back of the hall and on the other side of the podium on stage. Hansen added a little defensively, "There're people here that I don't even know. That *never* happens in these meetings. The TV crews are setting up in the aisle," he added, frowning. On the stage the chairman was briskly rapping his gavel for order. A flicker of lightning dashed at the windows.

"Later," said Sal, whose hand was beginning to burn from holding the coffee. The secretary, orange-haired Gertrude, rustled minutes of the previous meeting and seemed determined to read them.

* * *

"First," said Skyler after the preliminaries, "there is some new business that, though it bears on the mining issues we have on the table, can be dealt with and put aside. I refer to the Reformed Brethren Church property along the Upper Chain of Lakes and the excavations there.

"Reverend Weathersill, will you tell us about the activity on this property? I realize that you may not have technical details at hand, but a summary will do. You have the floor."

Weathersill, who had come in garb as ecclesiastical as he could find, rose, took a microphone that someone thrust at him, and cleared his throat. "It's just preliminary exploration," he said, watching Ross and Wicker from the corner of his eye, "that, um, should provide samples of ore or minerals . . . ." He was quoting from the mining company lease and trying to sound casually knowledgeable but not as if he were on the Random Mining team. It was hard going.

One of the township supervisors interrupted. "Question, Reverend Weathersill?" Weathersill nodded.

"The company is taking samples all along the property, right?" Weathersill nodded again, and Ross tensed to spring. "What have they turned up? I mean, so far."

"Well, all the holes immediately filled up with water," said Weathersill, "so I really couldn't . . ."

"I can speak to that," said Ross, quickly rising. "This is purely preparatory work; it amounts to clearing, site selection and some extraction before we can begin any substantial digging." Weathersill turned to him, surprised.

"Purely preparatory?" he asked, a looking a little stunned. Ross was beginning another paragraph of explanation, but Skyler rapped to interrupt.

"Ok," he said. "We've got the picture, but all this may turn out to be moot." Larry Bear and Judge Press rose and looked inquiringly at Skyler and the council.

"Chair recognizes, et cetera, et cetera, go ahead," Skyler said.

"Larry Bear and I are doing a tag-team presentation," Press said to the room. "This is a good time to mention that the Outgamie Chippewa, who beat us here by a thousand years or so, hold a 1872 game, timber, and fishing rights claim to the Upper Chain of Lakes shore line calculated, I believe the treaty says, a still-wind bow shot from the bend with the three great stones. As you campers will know, these stones next to the Rolling Log flowage mark the boundary of the National Forest. The treaty is still valid." He turned to Larry Bear who continued.

"Now, even with a brisk westerly," Larry said to the room, "that well-shot arrow takes in most of the church camp property. This checks out with the old maps in our records, and the documents that Judge Press found in the state capitol."

"This claim," said Press, "puts the ball in the Chippewa park. First, it's already established by law that the Chippewa can fish anywhere in these waters, any time of the year, day or night. You'll all remember the unpleasantness at Flambeau Flowage a couple of years ago."

Every one remembered. Torch-bearing Indians, exercising their right to spear fish by firelight were confronted by a group of outraged locals who foresaw the tourist trade and their livelihood shrinking in direct proportion to the remaining available catch. They squared off at a public landing. The ensuing scuffle was Keystone Cops material—a game warden was tossed into the lake and one feather headdress caught fire—but the story made both national papers and local television, and resort owners across a thousand square lake-studded miles shook in their fishing boots, clutching their booking calendars to their flanneled chests.

"Therefore," Press continued, "it is my free legal opinion that mining activity in Indian territory and next to a national forest is illegal in ways we can only begin to imagine, and that would generate lengthy litigation while everyone tried to find out."

Larry Bear turned to Reverend Weathersill who had quietly folded into his folding chair, and said, "We'd like to discuss some interim arrangements with the church, until we can sort out who owns what and since when. So no digging please."

Reverend Weathersill nodded. "It was really more an exploratory kind of thing," he began, and lost his train of thought, seeing vanishing profits replaced by horrible cleanup costs. Maybe the tribe could do that. In the gym, the lights flickered; outside the wind picked up twigs and gravel and slung them against the windows with rain.

"Now look here," said Ross angrily, rising. "We have a perfectly valid lease for this work that represents no little . . ."

"Not the point," said Judge Press, who was still standing. "Your lease may be shipshape, but the Reformed Brethren Church's legal title to the land is in serious question." Maxwell Skyler tapped his gavel for attention.

"You will all have ample opportunity to discuss this later," he said, "but the Reformed Brethren Church is not the only party concerned with the Random Mining Company's push into this area."

* * *

Much later, when Sydnor tried to describe the evening, her image was of an opera. Not grand, but opera. There was a prelude, voices were raised, the plot unfolded with motives declaimed and/or exposed. Accusations were made and motives were furiously defended. Everything was exclaimed upon solo or in chorus, and it was very long. The finale was something of a stunner, with the resolution practically off stage—though there was hardly any stage.

* * *

"New business," Maxwell Skyler had announced, finally, and it grew quiet. "The primary purpose of this meeting is to hear the pro and con sides of the mining proposals make a decision, and to act it." There was a sound of 437 people inhaling simultaneously. "We're all familiar with the documents; we've all read the letters and the editorials in the paper, many of us have been to the meetings." A television crew readied its camera. "At the end of this session, any decision we make—one way or another—we have to live with."

Webb leaned toward Sophie and whispered, "There's nobody here from Natural Resources."

"Maybe they figured the Environmental Impact Statement was enough representation," Sophie whispered back. "Plus it's raining."

"It's Natural Resources; they're above mere weather," said Webb.

"Or they're putting some distance between the department and the mining flap," Sydnor whispered.

"Maybe it's a sign," Sophie said, with hope.

Max Skyler was pontificating. "We—the Council—have been busy doing our homework and talking to various interested parties. We will hear from them, that is, you will hear from them before adjournment. This is an opportunity for people to, if they have decided one way, to change their minds. It is incumbent upon us to present the matter as it presently stands.

"As you see, Mr. Ross and his associates from Random Mining are here; there is a delegate from the Sierra Club, we have technical experts—as I'm sure does Random Mining—and there are others here from the Outgamie Chippewa. The Chair recognizes Mr. Ross; you have the floor."

A heavy chuckle of thunder repeated several times and raindrops pattered against the windows, darkening the mood in the room. Sal nudged Victoria and whispered, "What do you want to bet there's a fight before 9:30." Webb glanced down the row at them and grimaced, lifting his eyebrows in mock scandal.

"Thank you," Ross said. He was feeling exposed. "My colleague Trenton Wicker, of Wicker, Tattersall and Wicker is with me and we both stress that the negative reports about the Random Mining Company enterprise have been vastly overstated. The critics have failed to grasp the magnitude of the potential waiting to be released here. This is an enormous opportunity," he added, growing enthusiastic, and covered, point by point, the profit for lessors, the substantial boost in area employment and businesses, and the remarkable strides in new technologies that rendered the extraction process clean, safe, and practically non-disruptive. Al Gustave, who was beginning to simmer, realized that the remarkable strides in new technologies were nowhere in the mining lease.

"One of our technical people, Tom Doppler, has been working in the area and can add to this," Ross finished and looked to the podium for approval." Skyler nodded to Doppler who had had traded the brown plaid shirt for a more academic-scientific looking costume. He spoke at length about capture and sluicing processes.

"Where do people find desert boots?" Sydnor murmured to Sophie. Doppler repeated much of Ross's information, but embroidered on strides made in neutralizing toxic aspects of mining wastes, since everybody in the room had already heard of them.

"The chemical processes are too lengthy to describe here," he finished, "but as responsible scientists, we would apply these appropriately and beneficially." Minnie whispered to Walter that it sounded like an insurance pitch.

"Are there questions? Comments?" Skyler asked. There were. Judge Press and said that Random Mining had heard some of his comments before, but that they bore repeating for the meeting.

"Counter to the claim that mining creates sustainable jobs, the Riverbend county unemployment figures for the period before that mine opened, during its operation, and after it closed, are practically the same. There was almost no change."

"'Almost' no change?" Ross inquired archly.

"'Almost' because unemployment rose briefly at the mine's closing and then leveled out to pre-mine totals. There were no permanent job gains, as Random keeps touting; in Riverbend's case, it was almost as if labor had been imported and then dispersed somewhere else when it wasn't needed any longer."

"Riverbend is—was—not a Random mine," said Ross stiffly.

"I'm not claiming it was," Press retorted. "I'm quoting public records, some of which show that there was no particular financial gain in that county's income during the operating period of the mine.

"If this is such a profitable enterprise, why are there no profits recorded? Who got the money? There should have been minor millionaires created and substantial improvements in town infrastructure, according to your promotions. There were none."

"All mines are different," Ross said, sounding annoyed. "You cannot compare an older mine in a different location that produces greater or lesser material with an theoretical mine here."

"Theoretical is the key word here," Press replied. "These are tip of the iceberg issues in some opinions, but they cast doubt on Random's promise of early retirement for a cooperative population."

Larry Bear rose again and said, "Mr. Chairman? If I could comment on Mr. Doppler's mining waste theories?"

"Your floor," said Skyler. Judge Press sat down and Tom Doppler's eyebrows shot up. He was being challenged by a Native American?

"We were all interested to learn that Random's mining wastes could be held for 9,000 years," Larry said, as various audience members chuckled, "and gave the claim about as much consideration as it deserved." Ross rolled his eyes heavenward; Doppler compressed his lips.

"What we need to know from Mr. Doppler is the length of time Random Mining has used these underground waste storage silos."

"That would be hard to say," Doppler replied.

"Why?" Larry asked. Across the room, Sal smiled. He knew Larry Bear's stubborn fits.

"Well," Doppler said, "because they were put in different places at different times. And the later ones were—more improved."

"Make it easy for us," Larry said. "When did Random Mining install its first underground silo for toxic wastes?" There was a little silence, as Doppler realized that neither Ross nor Wicker was going to bail him out.

"Seven years," he said.

"So they haven't been in use for even a decade?" Larry asked.

"Not by us," Doppler said, resigned.

Wicker, heretofore silent, rose. "Mr. Chairman?"

"The floor is yours, Mr. Wicker."

"Strides in cleanup processes are being made every day. Random is in the forefront of this research, and we find ourselves in the position similar to that of a typical development company—the technology takes a long time to be applied in the field." He smiled at the audience, as if delivering a precious bit of wisdom. "But," he gestured around the auditorium, "it is ready to use here," and sat down.

"Then," said Larry Bear, who was still standing, "that must mean you've incorporated drainage pipes into the things, since the current models don't have any. But that's actually handy, because if they don't have drainage pipes, then nobody needs to clean them out when they clog and the silo starts to ooze."

Wicker threw a startled look at Doppler, who pretended not to see it. "We continue to make improvements," Wicker said, stubbornly.

Arthur Rosenheim, from is seat in the front row, silently applauded Larry. Arthur could feel the audience's dismay at silos oozing toxic wastes. But Ross hadn't forfeited the round. "Mr. Chairman," he said, "I'd like to remind this assembly that all of these issues have been raised and have been answered to the satisfaction of the Natural Resources Department in its Final Environmental Impact Statement," said Ross. "When this state's own organization that is dedicated to serving the environment accepts the care we have taken and conditions that we have struggled to establish, it seems to me that more far-reaching decisions take precedence over local squabbles."

Al Gustave snapped. He leaped to his feet, turned to the audience, and said, "And since Natural Resources was paid off to the tune of $100,000 by Random Mining lobbyists, you can bet your boots that they accept Random's conditions, which are to sit down, shut up, don't ask tough questions, and get smiley-face pictures taken arm in arm with Mr. tassel loafers here! Anybody from Natural Resources in this room? No!

"Don't you give me that beady eye," Gustave, practically spitting, said to Ross. "We got contributions to the Natural Resources big-wigs documented for anybody to see. And some of 'em admit it. You bought that Impact Statement; it's not worth a pile of horse manure!"

A roar from the audience: applause with laughter, some boos, some people stood up in the back row and clapped. Gustave nodded and sat down. "Oh god, he's going to have a heart attack," Sophie said.

"I don't think so," Webb replied, watching Gustave across the room. Maxwell Skyler was pounding his gavel for order. One of the reporters was scribbling furiously.

Victoria said to Sal, "I haven't heard anything like that since the anti-war demonstrations on campus. Does he live near you?"

"Yes," said Sal. "And I'll bet he's a big fan of the blue heron, too."

"Let's have some order," Skyler said loudly. "I think that exchange has concluded. We really have to move on. I'd like to turn the discussion over to Parker Hedges of the Sierra Club, with the Council's permission."

The stranger stood and introduced himself. "My organization has been examining the trail that the Random Mining Co. has left across the U.S. and some foreign countries," he said. "You can judge if it's something that you wish to be part of. I have a list." Here Wicker started to rise, but stopped at a gesture from Ross.

Opening a folder, Hedges described mines ranging from relatively small operations with associated small blunders—ecological disasters such as fish kills and poisoned well water, through several suspected of bequeathing non-specific illnesses to the local population, and finally, a worst-case scenario involving ocean dumping and its disastrous effect on the local food chain.

"Even though," he continued, "the organization was dumping mining wastes in the ocean, contaminating the source of the native population's food supply, the companies—it was a joint venture—denied that the subsequent cancers and illnesses were related to mercury and arsenic poisoning. I have photographs here, and if the council would permit, I'll pass them to the audience."

"I object," said Ross angrily, leaping to his feet.

"Please, Mr. Ross," Skyler said. "This is not a courtroom, merely a council meeting. Logically, I suppose you could present photos showing opposing views, so to speak." Ross sat down, seething.

"There is," Hedges finished, "one mine that seems not to menace anything except lizards and some spectacular beetles. It's in the high desert of Chile. Thank you." Photos were quietly passed from hand to hand. Hedges knew they'd be returned; no one wanted to look at them for very long.

"The council must be aware that Random is cognizant of these historical problems," Ross interjected. "And I say historical, because these sorts of problems have been dealt with. Indeed, our files are as thorough as those of Mr. Hedges' agency here." Hedges looked at Ross pityingly.

Arthur Rosenheim got up so quickly that he nearly knocked over his chair. "Mr. Chairman, permission?"

"Yes, yes, Arthur."

Arthur Rosenheim, unlike the others, strode to the front of the audience, though he directed most of his comments toward Ross. "Your Mr. Mactate would be familiar with the ORW—the

Outstanding Resource Water law that was mandated by the Federal Clean Water Act." Arthur said. "But since he's not here," (Ross mentally cursed Mactate and all his works or the lack of them), "let me explain."

And, Arthur, clearly and succinctly, described the Law. "This is a 'return it the way you found it' law involving waste water," he said. "It simply says that if you're tapping into an Ourstanding Resource Water—these are the state's most important rivers and waterways—for any reason, and then returning the water to that source, it has to be returned as clean as it was when you took it.

"Those holes in Reverend Weathersill's church camp land along the Upper Chain of Lakes," Arthur continued, "filled up with water, because the water table's only about 10 feet down, as it is almost everywhere in this part of the state. The Upper Chain is part of the Outstanding Resource Water system—*our* outstanding resource water; we use it, we're drinking it. And for mining, you'd need that water to process the ore.

"The sludge goes into Mr. Doppler's big underground silos, but what about the thousands and thousands of gallons of contaminated processing water? It has to go someplace. Where?

"Not back into the Upper Chain and the river; they're both Outstanding Resource Waters," Arthur continued, "unless the wastewater can be purified back to its original state.

"The question for Mr. Ross and Mr. Wicker is this," Arthur said. "Which of your sites return clean, toxin-free processing water to the source, as mandated by the ORW laws?" The quiet in the auditorium made the wind rising outside sound increasingly threatening. A flash of lightening punctuated a murmur from the audience, and the rain began in earnest.

"I can speak to that," said Hedges, abruptly. "If any U.S. mine, Random included, has been able to meet that test, we have not heard of it. They don't. They can't. And if they could, they wouldn't keep it a secret."

Wicker glanced at Ross who looked like he might crack walnuts with his teeth.

"So we can take it as given," Arthur said, "That Random Mining does not and cannot meet the state's Outstanding Resource Water requirements. They are," he finished, "up the creek without a paddle." The comment generated a sudden snapping of flash bulbs from the front row. Skyler banged his gavel and the photographers stopped, leaving one television camera humming in a corner. In the audience, Judge Press turned to Larry Bear and said quietly, "Let's see if we can get a copy of that tape."

"If there is no more discussion," Skyler said, "We can begin . . ." and the rear gym doors burst open.

Any schoolchild who had played cowboy and Indians, any grownup who had read "The Last of the Mohicans," and any movie buff who had watched war-painted warriors hurl hatchets in the heat of battle, would have experienced a jolt of recognition at the legend standing in the doorway. A Native American Indian Chief, in full ceremonial rig and headdress, stepped into the room and raised his arms. The television cameras swung around instantly, illuminating Nelson Two Snakes.

"Oh god," said Larry Bear, under his breath. The headdress was amazing; it was a three-foot crest of quivering eagle feathers, and had taken on a life of its own.

"I speak of the sacredness of the land," thundered Nelson Two Snakes to his stunned audience, his voice penetrating the furthest corners of the room. The TV crews nearly fainted from joy. "I speak of the care of the animals, and the promise to the Great Spirit to keep them safe." Nelson moved up the center row, addressing one side, and then the other. He swung around, facing the audience, his back to the council members.

Hitting his stride, he celebrated the fish in the rivers, the never-ending sunrise and sunset, and the need to protect the gifts of the land: the forests and the creatures that sheltered there. He was mesmerizing.

Pausing next to Ross (who was trying to avoid any contact with this invocation), Nelson Two Snakes next considered humankind. His voice dropped, becoming intimate and profound.

"We are named the keepers of these forests and waters and their creatures. This is the greatest treasure the Great Spirit has given us. Who is it that has seen the eagle soar who cannot rejoice in his flight? Who are those who cannot celebrate the first fawns, new in the bracken? And those who cannot see in the sunset the promise of a beginning after the ending: those are hollow creatures, whose oneness with the earth has been sucked from them." (Several people dabbed at their eyes.)

Scarcely pausing, Nelson Two Snakes turned and turned silently, through north, east, west, and south, then lifted his hands and eyes to the gymnasium heavens and gave a cry that raised the hair on the back of his hearers' necks. It was the beginning of a chant to the spirits of the earth, which, while interesting on film, in 12-inches-away reality passes beyond riveting and into the realm of powerful, dangerous medicine. He hit a particularly strong note, and, in terrible harmony, a great crack and alarmingly intimate ripping sound of a nearby lightening strike plunged the gym into darkness as the thunderstorm hit and the heavens opened. The last note of the chant was in pitch blackness.

A little reflex scream came from the rear of the room and someone knocked over a chair.

"Yikes," said Victoria, clutching Sal's arm hard.

"It's nature's vengeance or something," said Sal.

Amidst subsequent peals of thunder, a conversation arose in the corner closest to the coffee urn, where a flashlight quickly appeared. While someone dug for emergency lanterns and people struck matches randomly and to little effect, a Rotarian walked a flashlight up to Skyler. Murmuring thanks, he held it lighted under his face. It cast his nose into a great pyramid while blackening the sockets of his eyes—a vision that, as Sydnor later described it, made Vincent Price look like the Avon lady. Everyone stared, rapt.

"We need to have our vote and finish the meeting," he said. "Ok with everybody?" There was a rush of yes's, interspersed with the far off crashing sound of someone hopelessly trapped in an unlighted gym toilet. Pupils dilated in the dark, the audience settled down. The lavatory trapee had fumbled his or her way out and was edging back along the corridor wall, knocking into regularly spaced trashcans.

On stage, a disembodied hand put a kerosene lantern on the table next to Skyler and another one on a table in the middle aisle. Nelson Two Snakes was discovered sipping coffee and chatting to the television people.

"Last item," Skyler said, loudly. "We've been handed a petition protesting mining in this county. It has been signed by 1,322 people, and I make that out to be—given the town's population and the number of property owners around the lakes—something like four fifths or more of the taxpayers. I'm impressed, and I believe I speak for the council that this genuinely represents the wishes of Washington County residents regarding the mining issue. May we have a motion?'

Someone made a motion that mining operations in aforesaid county, if begun, be stopped and that further mining operations be refused. Or made illegal, or both.

"That's about three motions," Skyler said. "Somebody fix it." Judge Press helped sort it out; the motion was moved, seconded, and an indefinite moratorium on mining in the county was loudly approved. There was spontaneous and sincere applause. The "those opposed?" query hung quietly in the air and floated away.

"Anybody who wants to see the signed petitions can," Skyler announced, carefully rising from his chair in the dark. "But please wait till the electricity's back on. I'm going to ask Mr. Hedges, Arthur Rosenheim, Judge Press and Larry Bear to hang around for a little while for any questions. Can we move another lantern toward the door? And somebody call for a motion to adjourn.

"It's late, the roads are probably a mess, and I expect it'll take public service a while to get the electricity back up. We'll take up any leftover township issues at the next meeting. Somebody please make an adjournment motion." Skyler got his motion, a second, a vote, tapped his gavel, and declared the meeting closed.

Judge Press, Larry Bear, and Al Gustave made for the stage. Wicker and Ross seemed to have left under cover of darkness, but could be heard berating Tom Doppler who had been trapped in the dark in the men's toilet. Maureen, Webb, Sal, Sydnor and others edged out of the building into the night, blown colder and crisper by the storm front. The Yellow Perch Lake group gathered in a little circle in the parking lot.

Some sensible people were lighting the lot with their car headlights, as drivers picked leaves and broken branches off windshields. "Well, hooray for our side," said Maureen.

"I'm exhausted," said Sophie.

"Maureen Hendrickson," said Sal, "Webb and Sophie Tintinger, Sydnor Feffer, this is Victoria Caruso."

"Congratulations on your Ph.D.," Sydnor said. "We were all interested in it too. I guess this evening is a victory for the blue heron as well," she added, glancing at Sal, who was holding Victoria's hand.

"It sort of pales compared to the adventure in there," Victoria said. "Sal told me what everybody's been doing." She seemed awed.

"Why're you all standing around in the dark?" demanded Al Gustave who materialized next to Webb.

"Victoria," said Sal, "you wanted to meet . . ."

"Actually, I already have," Victoria said, "while you were getting coffee, Mr. Gustave introduced himself. He said we should paint camouflage colors on my jeep."

"Spruce it right up," Gustave said. "Girl of the Limberlost and all that." Everyone gazed at him in disbelief. Was Gustave undergoing some kind of personality change?

"That was a terrific pitch you did in there, Al," Sydnor said to test his reflexes. He seemed extremely happy.

"Aw," said Gustave. "Well, you know."

"Ok folks, let's roll," said Webb. "Drinks at the Presses; we double checked with Adeline; it's a little celebration."

The town was dark from the power failure, but the main street was cheerful with kerosene lamps in the five restaurants and bars that kept late hours. A group of campers who had been ejected by the power outage from the late show at the Arbor Vitae Theater and Bowling Alley had gathered in the parking lot and were arguing about whether or not the evening had peaked. Limbs had been broken off trees by the storm, and various householders were dragging the wreckage off side streets and driveways, making unhappy clucking sounds. Candles burned in some windows and pinecone litter was everywhere.

Moonlight was beginning to show through ragged clouds as Sal and Victoria started home. They'd excused themselves from the revels, pleading too many hours on the road. "We're bunking in the boat house," Sal said. "I don't think Tamarack Lodge expects to see you tonight."

"Or maybe ever again," Victoria said. "They probably rented the cottage."

On the road, they passed two motor cyclists and a U-Haul driver tugging a broken jack pine out of the left lane; a quarter-mile after the turnoff onto the Yellow Perch lake road, they had to do the same with the top half of a birch sapling. At the Constantini drive, Sal lifted a battered branch and wove it around a popple as one would stake a tomato plant.

"And people think all these odd tree shapes are from Indians marking trails," Victoria said, taking Sal's hand as they picked their way to the stairs down to the boat house.

27 AFTERMATH

Later that same night, Minnie Rosenheim taped a "Do Not Open" sign to her deep freeze, safeguarding two dozen cheese cakes against premature defrosting.

"It should be all right," she was saying to Walt, "These power failures never last longer than six hours, tops." He was adjusting the wick on a lighted kerosene lamp; kitchen cookware shadows lengthened and shortened like little demons dancing.

Minnie gathered some cookies for a midnight snack. "How come," she inquired, "nobody said anything about how bad the mining thing would be for summer tourist business? For heaven's sake, I'll bet the town could've lost thousands, maybe hundreds of thousands of dollars."

"Well, I guess everybody knows. The businesses do, anyway." Walt was deciding among molasses, chocolate chip, and oatmeal-raisin. "But it'd take a long time to make the case and get the dollar figures—you'd have to calculate an average over five or seven years, say, of the annual revenue from tourist business, and then you'd have to defend the numbers."

"And on the summer people's side," Minnie mused, "they've got investments here too. Some of their places are maybe nicer than the ones they live in back in the city. Well, in nicer outside surroundings, anyway" She fired up a tiny wood stove to heat up leftover coffee.

"So I guess they all pretty much believe what Charlie and I talked about earlier," Walt said. "A vacation in a mining town, unless it's stopped being one about 100 years ago, doesn't seem all that wonderful." The coffee had begun to steam.

"And anybody who might have wanted to vacation in a mining town didn't come to the meeting. If there are any," Minnie finished, pouring leftover whipping cream into the coffee cups.

"Min, I don't understand how you could have sailed these cookies across the shop. They're the wrong shape, for one thing." He stared at his oatmeal-raisin cookie as if he'd never seen one before.

"Fury," Minnie replied, and laughed. "Pure fury, and maybe the walnuts were ballast. I think more people are coming in, hoping I'll do it again."

* * *

At the county courthouse, Charlie Haney, armed with a flashlight, felt around his top desk drawer, again found his checkbook, and tucked it into his shirt pocket. The Upper Chain of Lakes file, listing the private properties there, lay on his desk, feathered with addendum, an exercise in speculative tax appraisal. It would be interesting to see what happened to the church property when all this calmed down. Because from a purely water frontage perspective . . .

He gathered up the bundle, tapped it briskly to tidy the edges and put the entire file into the bottom drawer of the old filing cabinet for the time being, where it joined two dead tennis balls used for wedging doors and a ratty-looking sweater. Haney zipped up his jacket against the night and peered out the window. Hard white moonlight shown. It'd take all morning to get the side streets cleaned up, he thought. And let himself out.

* * *

In the following days, Larry Running Bear wrote to several universities for law school information. After the meeting, he had talked for a time with Hedges and Judge Press. Maybe, he ruminated, a Native American lawyer would be a real asset. Hedges's environmental work was often an uphill battle, but boy, when you won, it was really something. And Judge Press seemed able to turn his hand to a worthy cause at the drop of a hat. Law. How long would that take? Then he considered Wicker and Ross. And how hard could that be?

Casting an expert eye over a pyramid of squash (under construction by bored summer help), Larry Bear was suddenly very hungry. Briskly, he locked the cash drawer, handed the key to his assistant, and stepped out into a light overcast afternoon for lunch.

* * *

Anyone interested could have seen a duo in woodsman garb, but wearing tasseled loafers, entering the First Community Bank one morning a week later. Their business seemed to be with a vice president, who settled them in front of her desk and went away to have a check cut to close an account. The two found themselves seated before bookends cunningly contrived from two large-mouth bass, frozen in mid-leap on highly varnished slabs of log. One fish had a small insect shellacked to its lip. The two men contemplated the desk accessories.

"Do you think they're real?" one asked finally. He was leaning forward to feel the fish teeth but retreated guiltily as the banker returned. Smiling, she presented the document with a practiced air of mild regret and graciousness.

"Have a nice day," she said.

* * *

Toward the weekend, Sydnor was invited to dinner with Lucia, Sal, and Victoria. Sydnor was delighted because it was a chance to examine Victoria close up; she seemed as if she might be a kindred spirit or, at the very least, interesting. It was also a great opportunity for gossip. Tommy and Nick were showing off around the pier with a paddleboat.

"Did you ever notice," Sydnor said, looking down from the deck, "that small wet boys smell a lot like wet puppies?"

"Yes," Victoria said. "It's true. It might be the damp bathing suits, or all that fun with worms. It probably goes away in the winter. Who are they?" she asked, lowering her voice as Dieter and Mrs. Vilnus appeared in the doorway with Sal.

"Ah," Sydnor said, "people you've missed. Too late to explain. Sit back and savor the experience."

The children had had dinner earlier, so the grownups were left with fried chicken, a wild rice and walnut salad, and apple pies. And they became merry with wine. Lightening bugs semaphored to each other over the dock, and tiny fish erupted in giant watery circles, snapping after gnats and mosquitoes. Lucia told the story about her mother's argument that bested the immigration man at Ellis Island and sent Mrs. Vilnus into a fit of laughter.

On the other side of the cove, Webb, inspired by a dry Manhattan (two olives), finished a short, straightforward account of the Township Council meeting for the lake newsletter. Everyone would know the outcome, he told Sophie, but the report gave him verisimilitude as chronicler. He said "verisimilitude" again, savoring the word.

The status quo, he wrote, is sometimes worth maintaining, though it does us a world of good to have to reconsider it from time to time. "Good citizenship is sometimes just paying attention. Sometimes it's good fellowship as well. So do not fail to attend the upcoming Yellow Perch Lake Association meetings. Coffee and donuts are always served. The small-mouth bass question is on the agenda: should we re-stock? Is anybody catching bass of any decent size? We'll hear further reports on the weeds at the north end. And please tell new neighbors," he scribbled, "that they are welcome to come—the more the merrier—and especially should consider attending the annual dinner at Rubchek's Supper Club."

Peals of laughter drifted across the lake from behind the lanterns on the Constantini dock.

"Soph, what do you say we take a walk around the lake? That sounds like Lucia's got enough revelry to share with neighbors." Sophie was already dabbing her wrists and ankles with mosquito repellent.

* * *

Mrs. Louise Garfield, poised behind great clusters of hideous ruby glass in her antique shop, considered the county's ore deposits as vindication of several of her theories. She had quickly printed a small brochure, "The Powers Beneath Your Feet," which she pressed upon surprised customers buying Victorian toothbrush holders.

She told incredulous friends and listeners that just being in the area had eased her rheumatism considerably, although some of the more cynical noted that Louise had never mentioned rheumatism until she had learned that the county's sub-basement was, so to speak, lined with copper.

* * *

On Saturday morning, as part of a grocery run, Maureen and Sydnor made a quick stop at the library to use the copy machine there. "I need to make duplicates of the cottage insurance declarations page," Maureen said. "I think I can get a less expensive policy out of town."

While Maureen fiddled with the copy size, Sydnor read the library's rules and copy rates on a sheet of paper thumbtacked to the wall above the copier. There were tacks in each of the four corners. It suddenly reminded Sydnor of something. She found a librarian who was collecting a dozen oddly shaped children's books.

"Excuse me," Sydnor said. "I was just wondering who services your copy machine. Someone in town?"

"Oh yes," said the librarian. "Well, not right in town but close enough, and a good thing, too. He does all he copiers in the area."

"Is it a company or is it a person?"

"Both, I guess," said the librarian. "It's Stan Wolf Copy Service. He's very good. Are you finding everything you need?"

"Absolutely," said Sydnor. "Thank you." She could hardly wait to tell everybody that she had identified the friendly mole.

* * *

The loons were gabbling to each other at the north end of the lake and the first sunshine of the morning was burning off the mist that rose from the water.

"I'm sorry I missed the meeting," Miranda was saying. "We've been completely out of it except for the petition adventure, but it's a good thing that Mason missed the storm. He would have taken it as an evil portent, and god knows, Mason's had enough of evil portents lately." Miranda Thrip and Evangeline Juska hunkered down under quilts tucked into canvas chairs at the end of the Thrip pier, watching morning begin.

The two women had originally cemented their friendship over mutual horror at the price of Bing cherries at the Co-op. At the lake, Miranda and Evangeline found that they were both early risers and prone to similar types of sinus attacks. Miranda was happy for Evangeline's company, now especially, as Mason was still in the city checking on business and sifting through boat papers and insurance policies.

"I've been meaning to ask," Evangeline said, "how you got the boat back into shape in time for Lucia's picnic. It seemed like an awfully speedy recovery."

"You don't know the half of it," Miranda said. She pulled her sweatshirt down over her knees and told Evangeline about the final straw. "Mason insisted that the propeller just needed to be replaced, and he and one of the Dockworks guys—talk about patience—wrestled the bent thing off and rigged up another one. I guess it was ok, I mean, the Dockworks people know what they're doing, right?

"So anyway, nothing would do but it has to go into the water to see if it works ok. Why they couldn't just turn the thing on while it was parked there is beyond me." Evangeline made sympathetic sounds.

"Mason backed the whole operation down their launching ramp, the one into the channel. And the guy from Dockworks says, 'You're fine, set your parking brake, put the van in neutral, hit the winch release, and ease the boat into the water,'"

"Well, he did, and the boat's easing back and easing back and it's suddenly filling up with water. So I said, Mason, something's wrong with the boat, which everybody's starting to notice by this time. And then the Dockworks guy starts yelling, whoa, it's filling up, whoa, stop the winch.

"It was sinking into the channel because Mason, in all that fussing with the winch and the dents and the propeller, hadn't replaced the drain plug. So there's this geyser of water shooting over the back seats and the engine is sinking fast. Evangeline, the air was blue with swearing. And some other customers came running over and one yells, 'Reverse the winch! Reverse the winch!'

"Mason hit reverse and the boat leaped out of the channel, water just streaming out and cushions flying off in all directions, and it is a good thing there is some kind of brake on that winch, or the boat would have overshot the trailer and punctured the rear of the van.

"So that was the final straw. I thought Mason was going to have a heart attack, he got so red. And nobody laughed, really, except a couple of the Dockworks guys were sort of choked up and smiling, but the one helping Mason kept a straight face the whole time. And it finished off the propeller shaft once and for all."

"Oh my," said Evangeline.

"So what you saw us in at Lucia's was a different Rolling Boil."

"Different?"

"Duplicate. Substitute. Mason was so upset he leased another boat just like ours—I didn't know you could do that—and had 'Rolling Boil' slapped on the transom and that's what's under canvas here. Avoided a nervous breakdown, I think."

Evangeline looked stunned.

"Ours never got out of the garage or the driveway," Miranda finished. "The only time it was in the water was at Dockworks."

"Oh Miranda, is it salvageable? Or insured? Or something?"

"That's what Mason's figuring out at home. Some of it, I guess. He's ready to pack it in, I'm afraid. He hasn't had the wonderful summer he'd expected. This is the first season we were able to get away from the city for any real length of time," said Miranda gloomily.

"Oh now, you need some therapeutic socializing. Why don't the both of you come to the lake association dinner with Ernie and me. It's a really good time and the food is just fine. It's not all boats and fishing. Well, maybe it's fishing, but it's not all boats, and there are lots of interesting people around. You saw the newsletter, for instance."

"What kind of dinner is it?"

"It's a once-a-summer get-together up at Rubchek's just at the lake road turnoff. There're grab bag prizes and we sort of toast out the summer, and it gets everybody geared up for what's left of the season and next year."

"I'd love it. We'll come," Miranda said, "if I have to carry Mason. Thank you. What . . . ?"

"The drain plug. Sorry, it's . . ."

"Yeah, I've been thinking about it. From a safe distance, it's pretty funny."

"Heh, heh, heh," said Evangeline."

Miranda wrinkled her nose for a moment to get control, and failing, giggled. The two women chuckled furiously in the morning sunshine, and their laughter, unrestrained, mixed nicely with the banshee cackling of the loons.

* * *

Reverend Weathersill, at work in his office, listened idly to the Monday evening choir practice. The hymn, if one could call it that, had been composed by members of the junior choir as part of a program "to show our teens that they can make a contribution to our ever-changing 20th century church." Weathersill's pronouncements often fell into patterns that made even the Sunday Bulletin seem to drone. He listened now to the harvest of this rashly broadcast seed.

"We are sheep, we are doves, we're the zoo of the Lord," the choir sang, goosing the melody with a sneaky rock beat. Weathersill turned his attention to a letter he was composing. "We are bear, we are li-ons," the choir yodeled.

"May your ark be safe from termites," Weathersill murmured and pulled the office door closed. "Bishop Manning Sturgis," he wrote, and scribbled furiously for a good eight minutes, rationalizing his decision to rearrange a good piece of the church camp topsoil and forest.

He paused, and considered the dust motes streaming in a shaft of light. The choir was worrying a refrain that sounded like thuk-a-walka, thuk-a-walka. It was hard to concentrate. He approached the next paragraphs cautiously, and avoided some still-difficult questions about the acreage that the church actually owned. He added a few virtuous lines about nature's remarkable ability to heal man's inroads. An unfortunate choice of words, he thought, and made a note to fix it later.

"The property has, unfortunately, much less potential than I had been led to believe." Modulated regret; that was the right tone. "However, after consideration, I wonder if a loose affiliation of our Midwestern chapter houses might not make use of the existing infrastructure" (a reach, but still) "along with the near perfect fishing opportunities provided, as a retreat facility." He suggested that fees could be levied and applied to tribal leasing arrangements as necessary. Oh, life should not be this complicated. He considered money, again.

"This would require physical improvements to the cottages and grounds; I know that you are something of a fly-fishing expert, and the waters of the Upper Chain abound in various species of trout." (He hoped this was true.) "Would not such a retreat site refresh the spirits of our colleagues? Perhaps special guest speakers might be invited to enjoy our hospitality in this wooded area and to share their thoughts on the many ways to serve the Lord . . ." and Reverend Weathersill wrote on, creating Camp Retreat, complete with prayer and tennis, quietly played, and meditations at sunset, next to a grill.

"We're all God's children great and small," the choir roared on, "We're all God's children short and tall, be we hairy, be we smooth, God's real happy we're in his groove."

28 THE DINNER

Each summer, Rubchek's Supper Club took a figurative deep breath, battened its hatches, and turned over its dining room to the Yellow Perch Lake Association for the annual dinner. Usually a 40-year old restaurant with a menu encompassing Friday Fish Fry ("perch or haddock, ask for seconds"), chicken liver dumpling soup, and various sauerbratens took this sort of event in its stride, and it did, but the Rubchek family members admitted among themselves that it was a strain.

For weeks in advance, lake residents pondered their choices ("walleye pike, roasted chicken, six pieces, and prime rib, each $15.00, includes salad, dessert and coffee"), and changed their minds a half dozen times before sending off the orders. One year Rubchek's substituted duckling for chicken and threw the lake population into a collective swivet. Would there be orange sauce or red cabbage? Could you serve chicken liver dumpling soup with duck? Were they Wisconsin ducks or Long Island ducks?

"You would think," shouted Angelo Rubchek to his salad girl, daughter Judy Rubchek, "that these people never sat down in a restaurant in their lives. It's none of their business what kind of liver I put in the liver dumpling soup!"

"Would it be better or worse if they knew that the chicken livers were from absolutely different chickens than the ones they were eating and were shipped in frozen from Portland besides?"

"Gah!" said Angelo, and stomped off to yell at his cheesecake supplier, vowing as he did every year that this was the last association dinner he was going to put up with.

* * *

In preparation for the event, Sophie was scrutinizing a small linen table runner inset with a crocheted eagle, a little blunted about the wings.

"I think this will be a perfectly nice grab bag gift," she announced to Webb. "Maybe too nice, in fact."

"Well Soph, the tickets are a dollar apiece. I think that's a pretty generous price for some of the stuff that gets handed out."

"There wasn't anything really awful last year. Maybe the fish bookends with the fuzzy little flies stuck to their lips . . ."

"I kind of liked those. I mean," Webb added hastily as Sophie gazed at him, shocked, "for a fishing cottage."

"I can't believe that somebody actually took them! I bet they're figuring out how to disguise them to slip them back into the grab bag again this year."

Next door, Sydnor was staring at a large broomstick dressed as a kitchen witch, her last year's grab bag prize. It wasn't so bad, she mused, turning it around to admire its tan felt wart and gingham apron, it was just so *big*. It had been stored in a bedroom closet and a small child, coming upon it unexpectedly, had screamed and had to be comforted with many roasted marshmallows. Using it as a broom was out of the question; it was equivalent to abuse or something. It was also absurd.

Well. Sydnor untied its apron and took off the pointed hat. Let's see, she thought, poking among the calico and broomstraw, how this critter's assembled. A new broom, she mused; a clean sweep makes the heart beat faster. And bent to her task.

Al Gustave, in his cabin around the point, worked in perfect silence. Fine tendrils of wood fell away from the small figure in his hands. Carving slowly and lovingly, he lifted out fragments and slivers, cutting delicately around a beak, a wing, the barest indication of a webbed foot.

Little rivulets of feathers appeared, and an eye. It was a small mallard, about one quarter scale, fully fledged. It emerged interrupted from the wood, head cocked, with an air of listening perhaps to the dryish noise made by a patient carver teasing the pine away from feathered wings.

Around the point and across the lake, Mason was resisting the lake dinner.

"I don't want to," said Mason Thrip. "I'd feel funny."

"Oh come on, Mason, it'll be a lot of fun and you already know the Juskas."

"You know the Juskas. I hardly know the Juskas. I said hello to Mrs. Juska twice and fell off their pier. They're probably wondering what we did with the boat."

"No such thing," cried Miranda, thinking the entire lake must, by now, surely know the Rolling Boil's disasters and would be watching for next installment in what looked to be an on-going soap opera.

"These are nice people. You know Webb and Sophie, you know the Constantinis. Aren't you curious about Al, the old guy who loses his lures and stands up in the boat and yells and swears? Well, maybe not all nice people, but interesting people."

"Randi, what would I *say* to them? We don't have anything in common."

"Oh Mason, stop fussing and just come. I want to go and I've made reservations for both of us. We've got both a walleyed pike dinner and a chicken dinner ordered and you can have either one you want."

"Is the walleyed pike from here or is it frozen and flown in from someplace else?"

"You can ask Rubchek's. We'll go a little early so the Juskas can introduce us around, and I want to bring a grab bag gift."

"At a dinner for grown-ups? A grab bag gift? What?"

"Those little mouse cheese holders."

"What little mouse cheese holders?"

"You know, Mason, that set of little silver mice with wire tails that stick straight up and you stick a hunk of cheese on each one. We never use them; I can't think why not, they're adorable."

"Uk," said Mason, by which Miranda knew that she had won.

At the Vilnus cottage, Dieter and Mrs. Vilnus were tidying up after a major filleting, pickling, and smoking project, all underway simultaneously. Many gleaming glass jars of fish bits were stacked on large rough shelves built along one side of the room.

In language of middle European origins, Mrs. Vilnus addressed her husband at length and ended with a query. Dieter considered for a moment and acquiesced. Mrs. Vilnus gave a quick laugh and responded rapidly in sentences fairly clotted with umlauts. She then paused and added, "grab bag." Dieter responded with several precise phrases and they both burst into appreciative chuckles.

Mrs. Vilnus took off her vast apron and Dieter stacked various knives and trays into an ancient sink, tossed in a handful of baking soda and left everything to soak, while they prepared, apparently, for the dinner.

There were no sartorial requirements for the lake association dinner; people came in fishing clothes (clean), vacation clothes (antique), and Sunday clothes that they were using up. This gallimaufry coordinated nicely with Rubchek's indigenous decor which ran to indoor/outdoor carpeting in the dining room, perpetual Italian Christmas lights around the bar mirror and dash of Cape Cod reflected in the occasional shell ashtray.

"Private Party To-nite," read the sign in front of the restaurant. "Yellow Perch Lake Assn." was scribbled in Magic Marker on what looked like a piece of shirt laundry cardboard. People began straggling in for seven o'clock cocktails at 6:30. Evangeline Juska, with her neighbors in tow, was in charge of the current grab bag gifts and late dinner reservations. She rustled up a card table, anchored it with an official cigar box full of change and the odd reservation slip, and handed her husband a large roll of orange tickets.

"Use your charm, Ernie," she said to her spouse, the genial Paul Bunyan and speed typist.

"Still a dollar?" he inquired.

"Full value at rock bottom prices," said Evangeline, adding, "Miranda, help me stash the prizes. We tally reservations against the master list; Rubchek's can handle five extra places, after that nothing but cocktail onions. Mason . . ." Evangeline noted Mason's hysterical air; he looked like a horse about to leap sideways into a ravine and break all his legs. "Would you get us drinks, please?" she asked. They make a wonderful vodka tonic."

"Certainly, certainly," said Mason, recognizing something he could handle and rather desperately wanted.

"Judge Press!" Evangeline said, waving her cigar box enthusiastically, "come meet our new Association members."

"Miranda. Splendid. Didn't we meet at Lucia's picnic? Welcome to the annual bash. My wife's just wedging the car into some poison oak, but she'll be right in."

"My husband's in the bar getting . . . oh my," Miranda said, as Mason, who had found his social grace, carried in a tray of drinks extensive enough to gladden the hearts of a band of marauding Norsemen.

"Gin and tonic, vodka and tonic," he said to the women, "Bass ale; you look like you might be a neat scotch," he said regretfully to Judge Press.

"I'm more your borderline Sassenach," said the Judge. "I'll take that concoction in the corner; it looks like Seagram's. Yes? Well grand, but you never know what Rubchek's slipped into those bottles; I swear there's a Cutty Sark label in the bar that may date from the time she was still running cargo."

And chatting into Mason's left ear, Judge Press steered him and the clinking drinks tray toward the dining room.

He murmured to Mason, "You think you can find anything in the bar that looks like a decent port? Lucia!" he called, and Lucia Constantini, draped in a glorious floral silk shawl, beamed and rustled toward them. Sal, right behind her, took a critical look at the supplies and towed the drinksmeister back into the bar. Victoria had an important job interview in the city, so Sal was at liberty and felt he owed himself a good, solid revel.

" . . . going to need about a pitcher of vodka," he was telling Mason; "and my mother drinks port at Rubchek's because she sends him a case every Christmas; it's an in-joke with safety features."

"Sal may not be able to resist asking about the boat," said Lucia apologetically to Miranda.

"Well, good. If he can get Mason to talk about it now, we can save thousands in therapy later on. I can just see your garden from the end of our pier," Miranda added. "What are the red flowers? They look wonderful.

"Oh, the zinnias have absolutely gone crazy. They've never done so well. Please come over tomorrow and see the vegetables too; the zucchini are as big as suitcases. It could be the fish heads," Lucia finished. "Sophie knows about fertilizing," she added, as Sophie, Webb and Sydnor arrived, carrying oddly shaped bundles.

"I always say bury everything but the scales," said Sophie without breaking stride.

"Nitrogen, nitrogen," Webb intoned. "Evangeline, where can we put these soon-to-be-burnt offerings."

"We're filling the closet next to the ladies' room. My, that broomstick looks like . . ."

"Don't say it, Ev," warned Sydnor. "The contributors guarantee that the product is completely different from last year. I see doubt; I say again, a guarantee."

"The grab bag has no memory," said Evangeline primly.

"Why is Al Gustave holding a newspaper bundle?" Miranda asked in a stage whisper.

"No need to whisper; can't hear yourself think in here," said Evangeline. I think he's brought a grab bag thing." Evangeline waved to him; she and Miranda started toward him past the noise coming from the bar.

"The difference," Angelo Rubchek was saying loudly, "between Armagnac and a truly fine old cognac is not just the region . . ." Angelo, Mason, and Sal were sipping Lucia's port and gesturing with their snifters.

"Just what is the difference," Sal demanded, "between Extra and Grand Reserve . . ."

"Oh," said Mason, "if you mean like X.O. and the next notch, I think it's the aging process. You take oak barrels, see, and . . ."

"Gascony! Gascony! It's the southern soil," interrupted Angelo, automatically uncorking another bottle of the Constantini port. He ignored the escalating series of shouts from Mrs. Rubchek in the restaurant kitchen.

Little galaxies of lake association members had formed in corners of the dining room and bar, charmed to find their neighbors in exactly the same positions as earlier in the day when they had conversed between boats or in the Co-op or walking to the Press's to deliver a *Milwaukee Journal* for the Judge to compare with the *Chicago Tribune*.

In the kitchen, Mrs. Rubchek directed her staff with a Napoleonic air, scattering salad girls and soup bowls in all directions. The help, borrowed from Kiley's Cabin In The Woods Eatery, thanked their stars that theirs was a lower-key business all around, one reason being that, after sunset, the Eatery was nigh impossible to find.

In the dining room, Miranda was saying earnestly to Al Gustave, " . . . ages before the propeller shaft is fixed and it'll be winter. It's just that Mason wants to be on the water and the other lease is up . . ."

"He ever tried fishing?"

"Not with me."

"You folks get any tackle with your place?"

"There's a bunch of poles and things in the shed, but we never..."

"Prob'bly worth lookin' at. Tell you what. I'll be by tomorrow before lunchtime. See what you got. Collector's items, I'll bet. Tell your husband. I'll take him out, show him the ropes, do a little casting; might interest him."

"Oh, good," said Miranda. "I'll tell him." And with additional pleasantries, each wandered off, full of fierce and secret delight. Something useful and a lot of fun besides had been pulled off.

Webb, who was talking with Adeline Press, had commandeered a table, and others were staking claims with jackets and sweaters. At one table, a bamboo walking stick was hooked across two chairs. Angelo Rubchek had been sucked into the kitchen maelstrom and Judy Rubchek had taken over the bar where, with damp and wild hair, she was opening bottles of icy cold Wisconsin beer four at a time.

Sydnor and Lucia Constantini were each holding a corner of Lucia's glorious silk shawl, the better to admire it, and the Thrips had been reeled into an improbable conversation on the uses of wintergreen berries with Ed Juska, Maureen Hendrickson, and Louise Garfield (who considered herself an association regular due to the location of her antique shop).

Those chatting closest to the door paused briefly as a trim bald man with a very tan forehead and a very white pate arrived. Maureen Hendrickson detached from her group and hooked her arm through his, thus telegraphing to fascinated onlookers that Milt Hendrickson had finally come in off the lake. Milt solemnly hailed Dieter Vilnus, who had saved the two places at his table across the room.

"Soup!" yelled Mrs. Rubchek to her kitchen staff, looking very much like the *Alice in Wonderland* Red Queen wrapped in an apron. And magically, everyone flowed into folding chairs to confront by-now-forgotten dinner choices. A small hubbub ensued.

"Are we still deciding?" asked Miranda of her husband.

"I could eat a table leg; my god, what port. Either one is fine, maybe the chicken; would anybody mind if I finished the relish tray?"

"Complements of the management," said Judy Rubchek, tucking a plate of sautéed chicken livers next to the salad dressing, "for serving drinks and because maybe you could use them."

"Answered prayers," said Mason and dug in.

"I've always thought the best part," said Adeline Press to Sydnor at a nearby table, "was the door prize grab bag adventure. Have you heard who's actually using those varnished fish bookends?"

"Listen to Sydnor laugh," said Maureen Hendrickson to Mrs. Vilnus. "I'll bet they're talking about the drawing. The stuff we have coming and going! Remember that collection of embroidered doorknob cozies for each season, with little faces and bells stitched on?"

"Ach," said Mrs. Vilnus, rolling her eyes.

"Well, Maureen," said Louise Garfield virtuously, "some of these things require skill."

"Skill I grant you," said Maureen, passing a plate of hot rolls. "It's the design that goes all funny; I think it's the same sort of talent that fills jelly glasses with seven old tooth brushes and a couple of sprigs of cedar and calls it a flower arrangement."

"What an interesting idea," Louise murmured.

"I myself am for useful," said Mrs. Vilnus with strong emphasis. "If you get prize you can eat, is both tasteful and useful, yes?"

Dieter Vilnus, who could have added to this exchange, was instead listening to Dennis Melton asking, "So what's the Reformed Brethren action on the upper chain property?"

"Cleanup campaign," said Milt. "Maureen says they filled in the holes, took out most of the downed trees and cleared out the rest of the wreckage," he added. "And there's a sort of dock somebody's building."

"Pretty quiet," said Dieter. "We keep watch. Good neighbors."

"Man, that was close," said Melton.

"It's not going to be the last time," said Milt thoughtfully. "They're still out there somewhere looking at our land. What's going to happen to your resort, for instance? I mean eventually."

Melton gave him a beady look. "It gets bequeathed to the Butternut National Forest Land Trust. In perpetuity and et cetera. So you can all sleep better." More hot rolls came unbidden to the tables.

"Hate to break this up," said Judge Press cordially, "but it's getting on and Melton's offered to help with the drawing." It was an outgoing committee head's privilege to distribute the grab bag prizes. As Rubchek's wait staff flung little chocolate sundaes frozen hard as diamonds on the tables, he began collecting his distribution team. Melton was the scrupulously disinterested number-puller.

Meanwhile, there was some disturbance in the bar. Judy Rubchek appeared, beckoned to someone and then pointed at the table Sydnor was sharing with Webb, Sophie, and the Presses.

"Who is it, Syddy?" asked Sophie, catching her niece's expression. Sydnor rose with such a curious air of surprise and pleasure that Sophie thought for a moment that she was going to climb right onto the table, but Sydnor only smiled and gestured to Judge Press's abandoned chair.

A tall beaming figure, balancing a drink and a large platter of salad, chicken thighs and pike, nodded thanks to Judy, swiveled around tables, dodged a set of mounted elk antlers, and slipped between Evangeline and Adeline Press. He just missed a hard knock from a large hurricane lamp Evangeline was struggling to hold on to.

"I would kiss you," he said to Sydnor, "but I have chicken liver crumbs all over my face."

"Do it anyway," said Sydnor. "Where ever did you come from?"

"Manila and Minneapolis. I've been back in the country 48 hours. The water still tastes strange. It's clean, for one thing."

"A hem," said Webb, in two syllables.

"Oh, god, sorry. Quinn, this is Mrs. Press, from around the point; Judge Press is doing the drawing. Magnus Quinn is an old friend. How did you ever . . ."

"Delighted to meet you. The damnedest thing. Got a sort of semi-legal military lift to Minneapolis when I remembered you'd still be up here. And Syd, you'll never believe this, but there were a couple Geological Survey guys at the airport in these little twin engine jobs like we used to fly crop dusting at home. We got to talking, and it turns out they do some sort of regular scientific instrumentation run around the top of the state to measure—I am not making this up—dips in gravity and magnetic fields or something, whatever that means, and I hooked a ride. Sorry about running on but the connections were utter bizarre luck. You look wonderful."

"So you're back," Sydnor said happily. "Are you really back? And can you stay?"

"I'm really back," he said, "and I can stay—up here anyway—for the rest of the week. No one knows where I am; I am concealed in a wrinkle in time. Why are those people carrying in a case of pickled herring?"

"You have," Webb interrupted, "arrived at the annual lake dinner grab bag drawing and will have to sit here and enjoy it with the rest of us, exotic travels or no."

"It isn't herring," Sydnor explained. "It's crappies; I'll tell you later."

"How did you find us?" Sophie asked him curiously.

"I was on my way to your lake and saw the sign out front; it's not total chance. Sydnor has been describing this to-do for some time." He turned to her. "Did you know that Bob's North Fork Chrysler rents cars on a moment's notice? This town is the last word in flexibility." There was considerable rustling and arranging at the front of the dining room. Ernie Juska carried up the broom swathed in brown wrapping paper at the business end.

"This is going to be interesting. Were they pickled crappies, then?" Quinn asked.

Sophie and Webb and Sydnor explained, all talking at once to save time. Quinn listened, delighted. "I think I'm going to need another drink," he said, "and a couple of tickets. Anybody else? Tickets? Brandy maybe?"

"Ask Judy if there's a decent port," Webb suggested. "I think you'll be surprised."

Quinn considered. "What happens if I ask for Armagnac?" he asked.

"Stick to the port, stick to the port," said Webb, as Judge Press banged a water glass with a fork to get everybody's attention.

The Judge had divided the grab bag prizes into female, male, and neutral categories. Thus, if winning ticket number 475727 belonged to Sal Constantini, he would pick from category male, and not select five matched potholders trimmed with miniature pinecones, painted white.

A kind of giddy anticipation percolated through the dining room, fueled by good humor, drink, and the idiotic festivity of Saturday nights in resort communities.

Ernie and Judge Press had set up an old hat box to hold the tickets. Melton was hanging back, pleased and embarrassed and eager to begin.

Some prizes were concealed, but the hurricane lamp was obvious as was the red five-gallon can of outboard motor fuel, premixed. Several envelopes represented free dinner certificates at popular restaurants and one from Sal and Lucia Constantini contained coveted Green Bay Packer tickets.

Among the lumpier objects was Sydnor's wrapped broom and a large black plastic leaf bag that held a short stack of chintz decorator pillows, which the Judge unhesitatingly consigned to the "female" category. A number of bagged and packaged prizes had been privately identified. The Judge, with his most professional poker face, assigned them to degrees of desirability in the heaps.

The only way to speed-soften a Rubchek's frozen sundae was by holding it firmly between one's thighs, and some of the more practiced association members had done that. Still, there were some feeble chopping sounds as Press nodded to Melton and called the first number.

"478358."

An exclamation from the woman with the pontoon boat degenerated into a hasty *sotto voce* discussion of who the ticket really belonged to. "Me after all," she said to the assembly. She bounded up and seized a small heavy oblong parcel.

"478402," said Melton, and the gentleman who took double-time sunset walks in all weathers took the outboard motor fuel.

"He don't have a boat," observed Al Gustave to Miranda.

"Maybe he just wants to blow something up," said Miranda, and Gustave looked at her with surprise and respect. A little shriek from the rear: the pontoon boat lady had discovered that she now owned eight little silver metal mice with erect tails designed to impale and present hunks of cheese.

"Concept by Julia Child, body by D-CON," said Miranda, and Al Gustave laughed out loud.

Number 478663 was a guest at Melton's resort; she got Sophie's wing-clipped eagle tea cloth and was thrilled.

Louise Garfield, 480112, bore off the chintz cushion stack.

"I refuse to buy them if they show up in her antique shop!" Sophie muttered to Adeline Press.

"I certainly wouldn't if I were you," she responded. "I only gave them up because the fabric's made from nettles or something and they scratch like the very dickens."

Several calls for 480331 and a nudge from his wife finally snapped Mason Thrip to attention; a little drowsy from the port, he had been considering a little nap in the back seat of the car. "Here, here," he said, waving his ticket. Contemplating the dwindling door prize heap, he took the only sensible-looking item—a squarish box in a shopping bag with handles.

"What is it, Mason?" asked Miranda, peering into the parcel. "Take it out and let's see."

Mason teased out the carton. "Oh my Lord," he said. "It's a case, an entire case, of pickled somethings!"

"Fish, Mason, they're umm, whitefish."

"Crappies," said Gustave knowledgeably.

"Pickled crappies?" Mason cried. Smiles of sympathy appeared at various parts of the room; Dieter and Mrs. Vilnus looked extremely demure.

"Takes a little getting used to," said Gustave, "like green olives or brains. I'd recommend them, though." Mason tilted a feeble smile at the Vilnuses, who were smiling and bobbing at him like mating prairie chickens.

Meanwhile, Mrs. M. Hayes McIntyre, from a cottage in the north bay, was the lucky holder of ticket number 477932. Mrs. McIntyre, who had a nicely developed sense of adventure, seized the largest item remaining, immediately ripped off the paper, and gave a squawk of either joy, terror, approbation, or surprise. Sydnor had transformed the kitchen witch broom into a broom upon which rested a vaguely female creature with bag lady overtones. It held a pinecone wreath that framed a small muslin banner with a "WELCOME" appliqued message.

Mrs. McIntyre returned to her table with an air of having done her duty, whatever that was. She was warmly applauded by the interested and relieved diners who now knew that their ticket would not land them with a broom disguised as anything.

The last of the grab bag bits were dispersed quickly with appropriate snide comments from friends, and Quinn, who was surprised to find himself with the last winning ticket number called, took the one small parcel left. He brought it back and carefully unwrapped it.

Sydnor, Webb, Sophie, and Adeline Press all watched.

"This is beautiful," said Quinn quietly, and Sydnor felt that among her table companions, if there had been any possible deficit in Magnus Quinn stock, it was erased forever. He was examining the small carved mallard with tender care; Sydnor watched him and glowed. Webb looked around for the artist, but Al Gustave had disappeared.

"Thank you everyone!" said Judge Press, in his best circuit court voice. "Till next year!"

29 HOME AGAIN

Quinn left his car parked under a pine at Rubchek's and climbed into Sydnor's, slinging a battered canvas bag into the rear. Scraps of laughter escaped from a corner of the dining room where Dieter and Mrs. Vilnus were telling shaggy dog stories in a Slovakian dialect to Angelo Rubchek and his wife.

A bright sickle moon hung in the southern sky.

"Want to drive?" Sydnor asked.

"My god, woman, it's all I can do to sit up. Fortunately, by carefully wedging my head against your car roof . . . This is so beautiful."

Sydnor slowed at a curve and in the gleam of headlights were two of her neighbors, singing at the top of their lungs.

"Shave her legs with a rusty razor, shave her legs with a rusty razor, earlee in the morning," wailed Sal and Mason, bonded by port and other fermented beverages. Quinn leaned out of his window and started them on the next verse. The enthusiastic and quite obscene lyric followed them around the next bend and faded into the night.

"Hark, the pickled angels sing," said Quinn. "Will they find their way home?"

She laughed. "Oh yes. They're both on this side of the lake. Either Miranda or Lucia will toss blankets over them wherever they fall. The hangovers will be spectacular. Port! Deadly! Could you have found the cottage, by the way?"

"I think so, unless you've destroyed your mailbox. If I can survive crossing a heavily fortified border under a full moon, Syd, I could probably find the cottage. What's in the refrigerator?"

"Oatmeal-walnut bread, muffins, a half-dozen eggs, coffee beans, grapefruit juice, all the usual condiment stuff and some smoked turkey. Why?"

"You are a wonderful woman." He absently kissed her right ear. "Because I want to sleep for twelve hours, on and off, and not have to forage for food or even leave the area. And a have a long nap in a lawn chair. Do you have one that sleeps two?"

"Where is the swashbuckling madman we all have come to know and love?"

"In here somewhere, but the batteries desperately need recharging. Let the word go forth," he began in a singsong, then stopped. "Believe me, I didn't fly from Seattle to Minneapolis and then make scientific conversation with a flying toolbox to scramble eggs. God, Syd, did all these trees get taller or is it just the way it looks at night."

"Everything's different at night. It's romantic but a little scary. It's the woods, I think. They breathe."

"What a night. What a night. Wasn't that a night?" Quinn mused. Sydnor killed the engine and coasted into a little clearing near the porch.

"You're home, James. Got your duffel?"

He climbed out, sniffing the air. "Smell the pine. It smells the same. The cottage looks wonderful." He regarded it with affection.

"Except I've turned the bed so the first shaft of sun doesn't get you between the eyes."

"It wasn't the sunlight so much; I kept bashing my elbow on the windowsill. It was purple and green for days."

"Here; the door's open. Would you like a fire?" Quinn leaned on the doorjamb and closed his eyes for a moment.

"Bear with me and don't laugh. I was going to muck up something sonnet-y to prove I could do it, but all I could do was remember all the famous bits, like 'Had we world enough and time,' and then my brain would slide over to that line where he says, 'I will make thee beds of roses...' but at least I didn't get all tangled up with Shakespeare." He stopped.

" My god. Two Restoration poets, and in your condition. I'm enchanted!"

"And then there's 'For god's sale hold your tongue and let me love. . . '"

"Oh Quinn," and Sydnor's eyes filled up. He gathered her into his jacket.

"It was a long trip; you can probably tell. When I'm stronger I'll tell you about it and I kept mumbling iambic pentameters wondering if the cottage timing had changed or something, and you'd left early."

"It's been one heck of a summer. You helped more than you know; it'll keep till tomorrow, though," Sydnor said, leaning back to look at him, a perfect imprint of a jacket button on her cheek.

"All right, and just for that I won't tell you stories to make your hair curl."

"It's natural," she said grinning. "So maybe you already have."

"Don't make a fire. We'd probably burn the place down. Why are you smiling that wicked smile?"

"There are ways and then there are ways to burn the place down."

"If I fall exhausted to my knees right now, will you lie for me and say we steamed the paper right off the walls with passion that melted the stuffed fish in your living room?"

"Absolutely. And since every night has a bottom and a top. I think we could make good uses of the top tomorrow, and by the way, various neighbors will probably be drifting by tomorrow to chat."

"I will spend the day nude and won't they be surprised."

"Pray for sunshine, come to bed, it's going to start getting light in a few hours. There's a mouse in the house; do you care?"

"My dear, you could have zebras and I wouldn't care."

30 FIN

Sunday morning was still and limpid. An early haze burned off the lake and little tatters of breeze plucked at the tree tops and faded. The woods gave up dampish nighttime smells and end-of-season puffballs split, exploding tiny clouds of brown spores. It was going to be wonderful. It was going to be hot.

In Sydnor's cottage, sleep had been untroubled and deep. Now it was nearly mid-morning and people around the lake were beginning to stir. Awakened by the sound of a nearby motorboat, Sydnor had quietly padded into the kitchen to check on breakfast supplies. She padded back.

"Orange juice," she said, handing Quinn a glass.

"Luxury," he said, pleasantly groggy among the pillows. She climbed back under the covers with him.

"That may be," she said, "but if you spill it on the sheets, it's all over between us."

"You're a determined woman," he said, downing the juice and placing the glass on the floor. "But pliant, pliant."

"It's gorgeous weather," Sydnor said. "What's your pleasure?"

Thoughtfully, Quinn stroked the back of Sydnor's neck. "In my travels," he said, assuming a profound tone, "I have gathered some bits of oriental knowledge involving certain sensitivities. Perhaps I could be persuaded to demonstrate."

"Jesus, Quinn, you sound like Charlie Chan," said Sydnor, alarmed. "Do I need to whip up a hookah? Arrange for an opium pipe?"

"This is not a caterpillar on a mushroom situation. This is the wisdom of ancient civilizations. And of some very attentive experts in the erotic arts. They can assume the shape of human pretzels."

"You want to make love to a pretzel? Wait a minute. Have you been making love to a pretzel? To a bunch of pretzels? What do you actually *do* on shore leave or R and R when you're not filing stories? Working out positions from salacious temple sculptures?"

"It's hard to get that close," Quinn said, "but remember, new experiences extend our understanding of other cultures, deepen our ability to express ourselves."

"I'm trapped in a summer cottage with *The National Geographic*," Sydnor cried.

"Come here."

"Hey!" she managed.

And Quinn, with a really long reach, dispatched leftover clothing, flung a quilt aside, and rearranged some preconceived notions about balance and access.

"Do you think Americans bend . . ." Sydnor started.

"Take deep breaths," Quinn said, and without a word about yin, yang, chakras, or the position of the nesting buzzard, created a sexual sensation that, when full power had been achieved, rattled the windows, unsettled the kindling, loosened the door jambs, and stopped little furry creatures in their tracks. Even the birds shut up.

Some time passed. One of Sydnor's sandals slid off a kitchen chair and onto the floor.

More time passed. Nearby, a crow cleared its throat, tentatively.

"You understand," Quinn panted, "that in the East you're supposed to progress toward this through meditation and levels of preparation."

"Golly Moses," gasped Sydnor who was drenched with sweat and tugging at a sheet, "then we should have started when we were seven."

"I think I've pulled a tendon," Quinn said, testing his right shoulder.

"Don't look now," said Sydnor, "but we've attracted the local wolf pack who are on the porch staring in at the screen door. We must have hit some decibel level specific to the lupus frequency."

"You lie," said Quinn, drawing her and the captured sheet closer.

"How did you learn to do that?" asked Sydnor, glued to Quinn's chest. "And I really want to know."

"With tetracycline," Quinn said. "Lots and lots of tetracycline."

* * *

Sophie Tintinger leaned forward at her kitchen table, absently stirring a half cup of coffee, and peered out the window at Sydnor's cottage. She was careful not to touch the curtain.

"There's no smoke from the chimney," she said.

"Too warm," said Webb, " and too early."

"It's 9:30," Sophie said.

"Still too early."

"I suppose so. When did we start getting up at 7:30? Why did we start getting up at 7:30?"

"Soph, it's programming. Remember getting up at six for work? And chopping ice off the bottom of the garage door? Remember the expressway? I say 7:30 is late and I salute it."

"We're old," said Sophie gloomily.

"It's habit," said Webb. " Don't spy."

"I'm just concerned."

"Be concerned in the living room. You want part of the Sunday paper? Do you suppose Sal and Mason ever got home?"

"I'd love to know. I wish I knew Miranda better so I could ask her."

"Ask Al Gustave. He's going over to give a fishing lesson and look around."

"A fishing lesson? Al?"

"New and wonderful friendship. Or you could walk over to see Lucia."

"She'll be at church. Thank you, I'll just read the paper and stare from right here. Don't you rustle the sports section at me, Webb."

At 10:45, Sydnor emerged from her cottage in what she had once described as her "utility" bathing suit, wandered into the lake for some distance, avoided the drop-off, and slowly sat down. The water reached to her chin. She contemplated the further shore for perhaps a quarter of an hour, then rose slowly and rambled into deeper water for some careless floating punctuated by an occasional backstroke. Finally staggering back to the pier, she scooped up her towel and returned to the cottage.

"Too bad there are no binoculars," said Webb innocently.

"They're at Sydnor's," said Sophie, missing his tone completely.

At 11:15, Quinn walked down to the lake in a garment that may or may not have been a bathing suit, strode into the water, dove off the drop-off and struck out for the center. His crawl was competent, and he swam for a while over what Webb suspected was one of Dieter's sunken fish structures, and drifted back.

Behind the cottage, hair wrapped in a dry towel, Sydnor tossed two wet ones over a line slung between birch trees.

"Let's do a barbecue," said Sophie.

Webb raised his eyebrows.

"Nobody's going to leave the lake today," said Sophie, " and we've got plenty of food. I'll send Morse code or something."

"Fine. You want the 'At Home' section?" Webb inquired, gently waving a sheaf of newspaper.

By 12:30, Sydnor had flung open all the windows, replaced the now dry towels with two larger wet ones, and she and Quinn hauled out lawn chairs, repositioned the hammock, and wandered onto the pier to squint into the blaze of sun on the water. Sydnor, in an enormous straw hat, was sipping a mug of iced coffee. Quinn had a cold beer in one hand and Sydnor's binoculars in the other. He had spotted something across the lake.

"Even without binoculars," said Sydnor, "it's Mason Thrip, I'll bet, out for his fishing experiment with Al Gustave."

"Right you are. Mason's a little under the weather, looks like."

"How so?"

"He's hanging over the side. Oop! Little more active than that, I'd say."

"What's he doing?"

"Throwing up. Gustave is rising above it with all sorts of dignified casting."

"Can you see all that?"

"Far too well. Wait. Their trolling motor's started. They're moving away from the spew site; hey! Gustave's got a strike. Amazing what attracts fish."

Tiny voices were raised and floated across the like to them. A small figure—Miranda? —appeared in the vicinity of the Thrip pier.

"How have you kept this from me all these years?" said Quinn, riveted to the binoculars. "The strike's brought Mason around. Al's pole is bent double, he's playing the fish."

Sydnor was rising up and down on her toes, squinting furiously across the lake. "What're they doing, what can you see?"

"Thrip's taken over the trolling motor, Al's hooked a leg around a clamp-on boat seat. I hope it stays clamped on."

"What's Mason doing with the trolling motor?" The engine sound increased a notch and began to whine.

"I think they're using it against the pull of the fish. Is that considered sporting? My god, Sydnor, it must be a pretty good size to pull a reversed trolling motor."

Next door, Webb leapt into a boat and shot off across the lake with two large nets and an enormous gaff hook. Sydnor could only just make out Evangeline and Ernie Juska tentatively pushing off in a rowboat one pier south of Miranda, whether for moral or physical support was unclear.

Fish vs. Gustave and Thrip was moving closer to the shoreline and the cheering section had gathered at a safe distance. Quinn kept up his blow-by-blow.

"It's under the boat. It's under the boat. Mason grabs Gustave by his belt. Gustave hangs on for dear life. There's your uncle. He's handing Mason the gaff. Mason doesn't know what it is. Your uncle offers to hit him on the head with it."

"You're making that up."

"Only partly. Gustave yells at him. Mason takes the gaff. He looks like a shepherd. Mr. Juska is yelling something. Syd, this is wonderful. The fish is under the boat again. The boat swings around, foiling the fish . . . wait! The trolling motor's hit sand."

A thin metallic shrilling rose amid the miniature babble across the lake. "It's frightened the fish. It's frightened Mason. The fish is heading right for the shore. It's taking the boat with him. The motor throws a rooster tail of sand. Whoa! It's popped off the boat. Good thing they're in shallow water."

Sydnor gave a little scream, matched by tiny tenor bursts of profanity from across the lake. It was amazing how sound carried over water.

"Gustave's mouth is moving but he's hanging on to the fish. Surprise, Mason's hooked the motor with the gaff; there's a new skill! The fish is towing them in circles. Ernie Juska's standing up and waving his arms. The fish has got Al, Mason's got the motor, Mrs. Juska's got hysterics."

"What?"

"She's holding her sides and rolling back and forth laughing fit to kill. Or maybe it's an appendicitis attack. The fish dashes toward deeper . . . Ole! Your uncle's got it in the net. No! Your uncle's got part of it in the net, Ernie Juska's got the rest in another net; looks like they're going to have to lean toward each other for the rest of the day. That's a serious fish, Syd."

"Let me see! Good grief, it's as big as Al Gustave, practically; it must be one of the legendary lake muskies."

"Do you want to row over?"

"No, everybody'll come by for drinks next door to rant and rave about it. Let's not spoil it; we'll be a fresh audience and can be properly dazzled."

"Are we invited next door?"

"I think about when the motor revved first, Sophie dashed over and put a note on the back screen door. Are you hungry?"

"Suddenly you know? I am. It must be all this fierce and exciting fishing."

"On to turkey sandwiches."

"And then naps."

The afternoon ebbed, but the summer sun shone hard on the lake, the moving water reflecting sunlight onto overhanging pine branches and sunburning the undersides of chins. The adventure across the lake sorted itself out and Webb eventually returned to make a fast trip to town for extra supplies—the evening's cocktail gathering would be large and celebratory.

Quinn pulled a lawn chair over, folded himself into it, and rested his feet in the hammock. Sydnor had intended to offer him part of the Sunday paper she had purloined from Sophie but, improbably balanced, he was fast asleep.

A languid quiet settled over the cove, punctuated only by the sound of small waves and Sophie emptying ice cube trays into a bucket. Sydnor, oddly energized, confronted several rich choices. First, she could tiptoe down to the hammock and watch Quinn sleeping, an indulgence almost too decadent to contemplate. Or she could rummage quietly in the garage for the missing copy of the property survey. She seemed not to have gotten around to it. That might be the thing. She did not want Quinn, waking, to find her before him giving off quite so much rank appreciation. Once she had watched a female praying mantis lunch on its mate with satisfied pleasure. It was the sort of thing, she thought, could put you off sex for weeks or months at a time. She headed for the garage, remembering to prop the back door so it wouldn't slam.

Unlike Quinn's life arrangements, which moved from anticipation, preparation, and on to high adventure, culmination, and then back to preparation, Sydnor saw her own existence as steady-state. If offered a choice between a long balloon trip over the French countryside and an entirely new septic system, Sydnor would argue mightily for both, but secretly yearn for the septic system. Still, she might decide the other way. A friend once called her a creature of habit, but got it wrong. Sydnor's creative imagination kicked in unexpectedly; she took risks. It was why Quinn was sleeping some yards away under a spindle of pines; no completely sensible person, she often suspected, would abandon herself to a situation with so little stability, even though he was "back," whatever that would come to mean.

It was family, she thought, that was predictable. Her father had been a caretaker type. She had documentation from this deceased parent; he'd left penciled notes all over the property—messages in kitchen drawers and on garage walls about important details like paint and sufficient putty supplies. Sydnor, moving the wheelbarrow out of the way, considered these communiqués for the hundredth time.

"Pump flange extras in strongbox," instructed the scribble in the kitchen drawer. Pump flange? Strongbox? Could those have been the little leather circlets disintegrating in the toolbox? The steel strongbox —empty—had been used as an anchor for several years until the weekend when, tossed into an unexpected depth of lake, its weight ripped off a strut, part of a boat seat, and the pulley that guided the anchor rope.

"It's proof that we're all compulsives," Sydnor had explained to a visitor surprised by a warning that the late Mr. Feffer had etched into the door of the kitchen medicine chest regarding the World War II safety razor that was still there.

"Duplicate key in Plymouth," read the efficient block letters next to a garage door no longer locked. The key had either oxidized into rust or was still in the Plymouth that now existed only in family snapshots. Sydnor found these messages comforting. They provided a conversation, a continuity when only family fragments were left. Though slightly faded, the notes sometimes carried a certain air of urgency.

"Plat in coffee can! F. Feffer," inscribed on the garage wall, was a puzzle. Anyone after chairs, oars, rope, and old inner tubes had read it. The coffee cans, arrayed like fat soldiers along the north wall, were full of nails.

"Plat in coffee can, plat in coffee can," small cousins chanted, skipping toward the lake with their minnow nets. While Quinn slept beneath a tree five times his age, Sydnor read the message with a fresh eye.

Slowly swiveling on her heels in the cool sand covering the garage floor, she looked, object by object, along all the walls and ledges. The toolboxes were cleaned out; some had been discarded. Two old storm windows and lengths of lumber were stacked in the rafters. Paper wasps had built a modest nest in a corner. Brush clippers, sickles, the old mailbox, and an antique electric lawnmower all lived at the rear. Opposite the wasps was a squirrel nest; a sledgehammer and several axes rested in hooks on the other wall.

Ah.

Disentangling one of the ladders, she climbed to the squirrel nest and the rusted Hills Brothers coffee can serving as its base, all shoved back into the corner on a crossbeam. The coffee can held four shredded acorns, a ball of mattress fluff and, on the very bottom, a squirrel-stained tightly folded surveyor's map of three adjoining lake properties—the legendary plat.

She unfolded it gingerly and the stain, brown with age, repeated at each fold like a classic Rorschach series in diminishing tints. Gripping the survey firmly by the corner—squirrel pee, even 20-year-old squirrel pee, was unendearing—she descended and found a coarse pencil on the window ledge.

"Plat no longer in coffee can," she wrote firmly under the previous message. "Plat in black book case in living room."

She signed and dated her message and carried the document into the cottage, her proprietorship secure in this era. There might still be time for a nap, she thought. A lovely late afternoon lay ahead. And then it would be time for supper.

ABOUT THE AUTHOR

Iris Poliski has worked in Chicago, New York, and New Jersey research centers.